FINALIST
2019
Royal Palm
Literary Award
Competition

YE WHO ARE WEARY, COME HOME

Sarah A. Younger

DEDICATION

This book is dedicated to Granny O'Steen.

CONTENTS

ACKNOWLEDGEMENTS

I hope Granny O'Steen is proud of this series of books, even though they are historical fiction based on her tales. The important thing to me is that she will never be forgotten because of these writings and many of her stories will live on. I am grateful that I had a grandmother like her, who taught me values, manners, the importance of heritage, a work ethic, sewing skills, immense love, and a strong faith.

I am grateful to friends, family, and readers who have read and appreciated these books. Thank you to those who motivated me to write a sequel book, especially my childhood friend, Ada (Shiver) McPherson. My friend, Elana Whitehead, has provided encouragement, support, and advice throughout the process of writing both books. Thank you.

Also, thank you to my excellent editor, Susan Smiley-Height. My gratitude extends to my daughter, Morgan Richie, who has been my project coordinator and has encouraged me every step of the way. I know that these projects would not have materialized without her help. And lastly, thank you to my patient husband, Doug, who spends every day with me and knows the time, research, and effort that goes into writing a book.

The picture on the front cover is Granny O'Steen when she was about eight years old. It was taken in front of the La Crosse Baptist Church around 1896, which still stands today. The church has been well-maintained and looks as I imagined it looked when it was brand new in 1882. Not long after this picture was made, Granny was run over by a horse and buggy in front of this building. She may have been traumatized but she was not injured physically. The members of the church celebrated its 136th year anniversary this year, 2018.

The frame quilt on the cover is a postage stamp quilt that I made in 2010.

A word about Watermelon Pond: Granny was a cane-pole fisher-woman and spoke about catching bream at Watermelon Pond on more than one occasion. She was a true Southern lady and I always wondered at her love of fishing, but admired that characteristic of her personality. Many times, as a young girl, I had to put the worm on her hook as that was not something she enjoyed.

Much of the historical information used in this book was taken from "History of Alachua County 1824-1969," compiled by Jess G. Davis.

PART 1

1888-1889

Yellow Fever

Chapter 1   *THE JACK*

"Thou shalt not be afraid for the terror by night......Nor for
the pestilence that walketh in darkness; nor for the
destruction that wasteth at noonday. Psalms 91:5-6

A June Florida night is sometimes so sultry it's hard to sleep. And sleep is often elusive to a nearly forty-five year old woman like myself. Sitting on the front porch in my rocker in the dark of night, I thought I heard a sound, the sound of a creaking axle heading down our dead-end road. That is not a welcome thought, so I grabbed the rifle just inside the door. As the creaking got closer, I called to Lani, my husband, who could sleep through a hurricane. Pulling his britches on, he stumbled to stand next to me.

"Sounds like the old carriage John and Suzanna left in, Sally" Lani whispered.

"They're not due back for a couple of weeks. Can't be them," I replied.

He stepped outside, barefooted, and called out as the carriage approached the driveway.

"John, that you?"

"Yessir," John answered.

"What the hell are you doing traveling in the middle of the night, son? It's dark and you have no light," Lani yelled.

John pulled the horses to a halt, set the brake and reached down to shake his wife, Suzanna, by the shoulder. As he stepped down, he said "Yellow Jack."

I ran to my son and hugged him to me, as Lani helped a groggy Suzanna down.

"Yellow Jack in Tampa, Palmetto, Manatee, and Gainesville. People fleeing by the thousands," John said. "The military is turning people around, blockades everywhere, quarantine stations. If we hadn't turned around, we might never have been able to get back. Couldn't wait to get home. Let's talk about it tomorrow though, as I'm beat down. We will have to take precautions, put up a gate with an armed guard."

"I'll take care of the horses. You two get some rest," Lani said.

As John and Suzanna trudged to their cabin by the lake, I followed Lani to the barn, my gown dragging in the dirt, feeling alarmed at the news. We had heard of yellow fever in Tampa but thought the army had it contained. The gossip was that it was carried in the air and swamp gasses and was highly contagious.

We had always felt safe here at the end of the road on our large ranch near the town of La Crosse, Florida, in Alachua County. The only thing we would have to be careful of would be leaving to buy supplies, and strangers showing up on the back step, looking for a handout. Church would be out of the question with so many people in the same building at the same time, but that's mainly where we got our news. In some ways it was good to live in an isolated area; in other ways we didn't always hear about the latest events. I knew I wouldn't sleep that night as on so many other nights in my life.

☼

There were times in those days when I dreamt, and the past would come to me. I was swimming in the warm stream near my childhood home in Lebanon, Tennessee, under the bright sunshine, or walking behind a lumbering freight wagon, headed south out of Georgia. Very rarely did I dream of fantasies; it was always extremely real. And when I awakened, I felt I was in that very time of which I dreamt, and it took me a few minutes to get my bearings. At those times, my husband's face was a stranger to me, asleep on his pillow. It startled me so that, many times, he awoke to see his wife's horrified face, lit by moonlight.

Now, I have been a blessed woman to have a compassionate man such as Lani (which is short for Lanier, his given name) for my husband, but I wonder that he does not think me daft at those moments. He usually smiles at me and I recognize him immediately. Then he takes me in his arms and kisses my face and relief floods my body. His strength then becomes mine and I have a love for him that transcends earthly love, as he is my rock at that time. But he is always my rock, and he says I am his also. I just thanked God that I didn't dream every night.

The worst dream I have had was of blood floating down a Georgia stream, diluting as it drifts. I am not proud to say that I killed a man who tried to rape my dear friend Elizabeth, and myself. But it is the truth, and had I not done it I might not be telling the story now. I believe God has forgiven me and I am working on forgiveness for myself. Even though I wake in a panic, I am always thrilled to not be dreaming that particular dream.

The year was 1888 and we were 23 years past the War of Northern Aggression. We had lived through it and had come out on the other side, but I believe once you have experienced war, you never recover from the horrors and I am speaking from a woman's point of view. Does a person ever get over killing another human being? Or seeing your neighbors' homes burned to the ground? Or going hungry because of the embargoes placed on ports and railroads? In our daily lives, we don't feel it as we are busy, but nighttime is when the hard thoughts come. And now we had another pestilence to deal with. How many family members and friends

5

would we lose to Yellow Jack? None, if I had my way. We would need to isolate our ranch until this plague passed. We did have big iron pots to contain the fires and cleanse the air.

☼

Lani and I ran the ranch, which was started by my first husband, Jacob, and myself. Suzanna and John, my oldest son, helped with the running of the ranch and were planning to expand the cabin by the lake, preparing for a family. It did my soul good to see my eldest be so gentle; there were times I had thought perhaps he had developed character flaws, but I could see he was becoming a good man, like his pa, my first husband, Jacob Henry Winston. Of course, this new development caused more fear for Suzanna, with death lurking around every corner.

My favorite child, Harry, lived in Colorado with his beautiful wife and three children, ranching there as well. He wrote once a month begging us to visit, but I couldn't leave now with the quarantines in place. And though I longed to see that part of the family, the thought of the train ride was daunting, as well as impossible due to the quarantine. My two brothers lived there also and I hadn't seen them since 1860, when they were little boys.

Then, there was Lizzie, or Mary Elizabeth, my youngest, whom I very rarely saw, as she lived in Newberry with her curmudgeony husband, who couldn't see fit to raise a child that wasn't his. Sarah, who had lived with me since she was small, was a blessing to me, so I tried to forgive them both. When the mail started running again, I would write to her, hoping they were safe from this pestilence.

Chapter 2   HALF-MOON NIGHT

*T*here was always so much work on the ranch, even though we employed workers. It seemed there was always a crisis. Abigail and Lester were former slaves who had worked on our ranch since just after the war ended. Abigail, who was the cook for the hands, had been feeling poorly lately. When I visited her in their cabin in the woods, I realized she was seriously ill. Her skin was ashen and her energy was such that she was bed-ridden. Lani made me wear a bandana over my face, which I'm sure didn't comfort Abigail.

"Abi, my dear, we must have a doctor visit you." I said.

"No, Missy. It too far gone. Probably the Yellow Jack. Please take care of my Lester and the girls."

Clearly, she felt she was leaving us. I held her hand and cried with her. She had been in my life for so long, I really couldn't think how we could stand to lose her. Lester came in then with some soup from the kitchen. Surprised to see me, he asked if he should come back later.

"Lester, no. Come in," I said, wiping my eyes with my sleeve.

He sat by her bed in the one-room cabin, which was so clean even though I knew she couldn't manage the housework. Her girls were dedicated to their work and their parents.

"She lookin' better today, Missy," he smiled at me.

"Lester, a doctor could help. Please let me send for the doc."

"Cain't 'ford no doc," he said, adamantly.

"Don't worry about the cost. Just say it's okay to send for him."

"You the boss lady," he whispered, his eyes watering. I don't think either of them felt it would do any good. They were just so accustomed to doing what they were told. But I sent a ranch hand, Tommy, for the doctor after I left them.

I waited anxiously on my front porch. Old Doc Johnson was getting older and I didn't know how long he would continue to make house calls, but I was anxious to have Abigail well again, if that was possible. When Tommy returned, he said Doc couldn't come but that there was a new, young doctor in Alachua, who also ran an apothecrary or some such word.

"And you didn't think to go for him?" I asked.

"No ma'am. I got chores to do."

Well, that steamed me but good and I was already mad about that old coot doctor. I knew why he couldn't come. This was my ranch but some hands were only good at taking orders from a man. When I told Lani, he saddled his horse and left for Alachua immediately.

"I'll settle up with Tommy later," he yelled as he rode away.

I headed back to Abigail's cabin with some fresh-made sour orange juice, sweetened with sugar cane nectar. Her two daughters, Fancy and Lucy, were there, changing her clothes and helping her to sit up. She was warm to the touch, with perspiration soaking her clean dress.

"Mr. Walton left to get the new doctor from Alachua to help," I said.

"Won't do no good. He won't treat no coloreds," Fancy said, bitterly.

"He will if he wants our business, which is considerable here on the ranch," I said.

Abigail's girls had taken over the cooking for the ranch in her absence. They had always helped, but now they were totally in charge and were doing a fine job.

☼

Later in the day, Lani knocked on the door and standing behind him was a young man who looked to be about 25 years of age. Slight of build with wispy blonde hair, he seemed far too young to be a doctor. I introduced myself and Abigail. He said he was Dr. Billings. His examination was thorough, which made Abigail uncomfortable, as she looked at me with fear in her eyes.

"She has the ague," he announced boldly. It would later be called malaria.

"Is it fatal?" I asked, almost relieved that it wasn't yellow fever.

"Not if she takes this cinchona bark. She'll never be rid of it but the powder will help with the symptoms. Caused by mosquitoes. All of you should rub down with vinegar or grapefruit oil before you venture out at night or near lakes or ponds."

"Bless you, Dr. Billings. So good of you to come this far out. What do we owe you?"

"A side of beef would be appreciated, smoked. And I would like your recommendations to other folks. People are hesitant to work with me since I'm from Pennsylvania."

"Done," I said, "and you can have all our business if you don't mind the drive."

"Thank you, Mrs. Walton. You have renewed my faith in humankind."

"And you have renewed mine. Some folks will not treat the coloreds."

"Well, then, they have not taken the Oath of Hippocrates, required by all licensed doctors."

"Lord God, that be some bitter powder, Missy," Abigail yelled.

"Don't fail to take the doses, or you will be sick again," Doc said.

"Don't worry. We can't do without Abigail. I'll make sure she takes it," I said. "And doctor, what of the yellow fever? What should we do to be safe?"

"I know the theory is that it is in the air, but I believe it to be carried by mosquitoes, like the ague, but it's a different type of disease," he said. "Try to empty all the areas where water stands, put dirt in the ditches and potholes. Stay away from the lakes and be in by nightfall. That's the best we can do for now. It's an unknown."

And so, the good doctor left in his buggy, with a side of beef from our smokehouse, wrapped in a burlap bag in the back. I knew we would see him again as we had many accidents on the ranch and I couldn't treat them all. This man had a good heart, I felt, even though he was a Yankee, and so very young. It was a confusing issue however, not really knowing where the fever originated. But he was a very smart young man and I had to trust him.

John didn't show up at my house until late in the day, saying Suzanna wasn't feeling well, which struck fear in my heart.

"Lord God, John, was she exposed to the Jack? Doc Billings thinks it's caused by mosquitoes."

"We only made it to Waldo, Ma, but they have shotgun guards at the city limits. We spent one night on the side of the road but we used mosquito nets. Most people think it's in the air. We could smell heavy smoke everywhere. Some honeymoon."

Lani came in the back door, poured a cup of black coffee and sat down at the table with us. "How in the hell did you travel in the darkness?" he asked John.

"It was a half-moon night. And I got good eyes," John replied.

"We got big problems, needing supplies. We need some health certificates from one of the doctors or we probably won't be able to get into Alachua." Lani said.

"We are pretty self-sufficient. I'll expand the garden and bring in more chickens. And we have the grist mill and the sugar cane press. John, you and Suzanna move in here, away from the lake. Lani, order the men to stay on the ranch. If they leave, they can't come back. Any stranger seen on our property cannot stay. And we'll post a guard at the fence we erect on the road." I said.

"Yes ma'am," Lani said with a grin.

"Sorry, Lani. I just know we have to take precautionary steps."

"Hell, Ma. Doc Johnson says it's the air, not mosquitoes," John said impatiently. "Excuse the bad language."

"Dr. Johnson is old. Dr. Billings is a smart man with recent training. I believe him," I said.

"Well, hell's bells, we'll listen to both of them. We'll get rid of the standing water and burn fires in the charcoal iron pots, too," Lani said. And it was settled.

A few days later Abigail was up and cooking in the ranch kitchen. When I saw her, I grabbed her and hugged her close, tears running down both our faces.

"Thank you, ma'am," she whispered. "Dr. Billings a good man."

"Yes, he is. We love you, Abi. Don't scare me like that again."

"No ma'am."

Loud voices spilled into the kitchen from the dining hall. I stepped into the room and several ranch hands were arguing.

"They can't make us stay here. I need to go see about my family in Newberry," Oran Mills shouted and then he saw me standing in the doorway. "Sorry, Miz Walton."

"You may leave, Oran, but you can't come back until the epidemic is over. We're trying to keep our compound safe," I said.

"We need our Saturday nights in Alachua. It's our only good-time," Tommy Emmons yelled at me, rudely. He was really steaming my starch. This was the same hand who didn't go for the doctor for Abigail.

I was sure the ranch hands went to the saloon in Alachua on Saturday nights, drinking that tanglefoot whiskey, and probably visiting the houses of ill repute, too.

"I believe we'll call a meeting," I said. "You can air your complaints and we will give you the rules."

As I was leaving, I heard Tommy whisper, "Don't take no orders from no woman. Don't care if she's the boss's whore."

He meant for me to hear that remark. And scorched as I was, I held my tongue, even if he was a little sidewinder weasel.

Chapter 3   THE BOSS'S MAN

"*H*e said what?" Lani yelled. "He is gone and right now. That son of a bitch won't call my wife a whore. What in the hell is wrong with him?"

He grabbed the bull whip off the wall outside the door. "No, Lani," I called. "Just fire him. Don't beat him, for God's sakes."

I followed him to the ranch dining room where he kicked the door open so roughly it dangled from a single hinge. But Tommy was not there. And the men who were there were wide-eyed.

"Gone to the lake, Mr. Walton," one of them said.

I stumbled after Lani, wishing I hadn't told him the story about Tommy. We found Tommy standing by the lake, his back to us.

"Get your things and be out of here in an hour!" Lani bellowed.

"Mr. Walton, I didn't mean nothing. I'm just not used to taking orders from a woman."

"Well, it happens that she *is* your boss. If you ever set foot on this property again, I will shoot you myself," Lani said through gritted teeth.

13

Tommy brushed by me and knocked me into a palmetto bush. As Lani was going after him, I grabbed his arm and held him before there could be another altercation. But he followed him to the bunkhouse, and Tommy left with a carpetbag. He was escorted to the new gate and angrily threw the gate open. I heard him whisper, "Whore" under his breath. I was hoping Lani didn't hear it, but when I took my husband's arm, he was shaking, angry to the core. A man not prone to fury, Lani was driven to it by a sorry good-for-nothing no account skunk. I was shaking a little myself.

☼

Blindly staring at the ceiling from my bed at night, listening to the hoot owl outside my window, I felt the tears falling and running down my cheeks, into my ears. This new epidemic was like shooting a pistol at an unseen enemy. All the so-called experts or doctors hadn't a clue; everything was a guess.

I could see our workers were starting to panic. Trying to think what we could say to them to calm the situation was as frustrating as the situation itself. People around me considered me strong, but I saved my tears for myself and mostly didn't cry in front of anyone.

And then there was Tommy Emmons, calling me names and not taking my orders. It was humiliating to me, even though I found him to be of low character. I wanted to pound the pillows with my fists, but I contained my anger, which was building, like I imagined a volcano would do.

Lani turned to me, saying, "Don't worry, my love. We've been in worse times than this."

He kissed my face, tasting my tears, even though I had tried to cry quietly. A man of great perception, he always knew what I was thinking. And he knew exactly how to distract my mind as he kissed me lovingly.

"And you know, Tommy Emmons may be right. You might be the boss's woman." I could feel him grinning in the dark.

"Woman, yes. Wife, yes, but not the other W word. AND you might be the boss's man." We both laughed heartily at that and it lightened my heart. How I loved my husband. Holding onto Lani

14

made me feel safe and vanished my sleeplessness. I then slept soundly through the night.

☼

The old rugged wagon was pulled into place by the round pen. Lani wanted me to speak first, mainly because he wanted the men to have respect for me, which I had assumed they all did. Most of the people I loved lived on our little ranch; Loretta and Samuel, my sister-in-law and brother-in-law, their daughter, Rebecca and her husband, Nathan, and their son, little Samuel. John and Suzanna had moved into our house, where we lived with Sarah, my granddaughter, even though she called me "Mama." Abigail and Lester and their two daughters were part of our family. And many of our workers had been with us for years, around 15 hands at the last count.

I stood on the wagon bed, next to Lani and John, and had my first case of stage fright. As I looked down at the faces of about 25 people, I decided public speaking was not for me, but I had to at least make a stab at it.

Swallowing hard, I began, "You are all important to the ranch and to me; most of you are like family. You help make this ranch what it is. We have always tried to do right by you and make your life as comfortable as possible. But now, we're facing an epidemic that could endanger all our lives. We must isolate ourselves from the rest of the county for protection. If you must leave, do so today, but know that you cannot come back until this tragedy is over. John and Lani will talk about the precautions we will take to prevent this scourge."

About that time, Dr. Johnson's surrey pulled into the clearing next to the crowd of people. He stepped down, taking his buggy whip with him, in a threatening manner.

"Dr. Johnson," Lani said. "What brings you way out here?"

"It is my understanding that, after all these years, you have employed a Yankee doctor as your official doctor." His face was beet-red and the veins bulged in his forehead.

"Well, that's not entirely true, doctor," I started.

"What *is* entirely true, Mrs. Walton?" he blurted.

15

"We have employed Dr. Billings when you cannot come this far out," I said, calmly.

I could see the disdain in Lester's and Abigail's faces, as they turned their shoulders away from the doc. A slight slight I would call it as no one else would have noticed it.

"I demand to have your loyalty now that the yellow fever is upon us. The planets are aligned so that the fever will destroy many lives."

"The planets are aligned?" came the voice of Dr. Billings from behind Dr. Johnson. "And how would you treat that ailment, Dr. Johnson?"

"You goddamned, sniveling pup of a Yankee. You don't belong here," he yelled, and took after Doc Billings with his buggy whip.

Doc Billings was young and spry and sprinted away, while John took the whip from Doc Johnson.

"Lord have mercy," Loretta whispered to Samuel. "Will our only two doctors kill each other?"

Lani took control of the crowd and calmed them down. After all, we had enough panic with the epidemic, without two healers going at each other.

"We will be using both doctors. There are many different ideas on what is causing Yellow Jack and we will hear both of them out," he said firmly.

So, the two doctors took the stage (or wagon) one at a time and put forth their ideas. I had to admit, Doc Johnson sounded like a quack, talking about the planets and burning charcoal pots the livelong day and night. Doc Billings made more sense, speaking about mosquitoes and standing water. But we had to consider everything. Nine of our workers left us after we talked and we were sad to see them go, as work would be harder with fewer hands. And we didn't know if we would ever see them again. We all shook hands and many had tears in their eyes as they thanked us.

For the ones who stayed, I reckoned it was because they were single men and would rather take their chances on the ranch, rather than traveling the backroads trying to get home, if they had a home. And I would bet they needed the money, small as a ranch hand's salary was. Room and board kept them fed and warm, even though they lived in a bunkhouse with other men.

The sound of horse hooves resounded from the pasture area and all heads turned to see Crandall Levins riding his horse full gallop, stopping quickly by the round pen.

"It's Bill the Bull," he shouted. "Someone slit his throat."

Running to the barn, I screamed at the top of my lungs, "No." Bill had been birthed by me in a pasture. I had raised him from a baby and he was as gentle as a lamb. Why would anyone kill Bill the Bull? He was like a puppy dog, never a threat to anyone, even though he was threateningly large in size.

Lani helped me saddle my horse. Tears were brimming in my eyes, but I brushed them away, barely able to see or think. As he saddled his horse, I turned mine and raced toward the pasture gate. Crandall rode ahead of me to show the way. In a far pasture, Bill lay dead, not butchered, just murdered. I stepped from my horse and fell to the ground, hoping to feel a heartbeat, but there was none. Anger was building inside me and I wanted to hit someone. I felt my heart had been ruptured. He was the sweetest bull, who followed me everywhere, even when he was older and I was in the pastures. Bill probably stood still while someone slit his throat, not expecting that anyone could do such a thing. And who would expect it? Only a damned coward could do that!

"Tommy Emmons," Lani whispered. "He will get his due. Sally, send John with some shovels and we'll bury him."

Mounting my horse, I rode the long way back to the barn alone, sobbing as I went. We were ranchers and butchered cattle all the time, so I felt silly, but Bill was my pet and Tommy Emmons knew how I loved him. I believe I could have shot Tommy myself if I had known where he was, the evil devil, who was probably a long way from the ranch.

When I reached the barn, only Loretta and Dr. Billings were left standing by the wagon. After I found John and gave him Lani's request, I joined them.

"Walk with me, ladies," the doc said.

Loretta and I joined arms and followed him down a path to the woods.

"You see those air plants in the oak trees? They hold water, places where mosquito larvae dwell. We need to cut down as many of those as possible, especially close to the house. My doctor associate in Tampa says he has noticed more daytime mosquitoes. If that's so, it's a new breed of insect, probably brought in to the Port of Tampa. We've talked about ditches and mud holes, but we can do nothing about the lake. Now, I brought you a gallon crock of apple cider vinegar. Use it often and spread it generously over your skin. That's about the best we can do for now. I'll check back with you in a month or so."

"Take what you need from the smoke house, Doc. And we can't thank you enough," I said.

"And that aloe vera plant, either cut it down or soak the water out of the center. It's no better."

"We need it," Loretta said. "I'll dab out the water. We use it for cuts and burns, of which we have a lot."

"And the smoky fires. They probably won't hurt, as mosquitoes don't like smoke," he said.

"Except we're going into July and it's hot as Hades," I said.

Doc Billings headed to the smoke house, and Loretta and I trudged to her kitchen, my salty tears still falling for Bill.

"I'm so sorry, honey," Loretta said. "What on earth was Tommy thinking?"

"Thinking? Do you really think a cretin like him has a brain to think with? Why, he called me a whore."

Loretta sucked in her breath and blanched as white as her hair had turned in the past few years. She was nigh onto 60, I believed. Still pretty as a flower, and a lady through and through, even though we had been through hell together, leaving Atlanta in the middle of a war, facing adversity, and losing many of our loved ones. She was my dearest friend, but we were both getting older. I knew we had a bigger battle to face now, with the Jack breathing

18

down our necks. Kissing her on the cheek, I hurried to my house, vinegar crock in hand, to check on my girl, Sarah. As I left Loretta, she was tying a dishrag to a long-handled wooden spoon, to sop water out of the aloe.

Chapter 4   HIS DUE

*O*n July 28, 1888, the population of Jacksonville was struck down with yellow fever. It was a town of 130,000 people and within a week only 14,000 citizens were left, and many of them were dying. Some left on trains, some by ship, some in wagons, and of course, the poverty stricken were walking. Georgia would not let them into their state and gave orders that the Floridians be shot on sight. This was information which we heard through the grapevine, from the postmaster and train employees who went to our church.

We saw evidence that many refugees camped in our pastures. Cattle were slaughtered, mostly the babies, because they were easy to butcher and carry away, chickens were stolen, the garden was raided, all in the dead of night. There were three dogs on the ranch at that time but they couldn't be everywhere; we could hear them baying in the distance in the dead of night. It reminded me of the days of the Civil War, when thieves (Yankee and Rebel) raided our garden and the smoke house almost daily. What bothered me most was not the theft, but the fact that if they were infected with the fever and were bitten by a mosquito, would that insect now bite one of us?

Or were they bringing the new mosquitoes with them? So many questions and so few answers.

Armed guards were posted in the pastures, around the chicken coops, and in the garden, but this was stretching our men too tight, as we were more than half the manpower we had been, so everyone had to take a watch, even me. John and Lani set about cutting down the air plants, leaning wooden ladders against the limbs and climbing up, machete in hand. They then threw a whole passel of the plants into the fire that we kept burning in the center of the clearing, with smoke billowing out all around like storm clouds. The fire hissed and spat at us, but I was hoping those larvae were frying.

One evening, Lani and I took the pasture watch, wearing bandanas, long sleeves, gloves, and vinegar on any exposed skin. On nights when it was just the two of us, I didn't bother with a skirt over my breeches, since just wearing clothes was scorching hot. We packed our bedrolls and a canvas tent just in case we got tired. Most of the cattle were still in the far pastures as that was where the best grass was at that time of the year. It was a low area and still moist from the rains – good for grazing, but not so good for insect control. We rode until about midnight with no trouble and then, as we were turning around to make another circle, an acrid odor filled my nostrils, the smell of burning green pinewood and moss.

"I smell it," Lani whispered before I even said a word. We both pulled our rifles out of the scabbards at the same time and turned our horses toward the smell. In order to get to that part of our land, we had to go through another gate and ride toward the river where it circled around. The closer we got, the stronger the smell, but flames could not be seen.

Down by the river, in a little clearing we could see a bedroll, which looked like the body of one person. As we got down, my horse neighed and we could hear a pistol cock.

"State your business," a man's voice came through the brush.

"Lani Walton, owner of this land. Who goes there?"

"Mr. Walton, I'm in a bad way. Don't come no closer. It's Tommy Emmons."

"Coming in, Tommy. Put down your gun, son."

I threw a couple of fat pine knots, stacked against a tree, on the fire so we could see what we were dealing with. Tommy's face was as red as the flames, glistening with perspiration, and he groaned as he turned toward us, grasping his back.

"My back hurts like it's on fire. I've got the Jack and believe I'm dying," he croaked.

Without thinking, we stepped away from him, gasping. "You need a doctor, Tommy," Lani said.

"Nossir. I need water. So thirsty."

Lani bent down and poured water from his canteen into Tommy's mouth. "Thank you, sir. I'm so sorry I acted badly and left your employ. And I killed the bull," he sobbed. "I am a worthless feller to do such a low thing. I am truly sorry, Miz Walton. I hope God will forgive me 'cause I'll see Him soon."

Lani said, "We'll stay until morning, away from the clearing. If you're no better, we'll send for the doc."

"I don't deserve no kindness, but thank you, sir."

Tommy closed his eyes and slept. While Lani unsaddled his horse, he said, "Sally, I'm ordering you to get on home, away from this disease. I can't have you here."

I continued unsaddling my horse and rolled out our bedrolls, a good thirty feet away from Tommy.

"Do you think I would leave you alone out here with a sick man?" I asked. "We're far enough away from him and we are covered from head to toe against mosquitoes. I won't leave."

"God Almighty, I am married to the stubbornest woman ever born," Lani said.

"Would you be thanking God Almighty or would that be a complaint?" I responded.

He smiled in the darkness, but no answer came from his mouth.

☼

Feeling good that my husband would not leave a man to die alone, even a polecat, made it easier to stay. We slept in all our

22

clothes on a hot August night, with a roaring fire. I pulled the bandana up over my eyes and slipped into a restless sleep.

Tommy was dead by morning, as sad a case as I ever did see. How many times in my life had I had to forgive someone who had harmed me or someone I loved? We buried him on the spot, using a spade Lani carried, so no one could catch what he had - if it was contagious, marking the place in order that we could put a cross up later. I reckoned he wasn't as evil as I had thought, just angry and misguided. And he was not of an adult age yet, too young to die.

"I'm sorry to say he did get his due," Lani said as we rode back toward the compound. "I remember the day Bill was born. I was riding out to find you and there you were, on the ground pulling that little calf out, with your new riding breeches on. Pretty as a gardenia blossom you were, and still are. But you didn't want anything to do with me, and I wanted you so bad I could hardly speak. I never thought you'd come around."

"I wasn't ready, nor over Jacob at that time. But I do love a persistent man," I said.

"You blew into my life like an afternoon thunderstorm, blustery and full of turmoil, but the first time you smiled at me, it felt like a cool breeze on a hot, Florida, summer day," he stated.

"You, my man, are a true poet."

"I feel a song coming on, but it was almost titled 'Everybody Loves Me but the Woman I Love'." He grinned at me.

I laughed but I knew it to be a truth. He took my hand and we stopped the horses for a few minutes. I looked into his eyes and recognized tired when I saw it and knew we would need to get on home. Leaning over, his lips brushed mine and then my horse side-stepped, but we chuckled and trotted to the gate that led to the barn. Since we had ridden most of the night, we had an excuse to go to bed right away, weary to the bone.

"Yellow Fever raged through much of Florida in the spring of 1888, after the mayor of Tampa announced that the disease was present in his city. Alachua County placed guards at all rail and road entrances to the county, and an officer at the county line had

authority to put off the train anyone without a health card or certificate. Nevertheless, Yellow Jack spread, reaching Jacksonville in July, then hitting Fernandina about August. In Fernandina, officials denied yellow fever was present, then called for state help when commerce stopped and looting began. He repeatedly denied yellow fever was in Fernandina, and so the Gainesville Guards were ordered to the stricken city. The guards, singing "We'll Hang the Yellow Jack to a Sour Apple Tree" boarded the Seaboard train for Waldo and Fernandina. Several guards died of yellow fever. Then, in September, yellow fever was declared epidemic in Gainesville. Fear was widespread, and families fled the city before a quarantine was set up and the county line sealed. No one will ever know how many persons died in Gainesville; many were buried in mass graves, and few records were kept. "
Printed in "Frank Leslie's illustrated newspaper" on October 6, 1888.

By the time we read this reprinted article in the local newspaper, all of these things had happened. The weather had finally cooled and we tried to relax, hoping we had avoided the deadly disease, except for Tommy.

CHAPTER 5   BEING A FOOL

"Memories of the past are no better than a dream." Sally Walton

*I*t was close to time for the painted buntings to arrive. Filling the bird feeder hanging on the old oak tree in the front yard was a pleasant task for me. I gathered seeds year round for this joyous event, collard and other vegetable seeds that we had in abundance, corn meal from the grist mill, and different wild flower seeds. Jacob had made me the bird feeder and as I brought it from the barn, my fingers felt his fingerprints on the warm wood of his handy work, and my thoughts were of him and our time together.

The tears flowed as I hung it on the lowest limb, a breeze caressing my cheek, feeling like Jacob's touch. My heart was pained at that moment; how I missed that man. The love in me was so strong, my fingers gripped the ridges in the rough bark of the oak. Had I opened my eyes, I knew I would find Jacob standing there, but to open them and not find him there would have been too big a disappointment. I squeezed my eyes shut and held on.

After a time, I headed to the front porch, where I sat in the rocker and cried. Hoping Lani wouldn't appear at that moment, I knew that sometimes, I just needed to be alone to spend time with my memories of Jacob.

At the very moment I needed her, Sarah came on the porch and sat on my lap, comforting me as only a 7 year old could.

"Are you thinking about Grandpa Jacob?" she asked.

"I am, my girl. How I miss him and the fact that he didn't get to see you as you are growing."

As I said that, a bunting appeared at the feeder. Jumping up, we both started laughing, which of course, chased him away, but we knew he would return. They were hungry from that long flight from the north. Joy replaced my sadness, but I hoped Lani couldn't read my thoughts, as he had a knack of knowing when I was missing Jacob.

☼

My mood was morose after spending time with my memories and Lani always sensed it, feeling that I loved him less than Jacob. I was bad about hiding my feelings. Usually, when he was melancholy he played sad songs on his guitar, but now that was quiet also. He avoided looking me in the eye, which was unusual for him. But I understood: he was living with Jacob's ghost, too.

For me, it was only occasionally, when something stirred a memory. Feeling rejected myself, I felt time would have to heal Lani's wounds. Truly, I loved Lani as much as Jacob, but in a different space of time. And we were all exhausted from the excess work and worry, which made it harder to think properly.

When I was a child and the worries of the world settled in on me and my family, I took to the woods. In these days of turmoil and chaos, the backwoods piney forests settled my mind. Slipping away from the concern of my family was not always easy, but I usually managed at noontime, while everyone was eating.

Saddling and riding my horse, Lem, was the hardest part of disappearing but it was the best feeling when we made it through the gate unnoticed and he galloped at full speed toward the back pasture.

The wind pulled at my hair, and soon it was flowing out behind me, freeing me physically and mentally, releasing the horse also.

Riding fast, we finally had to slow when we came to the gate that led to the lower pastures. I could hear the flowing of the waters of the Santa Fe River as we neared the place where Tommy Emmons had died. Thinking of that night, I wondered if he had family, but now we had no way of knowing. The white cross Lani had placed on the grave was leaning to one side. So, I stepped down and righted it. When I did, I heard a grunting sound, and looked up to see the biggest gator I had ever seen in my life, swimming toward me as I backed up, tripping over the cross I had just straightened. As the gator lunged out of the water, I moved backward like a crab, knowing my time had come. The gator stopped not three feet from me, its pink mouth opened wide, hissing and showing huge teeth, the vile breath spewing toward me. Taking advantage of the moment, I jumped to my feet, with Lem snorting and backing away, catching his reins in the branch of a swamp maple, but I grabbed the reins and literally jumped onto the saddle, turning him away from the sound, dragging the sapling with us. With Lem neighing, breathing hard, and bucking and farting some, I could see he was just as horrified as I was and I steered him toward the piney woods, both of us looking backward the whole way.

The trembling in Lem's body matched my own as we moved away from the river. We rode for a ways until I could feel he was not as jumpy, or myself for that matter. And as we entered a field of golden marsh daisies, Lem began to calm slowly, allowing me to slip my feet from the stirrups and ride with my hands out, my face turned to the warm sun. It was a moment of ecstasy, renewing my spirit and heart. Lem stepped carefully, so I knew he was gaining peace too.

It was not my intention to rest, but to compose my mind for the oncoming yellow fever onslaught and to recover from the encounter we had just had, and to guide my family as I had on the trail out of Georgia.

Spreading my bedroll on the cushiony pine needles, I ground-reined Lem, my thoughts on the trip that I had traveled with my family during the war. Anytime we had slept on the pine needles, it had been a good night's sleep.

The odor of the pine tar wafted on the air and the song of the pines was blowing in the wind, the dappled sunlight shining on my face, which caused me to drift into a half-sleep, where Jacob stood in the trees, calling to me. He was smiling and motioning for me to come to him, but I couldn't move my legs. I called to him, "Jacob, wait for me."

"Sally?" Lani said. "What are you doing out here?"

I awoke with a start, thinking to see Jacob, and sorry to be disappointed in seeing Lani. He saw the look on my face and read the meaning.

"I. I was needing some alone time," I ventured.

"Clearly I can see that. Are you done with me, Sally?" he said, quietly.

Standing, I brushed the needles from my tangled hair, which was hanging to my back side. I tried to wrap it up and tame it some, but it was useless.

"Lani, it's just a passing memory that won't let go. You are my husband now."

"I fear you don't love me as you did him."

"I do, but sometimes the memories are so strong, I can't help how I feel, but it won't last."

"What shall I do if it does, stay with a woman who lives in the past?" he whispered. "You were calling to him."

His heart was beating fast as I stepped to him and put my hand on his chest. He took my hand and held it to his cheek.

"You've got to be mine alone. Jacob is not here, Sally."

"You would leave me?" I asked, anxiously, afraid of the answer.

"I can't leave you, but I can't have half a woman. And that's what you are right now. There was a time I would have accepted anything from you, but not now that I have known what you can be fully," Lani said wistfully.

Standing on tip-toe I tried to kiss him, but he turned away. "I see," I said.

"It's dangerous out here. Ride back with me," he said.

"I love you, Lani. Please give me a little time."

Not a word was spoken as we trotted back to the barn. Missing my old Lani, I realized I would have to be the one to change. After all, memories of the past are no better than a dream. And I realized I had enjoyed living in the past; it gave me time with Jacob. I was a fool…again.

At the ranch, Suzanna had not been her cheery self since she returned from the so-called "honeymoon." Her mornings were filled with hanging her head in a bucket until she could hold down some mint tea. I certainly remembered that dreadful feeling but I had to say, I was overjoyed that I would have another grandchild.

"Does Auntie have the Jack?" Sarah asked me one morning. How that made me laugh.

"Not quite that serious, my honey-girl," I said, as I cooked breakfast.

John came in from the barn looking worn-out from riding the pastures all night. He had not been pleasant lately, what with the excess work, Suzanna's sickness, and wanting to return to the cabin for some much-needed privacy.

"When can we move back to the lake house? There's always mosquitoes unless we have a hard freeze. We can't live here forever," he said as he poured his coffee.

"Well, you certainly can't take a chance with Suzanna now that she's in the family way."

That brought a smile to his face at last. "Aw, you're right, Ma. Thanks for reminding me."

Suzanna stepped into the room just then, pushing her red hair out of her eyes, walking to John and putting her arm around his shoulder as he sat at the table. He pulled her to him and hugged her, saying, "I need to count my blessings more. You are my biggest blessing, Suzanna."

"And soon to be a bigger blessing," she said, laughing. We all laughed.

Chapter 6 POLLY MILLER

"Miz Walton, come quick. There's a sick boy by the gate," Crandall Levins called to me from the back porch.

Throwing a shawl over my shoulders and grabbing a bandana for my face, I followed Crandall to the front gate.

"Says he has a letter for Mr. Walton. But he looks like he has the Jack to me. Better steer clear of him."

"Well, I can't very well do that, now can I?" I said, perhaps too harshly.

On the other side of the wooden gate, in the edge of the bushes, lay a small boy, maybe eight years of age. His breath was ragged, he was drenched in sweat, and could barely lift his head. I knew it was the Jack and yet I couldn't turn away from him. Kneeling beside him, I pulled the bandana over my nose and mouth.

"Son, what's your name?" I asked. He just blinked his eyes and turned his head away, probably thinking I was a bandit.

Well, here was a dilemma: How could I care for this boy and not risk the lives of myself and my family? But I couldn't let him die here alone either. I had to develop a plan quickly.

"Help me get him to the lake cabin, Crandall, and then send someone for Doc Billings."

"But Miz Walton," he started.

"If you're afraid, then go get someone else," I said sternly.

Pulling his bandana up over his face, he lifted the boy and carried him through the gate.

"Mr. Walton won't like this," he said.

I followed after the two of them as we headed down the path toward the lake. The cabin was isolated enough that I could tend to the boy, hoping I would not be exposed. I knew Mr. Walton would not like it either, but it was done now.

Crandall laid the boy gently in the brass bed, but then left immediately to send for the doc and, I'm sure, to notify Lani of my breaking the rules. Sometimes, men rankled me as I was the boss, even though I knew this might not be the best decision. As I was stripping the boy's ragged clothes off, Lani threw open the front door.

"Get away from him, Sally. More'n likely he has the Jack. What are you doing anyway?"

"Before you make any accusations, Mr. Walton, you better read a letter he has for you."

Lani picked up the note that I threw at him. Even though I hadn't read the letter, I suspected the content of it. He ripped it open in a fury and sat in a chair to read it.

"No. No. This can't be," he whispered.

When I picked it up, he stared at the sleeping boy.

Dear Mr. Lanier Walton, This is your son, Jasper Miller, my last name, born May 15, 1880. I am dying of the yellow fever and you are the only one I can send him to. Please take good care of him, as he is a sweet little fellow. Sadly, Polly Miller

Well, I had to sit down myself, even though I suspected something like that. Who was Polly Miller? I had to count back the years and remember when Lani and I started courting, but in 1880 I was still married to Jacob.

"Water, please," a little voice croaked, and I ran for a bucket of water at the well by the barn. When I returned, Lani was sitting on the bed, wiping sweat off the boy's head. I poured a glass of water and handed it to Lani and he held the boy up and helped him to drink. But he collapsed back into the feather pillow, his little head almost disappearing.

We took turns mopping his forehead with cool water, careful not to make eye contact with each other, but I was seething inside. Hadn't he always told me I was the woman he loved? How irresponsible was it to have a child and not take care of him? I was fit to be tied.

"Sally, let me explain," Lani whispered.

"I'd say we're about even right now. At least I've been honest with you," I said through clenched teeth.

"I didn't know about the boy. Polly Miller was the widow I used to visit in town. She never told me about him and then she moved away."

"You were married to Jacob at the time," he continued. "I thought there would never be a chance for me. I am a man, you know. She was a very sweet lady and was missing her husband, but she knew I didn't love her."

Even though what he was saying was the truth, I was steaming. My feelings didn't make any sense atall and I just wanted to slap him. But this boy was sick and I was hoping I hadn't killed off all the people I loved by bringing him on the ranch.

"Powdered cinchona bark. Mix it with a little guava jelly to counter the bitterness. That's all I can offer to help the symptoms. Same thing we prescribe for the ague," Dr. Billings said. He looked so very tired that I reckoned folks didn't much care if he was a Yankee when they were sick. People aggravated me when it came to common sense, but then I was aggravated long before the doctor arrived.

"Will someone stay with him? He needs constant care, especially since he's so young. Where are his parents?" the doctor asked.

"We'll take turns watching him. His mother died over in Waldo and sent him to us," I said.

32

"An orphan then? How very sad. Just try to keep him cool and keep your mask on."

Lani walked the doc back to his wagon while I decided how this should be handled. When he returned, he said, "If he's my son, I will be responsible for him."

"What do you mean if?" I asked.

"Sally, I do not know for sure if he's mine. But nonetheless, he's my responsibility. I'm trying to understand why you are so angry as this happened long before we courted."

"I don't know why I'm so angry. I just thought you were always in love with me."

"I was, since the first day I laid eyes on you. But you were not available. Polly Miller was not the only woman I spent time with. There were others. I told you that."

"And since we married?"

"You know better than to ask a question like that. We have not been apart since we started courting. Gol-durnit, Sally, you do take the starch out of a man."

He stormed out of the cabin and left me with a very sick child. We now had turmoil on the outside and the inside. But I was not backing down, as unreasonable as I seemed, even to myself.

Two startlingly blue eyes stared at me as I entered the cabin, taking my turn at watching Jasper. They were sunken in his head but had mostly been closed for the last week. I walked to the bed and felt his forehead, which was cool to the touch, making me smile at him.

"Hello, Jasper. Are you feeling better?" I asked as I removed the bandana from my face.

"No ma'am. I think I'm dying."

"Well, your fever's broken. That's a good sign. Let's see if we can get some broth in you."

"Won't do no good. The Jack took my ma," he whispered.

I took his bony hand in mine, light as a bird's wing. "I believe you might make it, Jasper. We just have to have a little hope." He squeezed my hand weakly.

Trying to see a trace of Lani in him, I studied his gaunt face, ravaged by the fever. "Can you sit up?" I asked.

Fluffing the pillows, I propped him in a sitting position, but he was not strong. The broth was lukewarm and he obediently drank from the spoon I offered. His blonde hair was dirty and his body smelled of sickness, but I was worried about bathing him until he was stronger. There were no smiles in him, but how could there be - a child thinking he was dying, losing his mother, and being in a stranger's house? I wondered if he knew Lani was his father.

"How did you get to our gate and where did you come from," I asked.

"I walked through the woods from Waldo. My ma told me how to come and said I must ask for Mr. Lanier Walton."

"That's not possible, for a boy to walk that long way by himself," I replied.

"My ma said Mr. Lanier Walton was my pa. I had to make it, to meet him before I died."

My breath caught in my throat as I listened to the child, thinking of the trials of making it on that long journey, knowing his mother was dying. What a brave thing for him to do. I felt a great compassion for him, at his young age, for making that perilous trip.

"Mz. Sally, am I an orphan? What is an orphan anyway?"

"Well, honey, an orphan is a child without parents, but I would say you are not an orphan since you have a pa."

"Does he want me?" the boy asked.

It was a question I couldn't answer, but I was hoping Lani would do the right thing. I said, "If he's really your pa, he has to want you, right?"

"Right," he said, smiling.

Lani came in then with the tin tub, kicking the door shut with his boot. We both jumped, Jasper and me, as the quiet of our soft conversation was interrupted.

"The boy smells like sickness. We need to clean him up and wash the bedding. Put your bandana on, Sally," Lani ordered.

"His fever is gone," I said.

As soon as I put the the water to boil on the cook stove, I went to Lani and hugged him to me, trying to make amends. He responded in kind, relaxing both of us.

"Sally, you're a good woman, the best. I cannot love you anymore than I do at this moment."

"He knows you're his pa," I whispered in his ear. "He's a good boy, Lani. We can take him in. He needs our family now and he's going to make it."

Standing back, I looked Lanier in the eye, trying to read his face. A smile broke loose and we both laughed. "I love you, Lanier Walton, more than you'll ever know."

"Only my enemies call me Lanier," he drawled.

We both smiled as we stripped the boy of his clothes and the bed of the sheets and covers.

Jasper was a boy of incredible stamina, weak as water and yet determined to regain his strength, once he realized he would not be joining his mother in heaven.

No one was allowed in the cabin but Lani and me, and we tried to steer clear of all the other folks in our compound. Lani stayed with his son at night and I stayed during the day. Not only tending to his physical needs, I also read to him and we had polite conversation.

Of course, I had to neglect Sarah at that time; however, I knew Suzanna and Loretta would be taking care of her. But Sarah was anxious to meet Jasper and, at times, I caught her down by the lake, trying to look into the cabin. She might have been a little jealous that I was spending so much time with another child. Shooing her away, I was not certain she knew how very dangerous the lakefront was just then.

Jasper was up and walking, though he tired easily. But he surely smelled better since he had a bath and looked better, too. Effortless charm are the words I would use to describe him, asking many questions and smiling at the answers, a smile to break a heart. Blue eyes had always been my weakness and all he had to do was look at me and I melted. Many times we sat in the sunshine on the dock. He had a yellowish look about him and I thought the natural light would help his jaundice.

Everyone on the ranch was anxious to meet Jasper, but I wanted to wait until the doc gave him a clean bill of health – just to be certain he was not contagious. And, I enjoyed our time together, just the two of us.

At the end of a month, he was better and I was in love with the boy. Loretta brought us some of young Samuel's clothes (now called Sam).

"My mama was a sewing lady and made clothes for the fancy ladies of St. Augustine. But she made me clothes, too, only I lost my bag on the way here," Jasper said, as tears filled his eyes to the brim.

"Oh, darling, I'm so sorry." I pulled him to me and hugged him, but he tried to be brave and wiped his eyes with his sleeve, which was much too long for him.

After Dr. Billings said he was our miracle boy, we moved Jasper into the main house, where he slept in the same room with Sarah. And I could see she wanted to take care of him, such a nurturing soul she was. Sam was happy to have someone to play with, but Jasper was not yet strong enough for the rough play that Sam liked. So, they had to take it easy with him, although Jasper didn't like to admit he couldn't keep up. I reckoned I was more protective of him than even my own children or grandchildren.

Chapter 7   *TIME IS THE GIFT*

*"Tomorrow is the new moon: and thou shalt be missed,
because thy seat will be empty." I Samuel 20:18*

*D*r. Billings issued only two health certificates to our ranch,
one for Lani as head of the ranch, and one for Samuel as head of the
gristmill. They were the only two people who could go to Alachua
for supplies. Usually it was the counties that issued the health cards
but some towns within counties posted guards, too. Alachua was one
of them. The cattle could not be shipped out, the cornmeal could not
be sold; therefore, our income was limited, not to mention the fact
that many calves had been butchered by fleeing refugees, which
would have been our future herds.

When Samuel rode by and waved, driving the old wagon to
town to buy corn from the farmers, a chill passed through my body.

He had become more and more crippled as the years went by, the old wound from the war always worsening. But they were stockpiling cornmeal for when the quarantine was lifted. As I waved back, I wondered why I worried about him. He could outwork any man, young or old, or able-bodied.

Loretta came through the back door as we were finishing supper, looking worried.

"I feel he should have been back by now. The sun is setting," she said of Samuel.

"I'll ride down the road aways. See if he's in trouble," Lani said.

As we cleaned the dishes off the table, Lani saddled his horse and followed the path Samuel had ridden earlier. He was tired from the long day's work, but he and Samuel had become close in the past few years and I could see he was worried. Of course, no one could take Jacob's place as Samuel's friend, but still, he and Lani were good friends.

It's funny how thoughts came to me so many years later and I realized that Samuel had to have been devastated by Jacob's death, and yet he never spoke a word about him, not even the mention of his name. Men and women are so different in how they carry their feelings; most women wear them on their sleeve and most men have them bound up in their hearts.

Loretta helped me wash the dishes and though she was a person much like a man with her emotions, she had come to trust me and we could talk about most everything. She was somber and I knew her thoughts were on Samuel.

"Five miles I rode, until almost midnight, with no light but for the moon, and still I didn't come across him. I'll strike out again in the morning," Lani said as he stumbled into the bedroom, just as the rooster crowed.

"There's something bad has happened since Samuel didn't return last night. He's never been away from me since the war," Loretta said as she came in the back door before the sun was up.

Lani was already dressed, drinking coffee. John was standing with him, ready to go also. I reckoned John would go as far as he could, hoping Samuel was between Alachua and our ranch, since John couldn't go beyond the city limits. But I also knew those laws would be broken, if necessary.

Pacing for a few minutes, Loretta and I then set to working, knowing we needed to stay busy. Suzanna joined us and sleepily asked where John and Lani were going.

"Looking for Samuel," Loretta said, sighing heavily.

"Oh no. Where is he?" Suzanna asked.

"We don't know. Didn't come home last night," I offered.

As I was stoking the cook stove, Loretta put her hand on mine. Tearfully, she said, "Time is the gift, isn't it, Sally?"

"Yes, it is. But you will have more time with Samuel," I said, not certain of my words.

"I don't think so, this time," she whispered.

Quietly, she slipped out the back door, ambling back to her log home across the clearing from us. As I prayed to God, I had a dreadful feeling about Samuel.

We heard the sound of the wagon before it arrived, Lani driving and John following on his horse. Samuel's body was laid on the bed of corn, all our fears confirmed.

The wagon wheel had collapsed, throwing Samuel from the seat, with the wagon and load of corn falling on top of him, crushing him to death. A stronger, more agile man could have jumped free of the wagon. The mules went over with the whole thing into a ditch, one having to be shot.

Loretta walked to the wagon, not a tear in her eye, touching the limp hand hanging over the edge.

"My Samuel, how I have loved you," she whispered, kissing his hand.

heavy-bellied Rebecca saw her father lying lifeless on the wagon bed. She was inconsolable, waddling, being in the family way. Sobbing as she walked, she pounded the wagon with her fist, collapsing to the ground and all the while, Loretta stared into air, dry-eyed. I knew the feeling.

"I'll prepare a place for him until we can bury him," Loretta said calmly.

Nathan talked Rebecca into leaving, with Sam holding onto her skirts, crying also. John and Lani carried the body into Loretta's home. My feelings had drained right out of me, like water through a broken dam.

I had known Samuel since I was 16 years old. Not a better, kinder man had ever lived. He was father to my best friend, Elizabeth, who had died our first year in this place. Quiet-spoken but wise when he spoke, Samuel's presence was always felt in a room, and his counsel was needed by both Jacob and Lani, along with my sons.

Rebecca wanted to blame Dr. Billings for not giving the health certificate to a younger, stronger man, but I knew that was grief talking. She was distraught beyond reason. Nothing could console her. Loretta, on the other hand, withdrew into herself, as she had done on many occasions. I couldn't fault either of them as I had felt both emotions and reacted much as Loretta had when Jacob died.

A plot of land had been set aside for the family graveyard, Samuel being our first occupant. Our small group gathered around the hole in the earth, Lani softly singing "Amazing Grace" while playing his guitar. The pastor couldn't come, so John and Nathan took turns reading scriptures, while I put my arm around Loretta, knowing it was not the comfort she needed. Still, she did not shed a tear. For as many tears as Loretta did not shed, Rebecca made up for, continually sobbing. She was, after all, her daddy's girl. The Biblical scripture Loretta chose was aptly from I Samuel 20:18. "Tomorrow is the new moon: and thou shalt be missed, because thy seat will be empty."

Sarah and Jasper held my hands as we walked back to the house. Their eyes were wide as they struggled to understand the hard emotions of the folks around them. As we sat on the settee when we returned, Jasper said, "I know why Aunt Rebecca is crying. It was the same for me when my ma died."

"Why Jasper, that's a wise boy who can figure that out. You have great compassion," I said.

"What's compassion?" he asked.

"It's a feeling for other people in your heart. Some folks don't have it."

"I have compassion, Mama," Sarah said.

"Yes you do. I am a blessed mother."

Jasper looked up at me and gulped. "Are you my ma now?" he asked.

"I believe I might be, a chosen mother. Nothing better."

His smile was big but shy, and he snuggled closer to me. We porched ourselves and found joy in the painted buntings. The three of us remained still and quiet as the birds buzzed in and out, feeding voraciously. Such joy and sadness had been experienced on the same day, but I knew that "life is for the living," as Loretta had told me so many times. So I pulled my children closer and reveled in the happiness of the moment, trying to shut out the persistent grief.

The children were taken under Loretta's wing once again. Sam, Sarah and Jasper walked to her house every day for lessons even though it was something she had not done in a long time. She was drowning her grief in work, the same thing I did when Jacob died. It's different when you live with someone every day and then they are there no more; it's a deep emptiness and a person tries to fill it any way they can. And once again, I was pleased she was there for my children.

"I know what you will say, Sally. Life is for the living. It was stupid for me to say that to you," Loretta said.

hope. You will be, too," I replied.

She managed a smile, but I knew how her heart was hurting and I missed Samuel, too. Just his presence had always been so reassuring; such strength in his quiet manner. I knew I shouldn't question God, but I did – to take a man as good as Samuel and leave some reprobates to do harm to others. How was that right? All I could do was try to comfort Loretta and her family without sharing my feelings about fairness. Life was not fair, and neither was death.

November was coming on and I was praying for a freeze, just so we could enjoy our world again. I missed my church friends and family and quilting guild.

In mid-November, my prayer was answered; a heavy frost appeared one morning and I knew it was enough to kill the mosquitoes. I rejoiced in the kitchen that morning while I made breakfast and Lani and I danced around the living room, even though he was not as convinced as I was that the frost would kill them. I think he was just happy to see me happy. The children began to dance and sing songs, which woke Suzanna and she then danced with us, too, while John grumpily pulled on his boots. Too much joy in the morning for that young curmudgeon, but I knew he would soon love moving back to the cabin.

By mid-December, there was no more yellow fever in Alachua County. The barriers were lifted, the guards went home, and I was overwhelmed with joy when I knew we would be able to see all our friends and family at the church in La Crosse. We all vibrated with happiness. It had been six months or more since we had been able to leave the ranch. Even Loretta forced a smile, thinking of the reunions that would take place. Hope drifted through our house like a welcomed summer breeze as Lani strummed his guitar in the parlor, a sound we had not heard in a coon's age, so to speak.

We had not seen David, Annie, and Jake and his family in such a long time and the mail had not run, so we didn't know whether they had weathered the Jack-storm or not.

Frantically I searched the house and compound for Jasper one morning, knowing he usually didn't wander too far from me or his pa. Rushing to the cabin, I found his little self, sitting on the deck, staring out at the placid lake. Hundreds of snowy egrets in the island rookery on the lake were squawking so loud I could hardly hear anything else. The weather had taken a turn for the worst, or best, whichever way a person looked at it. But it was freezing cold and Jasper looked to be shivering. I wrapped my shawl tighter around my shoulders and grabbed him up and rushed him into the cabin where John had built a fire, hoping to warm it so they could move back into it.

"Jasper, what were you doing out there in the cold?" I asked as I added wood to the blaze.

"I was ruminating," he said.

"Ruminating, huh. Where did you learn that big word? From Aunt Loretta?"

"No. Sarah taught it to me. She knows lots of big words."

Taking his shoes and socks off, I rubbed his feet between my hands. Still smaller than the other children, his coloring was never quite healthy-looking and I worried that the Jack had damaged his organs. The only thing I could think of to treat him with was Thedford's Black Draught.

My medicines consisted of aloe for the skins and cuts, Black Draught for the intestines and liver, and whiskey for pain. Sometimes Abi would mix up some herbs for me, but I didn't know what was in them.

"My mama, I can't remember what she looked like," he said, sniffling.

"Why, darling, I'm sure we can locate a picture of her somewhere. Are you missing her?" I asked.

"I loved my mama, but I love you, too. I don't want her to think I love you more than her."

with your pa and me. She knows I love you as much as if you were my own, and you are my own now. Don't you worry, my boy. She guided you to us. I will write to that photography studio in Alachua and see if he took a picture of her. You just need to know that we love you so much and you belong in this family. And Christmas is coming and we're going to church and you will get to meet all the rest of the family and our friends."

And by saying that, it gave me great comfort, too. Those huge blue eyes stared back at me, melting me, and I hugged him close for warmth and encouragement, for both of us.

Later that day, I mentioned the conversation to Lani and he said he had a picture of Polly in his treasure box. Well, that floored me again. But I guess we both had ghosts we had to deal with.

"She gave it to me, Sally. I didn't want to throw it away. And she was such a pretty little thing," he said with a wicked grin.

"Lani Walton, you are a scoundrel for sure. But let's get that picture framed for that boy. And please, let's not discuss your relations with pretty Polly again," I said.

"You really love that boy, don't you, Sally?" he asked.

"I'm afraid I do, madly, just like his pa."

"I have never met a woman like you. You tear my heart right out of my chest. Guess I had better write another song."

He hugged me to him and I melted into his arms. Love sure was a fickle thing.

Chapter 8   *JOY, GREAT JOY*

*M*y quilts always came in handy on the carriage rides, especially for the excited children sitting in the back seat. Sarah sat in between her cousin, Sam, and her "chosen" brother, Jasper, holding each of their hands. They talked and laughed constantly and my heart swelled with love for each of them. Lani drove with a smile on his face, contented with our new family.

"I just never thought I would be blessed with children and a wife," he said quietly.

"You are a blessing to us, Lanier Walton. I love you so very much," I replied. Leaning into me, he kissed me on the top of my head.

It was Christmas Eve day, 1888. We had come through the storm once again and had emerged on the other side. Our enthusiasm was as high as our childrens', but we were quieter. My heart was beating out of my chest to see all my friends and family. As we pulled into the churchyard, people ran to us, calling greetings and there, in the midst were David and Annie, Jacob's brother and sister-in-law. Lani helped me down and I rushed to them, crying as I went, so happy they had not been harmed by the epidemic. Annie and I could not let each other go, sobbing into each other's shoulders.

Lani, who had been David's foreman for many years, shook hands with him and they were reluctant to release each other also. Then Jake, their son, and his wife and three children came up and we started hugging all over again. Sam jumped down and ran to Jake's children, while Sarah and Jasper looked on from the seat in the carriage.

"Who is this handsome young man?" David asked.

"Why this is Jasper, Lani's son, and now my son, too," I said.

Eyes widened and Annie said, "We have some catching up to do. So glad you made it through the fever. Can you stay the night?"

"We were hoping you'd ask," Lani said.

Just then, Loretta and her family drove into the churchyard and we began the greetings all over again.

"And Samuel?" Annie asked. We could not bring ourselves to say the words. The tears flowed from every eye, and silence engulfed us.

Annie said, "We will talk later."

As the singing began inside the church, we hurried into the warmth and I thanked God for his many blessings instead of questioning Him about Samuel's death. Lani and I held our children's hands and sat in the back pew since the church was packed full of folks, smiling and singing carols. I was certain Annie would give me the low-down on who passed during the epidemic. I did see Dr. Johnson and his wife on the front row, though he wouldn't look me in the eye, the old coot. Then, I had to ask for forgiveness – being in the Lord's house and thinking that way about our town's healer. I never could seem to bring my thoughts in line with the proper teachings of the Bible the way some folks could, but I was trying.

☼

As we stood on the church steps, I held Sarah's hand in mine while Jasper and Sam ran to play with the boys in the meadow across from the church grounds. Sarah had just pulled her hand from mine and bounded down the stairs toward the boys when a horse and carriage came flying by the front of the stairs. I screamed "Sarah" but it was too late. The horse's chest knocked her down and she rolled into a ball between his legs. Luckily, he stepped wide to avoid her, but she was under the carriage and we couldn't see if the wheel had hit her.

Lani ran to her like a mad man, picked her up in his arms, and carried her inside the church, placing her on a pew. Dazed and disoriented, she called to Jasper, who took her hand. Her arm was bruised and had turned dark almost immediately.

Dr. Johnson came running in and told everyone to step aside while he checked her eyes. "No brain bruising, which is good," he said. "But that arm looks badly bruised. I'll put it in a sling."

"Damn fool, driving like a maniac!" Lani yelled as he paced in the aisle. "Who was that scoundrel?"

My heart was beating hard, knowing I could have lost my girl, but she was smart because she was aware of horses and had missed his feet, and the wheels. She smiled at me, "I'm okay, Mama. That was a good horse."

It happened that the boy driving the carriage was just learning to drive and the horse had gotten away from him. Lani read him the riot act, along with his parents. He was red in the face when he came back into the church. Sarah was his favorite and I could see he was shaken.

As we were leaving to go to David and Annie's, Dr. Billings, whom I hadn't noticed, whispered in my ear, "Cold compresses." I smiled and thanked him. He had to be careful around Dr. Johnson, but I liked that young man immensely.

Chapter 9   ALLIGATOR PEARS

Sarah was more traumatized than hurt physically, although the bruise on her arm was as dark as a stormy thunder cloud. Once we reached David and Annie's, I pulled a bucket of cold water from the well and soaked a cloth in it for a compress, which I changed as soon as it warmed up. Annie insisted we put Sarah in bed to rest so she wouldn't develop the humors. I could hear Lani tuning his guitar as he and Jasper kept Sarah company. He began to sing: "Go to sleepy little baby. Go to sleepy little baby. When you wake, you shall have a cake. So, go to sleepy little baby." Jasper and Sarah giggled and Jasper said, "She's not a baby."

That song was so nostalgic for me. My mother had sung it to all her babies and I sang it to all of mine. I remembered Elizabeth singing it to baby Jake when he was small, also.

"I love that lullaby, don't you, Sally?" Annie asked me.

"Oh yes. I just hadn't heard it in so long. I thought my mother made it up, but I guess not," I said.

We set the table and John unloaded our wagon with the pies and smoked turkey we had brought. I tried not to think about our first Thanksgiving in this land, before the war was over, not wanting to drift back to those early days again, when we were so blessed today.

Loretta and her family had gone back home as Rebecca's baby was due any day and they didn't want to be on the road when the baby came. I was hoping they had notified Doc Johnson, since Rebecca blamed Doc Billings for her father's death and wouldn't let him near her. Frankly, I thought she was silly; I trusted Dr. Billings far more but maybe that was my mistake. But no matter, we were happy to spend time with the family and we were all ravenous.

After dinner, I noticed some large seeds sprouting in jars along the windowsill while we were washing dishes.

"What are you growing there, Annie?" I asked.

"Those are alligator pear trees. I'm gonna set 'em out in the spring. They have a very interesting fruit that is not sweet at all. I tried one down in Gainesville last spring before we were quarantined. I liked it a lot and the grocer told me how to sprout it. Take one home with you. The trees get real big but it takes a while before they bloom," she said.

"Thank you. I would like that. That can be my Christmas present," I said.

She smiled. "I can do better than that."

I was thrilled with that idea as we are always looking for new ways to grow food. My pa always said, "If you can't eat it, don't grow it." Smiling at that thought, my pa's face stood before me and I missed him so much at that moment. He had taught me everything I knew before I left home. I guess I couldn't push that memory out of my mind and a tear rolled down my cheek.

Trees had always been a favorite thing of mine. I gathered tree seeds and pinecones and started them in a glass of water and then transferred them to a pot of dirt until they were ready to go in the soil, whether they were edible or not. Alachua County did have some cold weather in the winter time and sometimes it dipped into the freezing temperatures, but not for very long. Wondering if the freeze would kill the alligator pears, I planned to have a whole grove; after all, they were easy to grow and free.

☼

Later in the day when it was just Annie and me, as the men were in the barn and the children were playing quietly in the bedroom, she asked me about Samuel.

"It was an unfortunate accident when the wheel broke and threw him into the ditch and the wagon and load on top of him."

"I reckon I'll have to have a talk with Jake and explain that Samuel was his grandfather," she said quietly.

Taking a quick breath, I said, "I thought he might have known. Does he know about his real parents?"

She sighed. "I just never found the right time to speak of it. David said I should tell him but I couldn't bring myself to do it."

"Oh my. I thought you had," I said. "Well, no need to tell him about Samuel then, except for his death. Perhaps this will have to be a forever secret."

But I didn't feel comfortable with a secret that big; I certainly knew I would never tell. David and Annie had adopted baby Jake when his mother, Elizabeth, and his father, Jake, had died in the first year we came to Alachua County. The older Jake was my father-in-law and Elizabeth was my best friend, with Samuel being her father.

At that moment, Margaret, Jake's wife, stood in the doorway. She had been quietly talking in the bedroom with Suzanna. Her face blanched as she said, "How could you keep this from Jake? You are not his real mother? Samuel was his grandfather? That's so dishonest!"

Annie jumped to her feet. "Margaret, you don't understand. I *am* his mother. Please, please don't tell him. Let me tell him in my own time." For myself, I felt Margaret was out of line.

Suzanna entered the room then, holding her belly, saying, "There's many types of mothers and the best are the ones that want to be a child's mother. If you open this can of worms, Margaret, there will be consequences."

"Still, it is something that should not be a secret," she added.

"Please give David and me some time. We should be the ones," Annie begged. "I know it was wrong. Let me make it right."

As the men came in the back door, Annie made a quick exit to the bedroom, I'm sure to hide her tears. I hoped she would do the right thing, eventually.

Later, David and Annie took a walk with Jake, I reckoned to give him the news before Margaret spilled the beans. When they returned, all three were smiling, which was a big relief to me.

"He already knew. Aunt Loretta told him years ago," Annie announced.

"I have the best parents in the world. I'm sorry my real parents died, but I'm not sorry that David and Annie have been my parents," Jake said.

He was really so much like his real pa, Jake, with his easygoing manner and sense of humor. He kissed Annie on the head and said, "Margaret, gather up the hooligans. We're going home."

We settled in for the evening, feeling content and happy. Sometimes the hardest lessons bring the biggest blessings. I have found that to be true my whole livelong life.

Since we hadn't seen our family in so long, we stayed on for a couple more days. The ladies, including Sarah, quilted around the quilt frame that Annie lowered from the ceiling. We gossiped and laughed, warmed by the fire and the company. Annie told us of all the folks who had died in the epidemic, which was cause for some tears as we knew many of them, especially our quilt guild friends. Since Margaret and Jake lived next door to his parents, Margaret was with us every day, and she and Suzanna were becoming close pals in just the short time we were there. Suzanna had never quilted because she had been a ranch worker, but she was now becoming a lady and was enjoying her new role. Annie was particular about her quilt stitches, so I reckoned she would remove Suzanna's stitches after we left but she didn't let on. She might have removed mine, too, for all I knew, but I was more careful on her quilts than on my own. I was, however, missing Loretta and knew we would need to get back before the baby came.

Jasper tagged along with his pa and the rest of the men as they rode out into the fields, talking new planting techniques and ranching in general. They didn't stay too long as the winds were starting to pick up and we were happy with our female time, warm and cozy and full of pecan pie.

☼

Feeling anxious as we drove home, I hoped all had gone well at the ranch. We so seldom left the ranch, that we worried when we did. As we drove onto the property, Nathan greeted us with, "It's another boy, praise the Lord."

And of all things, Loretta had delivered the baby. She was as proud as a peacock and I was as surprised as I could be. I never thought I'd see the day.

"That old coot, Doc Johnson, couldn't make it and Rebecca won't allow Dr. Billings in the same room," Loretta said, beaming.

We stood around the bed, admiring the newborn and I was proud of Loretta, as she had fainted at Rebecca's first birthing. Another boy to help with the grist mill: that's what Nathan was thinking. As long as they didn't name him Jacob or Samuel, I would be pleased. And so it was Daniel David, directly from the Bible.

Chapter 10 *HARMON MURRAY*

*I*t was January, 1889, and it was as cold as it could get without freezing. The wind swept down on us bitterly, chafing our skin and leaving us shivering. We had had more losses in our herd, and the interlopers always seemed to target the babies, our future herd. We had determined not to ride our men all night long like we did during the epidemic as it was too hard on them.

Lester came to the house early one morning, eyes wide, carrying a rifle, so unlike him.

"Mista' Walton. Think somebody sleepin' in the barn," he said.

Lani jumped up from the table, kicked the chair back, and grabbed his pistol as he charged out the back door, Lester on his heels. I was still in my robe and slippers but I followed them to the barn, shaking from the cold weather the whole way. Lani climbed the ladder to the loft, aiming his gun at the empty space.

"Looks like they lit out. I can see where they slept though. Have to keep an eye out, Lester," he said.

Lani climbed down and wrapped his arm around me as we walked back to the house. "What are you doing out in your night gown, Sally? Do you want to catch your death? Be sure you lock the doors today and I'll put a guard on the gate again. I didn't want to scare you but there's some outlaws running through these parts. Black men. Do not feed anyone who comes to the back door. I mean it now," he said sternly.

"Yessir, Mr. Bossman," I whispered. He pulled me closer. But I knew I would clean my pistol today and wear a dress with a pocket so I could carry it with me again.

Lani and Lester checked the barn every morning and sure enough, someone was sleeping there and leaving long before daybreak. We warned John and Suzanna and especially Loretta, as she was a woman alone. But I knew she could use her rifle, too. Lani and John determined to put a lock on the front and back gate to the barn. Of course, anyone could climb over them but it would make it a little harder.

"Damn gutsy to come in here under our noses, sleeping in our barn, and probably killing some chickens, too," John said. "Found a pile of feathers in the back pasture."

"Maybe we should go after the sheriff. I wouldn't want any of us to shoot them," I said.

"Hell's bells, I'll shoot their asses," John said.

"Well, John, just be certain what you're shooting at," I said. "You might shoot someone you don't want to shoot."

"Hrrmph," he mumbled and walked away.

"I don't know where that boy came from. He is too grumpy to be my son," I murmured.

Lani smiled down at me, a glint in his eye.

"I am not a grump!" I said and huffed off. Well, maybe I was a grump if I was called one, feeling truculent, as Loretta would say.

Rain and wind whipped through the compound. The cattle huddled together for warmth near the fences and we huddled in the house, keeping a fire blazing in the fireplace. After I walked the children to Loretta's, I returned and prepared my quilt squares so we could get the quilt top put together for the quilting guild. It would be our first meeting since the epidemic and I had much work to do, with not one square stitched to the next one. The fire was warm and my chair was set up with my sewing table and supplies next to it. Life was getting back to normal.

When I heard the rapping at the back door, I laid my sewing aside, rushing to open the door. My pistol bumped against my leg as I hurried. Outside in the weather stood a black man about my height, drenched to the bone, trembling. I felt for my gun.

"Awful hongry, ma'am," he said. "Can you help a poor feller out?"

"Have you been sleeping in our barn?" I asked.

"Yes'm. No place to get in out of the storms," he said.

"Where are your pals?" I asked.

"Gone on to Gainesville. My leg is injured and cain't walk too much since I jumped outta the barn loft."

His eyes were hard, his stance threatening, even though he was rain soaked through and through. I fingered my pistol, feeling some fear, but it was hard to let a man starve.

"Wait here. I'll bring you something," I said.

Wrapping up some cold fried chicken in a dish rag, I unlatched the screen door with my left hand, sliding the package through a slight gap. Feeling that was a mistake, I felt comforted as my right hand touched my gun. The man's eyes immediately softened; that's what the smell of food will do to a famished person.

"God bless you, Missy. Nobody ever been that kind to me."

"Don't come back here. Keep moving on to Gainesville with your buddies," I said sternly.

"Yes'm. And thankee. Name's Harmon Murray. 'Member dat name," he said, as he turned to leave.

He did leave and didn't return again. We didn't hear about Harmon Murray again until 1891 when he was shot by another black man. His body was on display for all of Gainesville to see because he had killed and robbed so many people. I was sick when I read that article in the Gainesville Sun newspaper. What a terrible chance I had taken, opening my door to him. But maybe the kindness I

showed him kept him from doing more harm…..or from killing me.
I never told Lani or John about that episode.

Chapter 11 *HELL'S BELLS ANYWAY*

*I*n April a letter came from Lebanon, Tennessee with no return address. I didn't know anyone left in that town but my sister, Beatrice, and I knew she wouldn't be writing to me. She had hated me my whole life and the last written word I had from her was to inform me she was no longer a sister of mine.

As was my habit when I wasn't certain of information in a letter, I placed it on the dining table and walked around it until I felt I could handle the bad news. In this case, I left it the whole day because I had much work to do. We were short of hands and couldn't afford to hire more as our finances were dwindling. Not having many cattle sales in a year and with our herd lessened by the loss of our calves, we were trying to recover. It did hurt to think of those little babies dying at the hands of killers, babies that we had delivered and some we had hand fed.

Lani had sent John and a couple of hands into our unfenced pastures to search for criollos, or wild cattle. And of course, they would go beyond our borders, but as long as they weren't branded, they would be rounded up and brought to the ranch. Lani and myself, along with a few other hands were moving all the Herefords into the larger pastures, leaving one small fenced area for the rangy, wild cattle.

The cracking whips could be heard as John and the boys brought the cattle in, 15 in all, which would be a start. They surely were a scraggly bunch, the cows, I mean; boney and skittish, having eaten only wild grasses and bushes. There was only one bull, but that would be enough and we would fatten them all up with sweet hay and oats. But they were wild-eyed and looked like they would charge right through a fence.

Lani used a whip to drive cattle, but I had not got the hang of that art and had ended up with some pretty painful welts in my attempts, so I just used Lem to herd the Herefords. At the end of the day as we rode back to the barn, we were both tired, but pleased. Working out in the warm sunshine and eating around a fire was very satisfying. And although our finances were worrisome, I knew we could build our resources again. Working hard also kept me from thinking on that letter, which I was certain bore bad news.

"What's on your mind, girl?" Lani asked me as we rode home. Goodness me, but that man was right inside my head. Was my face that readable?

"Just a letter from Lebanon."

"What did it say?"

"I didn't open it."

"You do beat all, Sally. Why wouldn't you open it?" he asked.

"I'm certain it's bad news," I said.

Laughing, he said, "You are a perplexing woman."

Well, I was glad to hear that; I thought he could read my every thought.

The letter lay on the dining table when we returned, but still I could not open it. Since we were so tired, we decided to eat with the hands. Abi and the girls were getting accustomed to us showing up, so they made extra food. Abi made a dessert out of clabber and cane syrup that the children loved...and the men. I, myself, had never cared for clabber alone, but Abi sure could fix it up right, a little sweet and a little sour. Jasper and Sarah loved listening to the stories the men told, eyes wide, grins big. Of course the men cleaned up their language around the ladies and children, thank heaven.

Crandall told the tall tale of the time he lassoed a twelve-foot gator, only to end up playing poker with him. He said, "But the gator lost, and now I have some fine gator-skin boots that I wear when I go to town."

Jasper laughed so hard, but I wondered if he didn't halfway believe the story. His blue eyes were as round as saucers. Boy, could those men spin some outlandish yarns. As pleasant as the evening was, I needed a bath and my bedtime, still leaving that letter in place on the dining table.

After we put the children to bed, I put the kettles on the woodstove and Lani pulled the two tin tubs off the wall. I sank into the warm water and had to fight to stay awake, but Lani was soaking there beside me, talking of the day we had just had, his voice a drone in my ears. When the water started to cool, I stood and he took a towel and started drying my hair and face. The night was dark and I was glad because we were two people standing, looking into air, not seeing but sensing the other person. And suddenly, I was not as tired as I had thought.

February 15, 1889
My darling sister,
I am so very sorry we have not corresponded all these years, but I have truly missed your company. As you may know, my husband passed away a few years ago. I have two sons but they have gone west to seek their fortune. They could not bear to help me rebuild the farm. So, now I am alone.
I am trying to hang on to the land that our grandparents settled but I am finding that the taxes are too much for me to pay. I have sold off some acreage, and have hired two local men to help with the planting and such, but the gains are few.
I do so need your help at this time. If you could see your way to lend me a hundred dollars in order to pay the taxes, I would so be in your debt. After all, these were your relatives, too.

Your loving sister,
Beatrice

Oh my goodness! Lord, give me patience. What a lot of hogwash. I counted the 'I's' in the letter and realized nothing had changed. She was in need of cash, and so now she could be nice to me. I slapped the letter against the table and left the house to feed the animals. At least that was rewarding.

Those little red hens always came running to me whether I had any feed or not. I threw corn on the ground for them and they gobbled it up. Curious to a fault, they made little soft noises and pecked around my shoes. I tried not to get attached to them as I knew we would eventually eat them when they quit laying eggs. But they were comforting to be around, as if they were trying to talk to me. And then there was that rooster, the meanest devil in the world, who thought the hens belonged to him alone. The crowing in the morning was always our wakeup call and always an aggravation.

John had thought to bring in bantams at one point but I wondered at the wisdom of that experiment. The eggs were very small and the chickens themselves were not enough to feed a single man, and they ate as much as a regular sized hen. Once the roosters went at each other, the problem was solved. Now we had only Rhode Island Reds.

"I think we can afford a hundred dollars," Lani said cautiously.

I was fuming and he chose his words carefully. "Maybe it's time to mend old fences."

"Lani, this is a subject you should steer clear of. This person, who is not my sister, has always treated me like trash," I said.

"I thought you said she was your sister. I'm confused."

"Men! You always think there's a simple solution." I left the house, boiling over. I knew there was a reason I didn't want to open that letter. Heading to Loretta's, I felt she could give me some female advice.

60

"Well, the Bible does say we should forgive, but that's a hard one," Loretta said, pacing. We both paced. "Maybe you should ask for a note binding her to the loan," Loretta finally said.

I reckoned I would have to figure this one out by myself. Everyone was trying to help, but I was finding no resolution. Maybe I would help the girls with the wash; that's when I did my best thinking - when I was working.

"Why, hell's bells, Mama. I sure would like some bacon with my grits," Jasper said, smiling politely at me.

"What did you just say?" I asked, in a strict voice.

"Don't be mad at him, Mama. He's been learning to ride with Papa and that's just how the men talk. He doesn't know any better," Sarah offered.

"Sam says hell's bells," Jasper said.

"Well, in this house, you'll get a switching if you cuss. This is a warning, but the next time there will be a switching."

His eyes pooled with tears. I was sorry I had spoken so harshly as we had never had any strong language between us, but he was now my son and I couldn't have him talking like a vulgar ranch hand. People would think we were low class. And I would have a talk with that husband of mine.

Jasper came to me and hugged me around my waist. "I'm sorry," he said. "Please don't beat me."

"No. There will be no beatings today," I said, but I smiled inwardly, realizing the humor in the situation. I knew I could never lift a hand to him; he was like Sarah in that they were easy to reason with and so wanting to please me. After all, that was one of my favorite cuss phrases, too, even though it was only spoken when I was alone or under my breath. But I had to make sure my children knew right from wrong, even though it was questionable in my mind also, not wanting to be a hypocrite.

"Sally, he's going to hear bad language if he rides with the men. I'll try to change my lewd language in front of him and Sam, but I can't control the workers," Lani said.

"Well, at least explain what words not to repeat," I said.

"Aw, hell's bells, Sally, you're as pretty as a lily in the new morning light."

Well, he did make me laugh as I rolled out of bed. "You are trouble, Lanier Walton. But I love you more than my horse."

Grabbing me by my arm, he pulled me back to bed. "Your horse? That's all?" he whispered.

"I said 'more.' I didn't say how much more."

"Wicked woman, you are. Now, let me tell you how much I love you. More than the moon, the stars, the sun, the rivers, my life. But not more than my horse."

I punched him in the chest and left the room, laughing, heading to the kitchen to shore up the wood stove and make some coffee. It was a great way to start the day, smiling. And, I had decided to send Beatrice the money. I would make a small quilt, sew the paper money in the batting and mail it off to her, no strings attached. Of course I would send a separate letter explaining what I was doing. It was such a relief not to carry the burden of anger and unforgiveness.

CHAPTER 12   AN UNWELCOME TRIP

$\mathcal{M}$ail delivery was unreliable since the yellow fever epidemic, but we had a nice little post office at La Crosse in the home of our postmaster. Usually, once a week, I had someone ride in to town and pick up the mail. One morning early, Lester brought the mail to me, a fairly tall stack of letters, some for the workers, but there was a letter from Mary, dated months earlier. She was also asking for money, since Joshua had lost his job and she needed food for the children. Panicking, I rushed to find Lani and tell him of the dilemma. In that period of time, they could have gone hungry.

"Well, pack up the children and let's make a trip of it. I hope they are still living in the same place," he said.

Hurriedly, I threw some clothes in a carpet bag, grabbed some bedrolls, and Lani hooked the team to the carriage. Abi put some food together for us and we were on the road by one o'clock in the afternoon. The children were very excited, but I could see a little worry on Sarah's face.

"Don't worry, honey. We're just going for a visit. You'll not stay with them," I said.

Her smile lit up her face like sunshine. And Jasper, he was just happy to belong to a family and be with Sarah. The adventure was secondary.

"Not a good time to be leaving the ranch short-handed, and with Suzanna's baby coming soon, but this is kind of an emergency," Lani said softly. "We may have to camp out tonight, if we don't make it by dark."

"Seems like all the problems happen at once. I just hope they're all right," I said.

☼

Even though we had a lantern on the carriage, the darkness enveloped us early on. The children slept, wrapped in quilts with their arms around each other. As we pulled into the driveway where Mary and Joshua had lived, I had a sinking feeling. The only light near the house was our light on the buggy.

"Hello, the house," Lani called out. No response. We waited anxiously until a man stepped out on the touchstone in front.

"Late at night to come a-callin," the man said. Being barely dark, I figured farm folks went to bed early, as we did at home.

"Sorry to bother you but we are looking for the Courtlands," Lani said.

"Why, they been gone about a month or so. He took a job at the Tomoka Farms down close to Gainesville."

"I see. Any inns we can stay at in Newberry?" Lani asked.

"Yep. One in town. But you can stay here in the field iffen you want," the man offered.

"We have children. Best to stay at an inn, but thank you just the same. You the new foreman?" Lani asked.

"I am. William Blanding's the name."

"We are the Waltons, parents to Mrs. Courtland, Mr. Blanding," Lani said.

"Were they all right when they left?" I asked.

"Well, seemed to be, although that Joshua has some temper on him. That's how he lost his job," Mr. Blanding replied.

"Oh my," I whispered to Lani.

"Thank you, sir," we both called as we drove away.

☼

At the Newberry Inn, we could only afford one room with two small beds. Sarah slept with me and Jasper with Lani. In the morning I awoke with a crink in my neck and my first thought was worry about Mary and her children. But we could not chase them all over the blessed country; we had our own concerns, both financially and for the people on our ranch. And there was much work to do. I determined to mail her some money when I returned. We were up early and on the road after we had a big breakfast. Jasper and Sarah smiled the whole time. At least the children enjoyed the trip.

Every time I thought of my daughter, Mary, I couldn't help but think of Sarah, my granddaughter. Although I was raising her as my daughter, I could never get over the idea that Mary could give her up without trying to see her every now and then.

Sarah was the perfect child, smart, obedient, hard-working. She loved to grow trees with me and we were both excited to get the alligator pear tree into the ground. When she was given a little bound notebook, she began writing. I had never pursued reading what she wrote, but I knew she was busy all the time. I called her "a sower of words and a planter of trees." And that little girl, who would turn 8 this year, had taught Abi's girls to read. They were so grateful to her, they would have done anything for her, but she was just a nurturing spirit and didn't expect anything in return. Imagine, an 8 year old teaching 20 something year-olds to read, and read well.

Lester and Abi had been slaves who had never learned to read because it had been illegal at one point. But I had a feeling their daughters would, in turn, teach them to read. Sometimes I questioned a world where people were not judged by their character, but by the color of their skin. We loved that family as if they were our family, and yet, when we left our ranch, we couldn't go to church with them and our children couldn't go to school with them. Blaming God got me nowhere; we simply had to live within a made-up set of rules created by other people.

CHAPTER 13   OH MY SOUL

$\mathcal{B}$y the time we returned, Suzanna had had her sweet baby girl, and a boisterous one at that. She could cry louder than any child I had ever seen, maybe because she was a redhead, like her mama. Dr. Billings had come out the day we left and was still there when we returned. Wondering how he was neglecting his other patients, I asked, "Is everything all right with the baby and Suzanna?"

"Oh yes. Big, healthy girl. I was just enjoying the company and decided to stay on a bit," he said.

"Well, you're always welcome here, Doc," I said, but I did think it strange.

John was beaming. Lani teased him about needing boys to work the ranch, but nothing dampened his spirits.

"I believe we can have more," John said.

"Hmmph," was all Suzanna would say.

I held little Fereby Faith, named after Suzanna's mother, and she stretched out in my arms, finally sleeping. She was big and tall for a newborn. Sarah and Jasper hovered over her, each wanting to hold her, but I knew they needed to wash up before they held her with their little grimy hands.

Doc walked with us to the kitchen to see if there were any leftovers from dinner. Abi's girls were cleaning up, but dished up some beef stew, which smelled delicious. I did notice that the young doctor had a hard time focusing on our conversation, seeming to be focused on Fancy, but I determined that was a catastrophe waiting to happen. My heart was in my throat and I was thinking, "No. No. Please God No."

Both girls kept their eyes glued to the floor and did not glance at me, but the doc was beet red, his neck splotchy. Lani had ridden out to the pastures immediately, so it was just the children and me.

"Why's the doctor's face so red, Mama?" Jasper asked.

"Jasper, be quiet," I said. But to the doc, I asked, "What is going on here?"

"I. I. I better be getting back into town," he whispered hoarsely.

Following him to his buggy, I held onto his thin arm and said, "That is a forbidden relationship, sir. You must not pursue this or risk your life and Fancy's. I won't have it."

"I understand," he said.

"I'm not sure you do. This is not Pennsylvania. It is the South and you could be hanged. Do you hear me?"

"I thought you might understand, being the kind, compassionate person you are."

"Have you been seeing her?" I asked, breathing hard.

"Not so anyone would know."

"Oh my God in heaven. You must put an end to it. I can't allow you to come back here and put her at risk. She is my responsibility," I said testily.

"I would marry her."

"Are you daft? Have you not been listening? Stay away from her."

"I can't. I love her," he said, plaintively.

"You must unlove her. I don't know any other way to say it. You are banned from coming on my ranch!" I nearly shouted.

"I thought you liked me," he whispered, a tear rolling down his pale cheek.

"Leave now. I forbid you to see her again," I said, angrily.

As he rode away, I felt like screaming. People were so stupid when they were in love, if that's what it was.

"Oh my soul! Oh my soul!" Abi moaned, sitting at my dining table. "She done gone and got herself in the fam'ly way with a white man!"

Well, I had said nothing to anyone, not even Lani, but I guess the good doctor was as headstrong as a bull. Or maybe Fancy was driving the relationship.

"She gone have a white baby, Missy. She say he gone marry her and take her to Pennsylvania. Oh my Lord. We'll never see her no more. She packin'. Hep me, Miss Sally," Abi begged.

How many catastrophes could I handle in a six-month period? We might lose our girl, Fancy, and our doctor, the only good doctor around. But I needed to calm Abi and Lester.

"Now listen to me, Abi. Pennsylvania is a good state for coloreds. It is the one state that outlawed slavery early on. They will do better there than here. She can travel as his servant, if they must go."

"But can they marry? My girl is a good girl," Abi said.

Lani walked in then, stared at the two of us for a few seconds, and then turned around and walked right out again.

And so, late at night, Doc Billings came for our sweet Fancy. They planned to take the train from Gainesville because there were more people, thinking they would not be noticed. Oh my Lord, what naïve folks we were dealing with here. She, of course, could not ride in the same car with him and it was dangerous riding in a boxcar with other coloreds.

Abi, Lester and Lucy were beside themselves, sobbing, while Fancy and Dr. Billings looked dumb-struck. I think it was just occurring to them what was really happening. Fancy had hardly ever left our ranch. She had no idea how other people would treat her. Lani and I stood by the gate as they drove away, listening to the mournful sound of a family being torn apart.

"I'll write, Mama," Fancy called as they left.

But Abi was not to be consoled. For days on end, she cried, even in front of the ranch hands, as she served their meals, washed their clothes, cleaned the bunkhouse. It was awful. I thought she would be all cried out by the end of the week, but no, she wasn't. I knew how she felt because my Mary had run away to get married, but the circumstances were a little different. The only thing I knew to do was pray.

Abigail became so run down, not eating, and not sleeping, that the dreadful ague came upon her again. The cinchona root alleviated the symptoms, but she became so weak the work had to be done by Lucy and myself. And we had no doctor to help us. Doc Johnson just wouldn't come and I cussed him under my breath. I swore I would never call that old coot to our ranch again, even if I was on my deathbed.

Within a month, Abigail was gone to heaven. I reckoned grief was just part of my life but I was surely tired of it, especially losing a sweet woman like Abi, who had been in our lives for so long. And then there was Lester and Lucy, who had not only lost Fancy, but had lost a wife and mother. We buried Abi to the north of Samuel in our family plot. We were all bereft.

Lani held my hand as we lay in bed that same night and we both cried softly.

"That Doc Billings is a damned fool! What the hell was he thinking, messing with a young black woman? He's liable to be shot dead, even in Pennsylvania," he said.

"Well, we must only concern ourselves with what we can control. And right now, we need to hire another woman to work the kitchen and wash. I cannot deal with one more problem. I still need to send Mary some money."

"If her husband has a job, why do we need to send money?" he asked.

"Because she asked me to," I said angrily and left the bed to go sit in the dark on the porch.

After a bit, Lani joined me, feeling his way in the dark. "I don't care if you send her money. We're getting ready to sell about 30 head of the Herefords to the butchers in Gainesville, so we'll be okay."

"Goodness me, it's been a hard year. I'm sorry I got mad. I'm just so angry at Fancy and the doc. It doesn't make any sense, but Abi was like a sister to me. She was such a wonderful woman," I said.

"I know, my darlin'. And she knew it. You were a blessing to her also, and to me and to everyone who crosses your path. Where would Jasper and Sarah be without you? Why, I'd probably still be chasing sorry women if it weren't for you."

"Lanier, you make me crazy, crazy with love for you."

"Come show me, woman." He took my hand and I stumbled after him in the dark.

Losing Abigail made me sadder than I had been in a long time, probably since Jacob died. She had started out a slave in a time when slaves were not always treated well, but what slaves are treated well at any time? It was a subject we talked about in the wee small hours before dawn, when she couldn't sleep and I would see the oil lamp burning in the ranch kitchen and I would join her. She brewed the best dark coffee and we would talk about insignificant things. Every now and then she would discuss being owned.

"It's a God-awful thing to be owned by other folk; you feels trapped like a coon in a wire cage, but there's nothing to be done without risking your life and your family. I wasn't treated bad, just no freedom," she said.

We cried on many occasions; I had my own sorrows, but thinking about the life of a slave made my problems seem insignificant. After she and Lester married, they worked for us and carved a little deeded homestead out for themselves, with a yard and small garden. Their girls had never known anything but kindness, with the exception of going to town and being treated as second-class citizens. My Pa always said, "A man should not own another man or woman." I hoped her time with us made up for her tribulations.

Lester and Abi had "jumped the broom" right before the war ended. They hit the road as soon as they knew they would not be shot by the landowner. Remembering Lester coming to my back door, I realized he was also feeding his wife. She said he hated to steal the chickens, but they were so hungry and were camped not far from our house. My Lord, I am so glad he stole those chickens, even though I was mad at him at the time. That was a story we both laughed over and she said that was the best meal she ever tasted. We just can't always know a person's intentions and what the future would lead us to – in our case, a lifetime of friendship. Although Elizabeth and Abi never met, I felt the three of us were kindred spirits. I wish they could've sat with me around the quilt frame and had tea with Loretta. Wishes are not reality, however, but that was a daydream of mine – to have my sister/friends working on our quilts, gossiping and planning socials or holidays.

I often wondered why they seldom left our ranch, except to go to church or if Lester was sent on an errand. The fear of going beyond borders was inbred in them at an early time of their lives and they seemed to never want to leave. Their girls were a different matter; with Fancy gone, I figured Lucy would leave us at some point.

Lucy had written to Dr. Billings to tell him and Fancy of Abi's death, but to date, there was no word from them. There was a lot of love in that family, and I knew Fancy would take her mother's death very hard. But I had to move on, as death was part of life and I had the responsibility of so many people on my shoulders, but thank goodness, I had Lani and the children. Jasper and Sarah kept me smiling, at least on the outside.

Jasper had such a different way of looking at things, so curious and interested in learning. Loretta said she had never seen a child who approached life from his point of view, saying he was extremely bright. When I mentioned that to Lani, he said, "His mama was a pretty smart lady. That's where he gets it."

"Oh good Lord. Pretty and smart, too," I said, smiling. Every now and then, however, a little jealousy slipped in.

Loretta said they drew pictures of kites one day, and Jasper drew his from the kite's point of view. All the children she had taught had drawn from the child's point of view. Maybe he would grow up and be a doctor someday. We surely could use one, at least a good one.

CHAPTER 14   THE JASPER TREE

*B*eatrice should have received her quilt and money, but of course, there was no thank you or kiss my foot or even if it had arrived. I was working on the quilt for Mary and had stuffed the hundred dollars in paper money in the batting when Lani arrived with a handful of mail. Five letters from Harry came, worried to death about all of us. I simply had not had the time to write and tell him we had weathered the storm, so to speak. How could I tell him we couldn't take the time to come out to Colorado with everything that was taking place on the ranch? I did long to see his face and that smile and those three grandchildren of mine, along with his pretty wife. Some of those letters would have to be read later as I had to get the quilt and money off to Mary.

Thinking that the weather was warm enough to plant the alligator pear tree and since it was about a foot tall with big green leaves, I thought maybe Loretta and her class of three would want to help me. She informed me that the scientific name for the tree was Persea Americana, also known as the avocado.

The man we bought the property from had planted a few citrus trees, mostly sour orange, but they were in a little grove down toward the pastures and were mature trees. The squirrels and raccoons were not fond of sour oranges and neither was I, unless sugar was added to the juice.

Jasper, in his old-soul wisdom, said the hungry squirrels might eat the alligator pear seed and pull the tree right out of the ground. Sarah said the cows would eat the tree if we put it in the pasture and Sam said it would never make it anyway, so it wouldn't matter where we planted the dadburned thing.

"Well, isn't that a positive thought? And watch your language, young man," Loretta said. "I think it should be planted close to our houses, so we can watch for critters. We can make a wire cage to keep animals away. And since school is almost over, we can all keep an eye on it."

"And take turns watering it," Jasper suggested. So, we planted the tree right outside the back door, about 20 feet from our house.

Jasper and Sam dug a little hole about ten inches deep for the long stringy roots and while Sarah held the tree, the boys filled the hole with dirt. And we all stepped back and admired our work while Loretta poured water around the base.

"According to my botanical book, it takes seven years to produce fruit, but it makes a beautiful shade tree in the meantime," Loretta said.

Jasper patted the base and looked so proud. "I'll climb this tree someday," he said.

"I know you will, Jasper. Now back to school. Last week for school and then Sam goes to work at the grist mill," Loretta said.

"What?" I said, a little too loud.

"Nathan needs the help and we can't afford to hire anyone at this time."

Well, I was stunned that Sam would have to go to work at his young age, just 8 years old this year. "Loretta, if you need to hire someone, we can help," I said.

74

"I want to work with my pa. I'm strong and smart, just like him," Sam blurted.

The children slowly followed Loretta home and I stood on my back porch, watching them and wondering why I hadn't thought of their financial predicament before now. With Samuel gone, the grist mill was probably not being run as efficiently. Nathan was not Samuel.

The avocado tree would become known as the Jasper Tree. Checking on it every day, he watered it and checked the shriveling seed so he could toss it away, which was the item the squirrels wanted. After that, the only problem would be the fruit but that would be a few years away. Sarah always helped, but she also called it the Jasper Tree.

A new puppy was delivered to our home by a neighbor down the road aways. He said it was a good hunting dog, a beagle. Of course, the children loved him and coddled him, which Lani said they shouldn't do because he would be spoiled and then wouldn't hunt. At night we could hear his lonesome howl from the barn, as he missed being held. One morning I found Jasper sleeping in the barn with the puppy, but I knew that couldn't continue.

School was out and Sarah and Jasper spent their days running through the woods with the puppy, not what Lani had in mind for his hunting dog, but he loved his children more than he did hunting. I felt badly that Sam had to work like a full-grown man and so I assigned chores to Jasper and Sarah that had to be done before they could play. Loretta was at loose ends with no classes and came to help us in the kitchen. But I still wanted to hire another person as I was tired of the endless cooking and cleaning. And Lani was starting to hire more men as the cattle increased and the herd was being culled to be sold.

As evening settled on our ranch, and we finished the dishes and put them in the cupboards, Sarah came running in and startled us all, yelling that there were three men at the house and to come quick. As I panicked and ran toward the direction of the house, Loretta followed behind, yelling, "Who could it be?"

Sarah grabbed my hand and ran with me, slowing me down. I worried someone would come to take Jasper, perhaps a family member on his mother's side. Throwing the screen door aside, we charged into the kitchen and rushed into the parlor. Sure enough, there stood three men, two strangers and my Harry, with Lani grinning ear to ear. My mind calmed some as I knew he wouldn't be smiling if there were trouble.

My heart surged, my breath catching, sides aching. My mind could not conceive of the scene before me. Who were these men standing with my son? Harry came toward me, smiling, arms open wide, while I tried to make sense of the scene. And then, my eyes began to seep, seeing this sweet boy who I thought I wouldn't see for so many years. We embraced and my body shook with sobs, while Harry cried as well.

"Mama, I want you to meet my uncles, Uncle Henry and Uncle John."

"What? What? No. It can't be. My brothers?" It was too much to ask of a woman to have this kind of a shock with no preparation. I ran to the two men who I could have passed on the street and not known who they were. We stood together, looking at each other, trying to see a semblance of the children we once were. And then we just embraced each other, all crying, grown men and me. There was not a dry eye in the room. My heart was racing since I had not seen my brothers since they were young boys, and for that matter, I had been a young girl.

John burst into the room then and walked to Harry, hugging him and pounding him on the back. When he was introduced to his uncles, he shook their hands and looked to me, since he had never met them.

"Well, this is a real reunion," John said. "I have an Uncle John and Uncle Henry. How did we not know you were coming?"

"The mail was interrupted during the Yellow Fever epidemic. I just now have received Harry's letters," I said. "Are you hungry?"

"We ate in Gainesville. And rented a buggy to get here," Harry said.

As we all stood looking at each other, I realized how strange it was that I had not seen two people that I loved so dearly in so many years. The miles and time that had separated us had not changed our deep affection for one another.

"You can't know how we missed you when you left home," Henry said. "We were left with Beatrice, who really didn't care for us at all. Of course, now we are her favorite brothers when she needs money."

"What?" I exclaimed. "She asked you for money, too?"

"Yes. We both sent her a hundred dollars."

"Ah. So did I," I said.

Then, we all laughed heartily, as we realized we had been hornswoggled.

As I put the children to bed on soft pallets on the floor in our bedroom, I could hear Lani playing his guitar and singing a new song, not yet finished. The words drifted into the room so sweetly, "I stood high on a mountain top, wind and rain they would not stop." I kissed Jasper and then Sarah, my loves, and my heart enlarged with the sound of music and my brothers and sons sitting in the next room.

As we sat around the table, I poured brandy for myself and the five men who I loved so dearly. And again, my eyes seeped from happiness and contentment.

"Well, hell's bells, Sally. If I'd known we would have made you so damned sad, we wouldn't have come," my brother John said. I had to laugh at that dreadful phrase from which it seemed I could never escape.

"Oh, be quiet, John. You know I'm crying from pure old happiness. I love you all so much." The brandy burned going down, but I drained the glass and then I cried from the brandy. We all laughed and talked into the late hours, while Lani sat on the sofa, singing, "I will only wait so long. But this lonesomeness hangs on."

What a beautiful background sound even though I couldn't even fathom lonesomeness at that moment. Smiling inwardly, I knew Lani had never seen mountains, even though he mentioned them in every last song he wrote. Maybe it was time to go see some mountains, as I had never seen one either, only Tennessee hills.

Midnight was a time we never experienced, but this night I didn't want to end, until I couldn't hold my eyes open. I showed the men to their bedrooms and then I followed Lani to bed, tipsy as could be.

Chapter 15 COLORADO DREAMS

*W*e had two full weeks with my brothers and Harry, but it was not nearly enough time. Each moment that slipped away was such a loss to me. Henry and John talked of the hard times when they first reached Colorado, with very little money and no practical experience with cattle. It took hard work and marrying into good families before they established themselves. The Indians had been a big problem initially, with the theft of their cattle, but they explained that the hostiles were hungry and many were starving.

By the time Harry had arrived, the hostiles were close to being tamed, or broken, as many had been massacred a few hundred miles from the ranch, at a place called Sand Creek. He did not have to deal with that problem, but there were years of drought and water rights conflicts.

"Different set of obstacles out west. But we don't have Yellow Fever or Malaria or mosquitoes or gators," Harry said with a grin.

"Does that mean you won't come back home, Harry?" I asked.

"It means I want you to see Colorado in all its splendor. We look to the west and there's mountains as far as you can see. It's glorious, Ma. Good hunting, good folks. You and Lanier need to come back with us."

"Lord have mercy, son. This ranch has taken a beating this last year. We can't leave here now," I replied.

"Summer of 1890! You, Lanier, Jasper, and Sarah. You must come and see your grandchildren."

"I just don't see how. John would have to take care of everything."

"He's capable. I need my ma to spend some time with me."

"I'll talk it over with Lani, but I can't see a clear way," I said.

We spent many nights just talking. It seemed we never ran out of easy subjects and always Lani played background music, jumping into the fray every now and then. Loretta always joined us and sometimes Rebecca and Nathan came for supper. John and Suzanna and the baby were with us at every meal. We all wanted as much time as possible with our Colorado family; I felt hungry for their presence.

My brothers were easy-going, like Harry. They seemed comfortable wherever they were and could talk on any subject, except the death of our pa and Jefferson, my oldest brother. I learned not to broach that item as they clammed up immediately. Sensing their pain, I realized I could never learn the facts. I only knew they died together, Pa and my oldest brother. And maybe John and Henry didn't have the truth either. Sometimes mysteries die with folks and I reckon that could be a good thing.

Lani said since we had a year to plan a trip to Colorado, he thought we could be prepared. Jasper and Sarah could not contain their childish excitement and practically packed their suitcases on the spot. Harry said, "You might not come back when you see those mountains!"

"Yeh, I'm not much for freezing my arse off," Lani said, glancing at me sheepishly.

As we sat around the parlor the last evening, it was the first time we were quiet. My eyes were brimming and I kept wiping my sleeve across my face.

Lani sang his latest song and my eyes leaked even more.

"I stood high on a mountain top
Wind and rain, they would not stop.
I watched your rig headin' out of town
Kickin' up rocks, hurrying down.
Chorus. Did you care that I stood alone?
Did you want to be long gone?
I will only wait so long
But this lonesomeness hangs on."

"Like the wind on a storming day
You blew in but could not stay.
And did you ever think of me
While you were searching to be free?
Chorus. Did you care that I stood alone?
Did you want to be long gone?
I will only wait so long
But this lonesomeness hangs on."

"I did not stand on a mountain at all.
Wind did not blow, rain did not fall.
It was a mountain of despair
The wind was love, blown in thin air."
Chorus. "Did you care that I stood alone?
Did you want to be long gone?
I will only wait so long
But this lonesomeness hangs on."

"That's a mighty lonesome song, Mr. Lani," Henry said.

"'Twas written when I was at my lonesomest," Lani replied.

Well, I was wondering where that song came from. Lani told me later it was when I pulled away from David and Annie's house after I had asked him to be my temporary foreman. Goodness me, men were indeed such a mystery to me.

81

"You have always been my favorite sister," brother John said with a grin, as we stood on the wooden railway platform in Alachua.

"Well, that's not much of a compliment, knowing the competition," I said.

"Yeh, well, I have a good mind to head north and see where she's spending our money," he said, referring to Beatrice.

"Except then you actually would have to see her and maybe talk with her," Henry said.

"On second thought, maybe not," John replied.

"Well, I love you, my brothers, and I thank you for taking care of my boy and thank you for bringing him home to me. And for coming to see me after all these years. Pa would be so proud of you."

"As he would of you, sister Sally. You have become a very fine cow woman," Henry said.

We laughed and talked and tried not to let each other see the pain of separation. But Harry and I held each other, smiling at the time we had had and looking forward to more time together. We were dry-eyed but only out of sheer determination. How I wish things had been different and that blasted Susan Marley, Harry's first wife, had never walked into our lives. But God had blessed us all and that's what I had to focus on.

"It's only a year," I said, touching Harry's cheek, my heart bursting.

Jasper held onto my skirt and said, "We could go right now, Mama, if you want to." I held him to me, with Harry on the other arm.

"Nice to know I have a sweet little brother and I'll see him next summer," Harry said as he mussed Jasper's hair, just like Pa used to do to me. It was the first time I had noticed Harry's resemblance to my pa. I don't know how I hadn't seen it before. No wonder he was my favorite.

Watching the train roll down the track, I was happy and sad at the same time, thinking I was a mystery unto myself. But we had much to look forward to. I couldn't wait to see those snow-capped

Colorado mountains. And, Lord knows, Lani needed to see a mountain or two, so he could write more songs.

On the ride home, I said to Lani, "I believe we should take a train ride up to Lebanon, Tennessee on our way to Colorado and see where our money is being spent."

"Whatever you want, my darling, but be prepared to be aggravated."

"I'm already aggravated."

☼

When we arrived back at the ranch, a well-dressed black lady stood by a surrey tied to the hitching post by the barn, holding a fair-skinned child. Lester was holding the horses and glanced up as we pulled into the driveway.

"What's this?" Lani called out.

"Fancy done come home for a visit," Lester called back.

"Why, mercy me," I said. "Look at that beautiful boy." He had light colored curls and skin the color of café au lait.

We climbed down from the wagon and Lester took our horses and unhitched the wagon. I took the baby and held him as he smiled innocently up at me.

"Why Fancy, why didn't you write and tell us you were coming?" I asked.

"Wasn't sho' you would welcome me," she whispered.

"Where is the doc? Did he come with you?" Lani asked.

"No. Things didn't quite work out as planned," she said with a shy smile, a tear brimming. "Turns out we couldn't marry. His folks disowned him and I knew it was better if I left, so he would be able to be a doc again. I hope I can work for the ranch again, ma'am."

"I knew there was a reason we couldn't find anyone else to work here. What say you, Lester, can you move into the bunkhouse and let the girls have the cabin?" Lani asked.

I never saw a bigger, brighter smile in my life. "Lawd, thank you Mista Lani," Lester said.

"I would like to see Mama's grave before I do anything," Fancy said. She and Lester walked slowly down the path toward our little lonesome cemetery, while I took the baby and Jasper to the house. Another little orphan child, but at least he had a good mama, I hoped. Somehow I felt we had not seen the last of the good Dr. Billings.

CHAPTER 16   LORETTA'S SONG

"*W*hat is that song you're humming, Loretta," I asked as we were quilting around the frame.

"It's just a song for Samuel that I made up to help my heart mend."

"It's a pretty tune, but sad. Does the sad song have words?" I asked.

"Yes," was all she said.

I waited for her to sing it to me, but she kept her eyes down, fingers moving rapidly over the quilt.

"I. I. You know I haven't cried yet," she whispered.

"Well, it's just the two of us here. You can cry or sing, either one would be fine with me...or both," I said.

"I'll sing." She cleared her voice.

Her voice was just as pure as when we were young girls, singing with Elizabeth around the quilt frame in our home in Georgia or on the trail south into Florida.

"Soon you'll be leaving
Soon I'll be grieving

85

How can I make you stay
When you had to go away?
When the sun comes up tomorrow
I'll reach and you'll be gone
My bed will be empty
And I'll sing my lonesome song."

Well, Loretta was still dry-eyed, but I was not. An overwhelming sorrow came over me, so strong that I felt weak, unwanted tears dripping off my chin. I never wanted anyone to see me cry, thinking it a sign of weakness.

"I'm sorry, Sally. I didn't mean to make you weep. It's just that it helps me to sing this song when I'm lonesome for Samuel."

"It's beautiful, Loretta. You must sing it for Lani so he can play the guitar for you. When you can sing a song like that, you don't need to cry for Samuel. Your voice does it for you," I said.

She smiled weakly and we hugged. But by then I was not in a mood to be quilting. Leaving my house, I headed to the barn to do some work and think about the words to that song, remembering all the deaths of the dear people I had lost: most recently Abi, Samuel, Jacob, Jake, and Elizabeth. That was a most powerful song to conjure up those kind of feelings and I went looking for Suzanna and that red-headed baby, Fereby Faith, to cheer me up instead of throwing myself into heavy work that someone else could do better than me.

As I walked down to the cabin on the lake, I could hear the beagle pup baying and I knew my children were running through the woods chasing a rabbit. I just hoped they didn't get struck by a rattlesnake or run into a panther. They knew to stay away from the lakes and rivers as gators were plentiful in the area.

The fall of 1889 was still hotter than Hades. I found myself looking forward to the summer of 1890, standing in the shadow of a snow-capped peak, with a breeze blowing down the valley. Never having seen a mountain, it was hard to picture. Harry had said some of them were over 12,000 feet tall, as he pointed out some heightened clouds and said the mountains were that tall. How could that be? As tall as the tallest clouds?

Lani worried himself about leaving the ranch to go to Colorado, saying I should go with the children, but that notion did not appeal to me atall. "Well, we'll all stay home then," I said testily.

"Allrighty. I won't mention it again. But we need to move John and his family away from the lake with the mosquitoes so bad and when the baby starts walking, who knows what could happen," Lani replied.

Well, I didn't know exactly how that subject had anything to do with Colorado and I wondered why hadn't I thought of that? Or John? I knew they wouldn't want to live with us, but maybe Loretta could give up her house and move in with us. Yes, that would work if she were willing. So, I said that to Lani and he thought that was a very good idea. And it became the plan, whether John liked it or not. He should have done this a long time ago.

"And by the way, I have finished Loretta's song for her," he said.

"Will there be mountains in the song?" I asked.

"Not this time," he said with a laugh, "but I'll sing it for you."

It was late in the evening and as I dressed for bed, Lani brought his guitar in and sat at the dressing table, his rich, sometimes gravelly voice, singing that melancholy song.

"Here's the last verse and chorus."

"As the coffee brewed this morning
I looked on down the road
Hoping to see you
Turn around and never go.
But you'll be leaving
And I'll be grieving
I could not make you stay
And you left to go away.
And you left to go away."

As haunting as the words were, the melody was even more

so, especially with the guitar's minor chords. As Lani always said, "You can't sing a sad song if you haven't been down that road."

"You, sir, are a genius. Loretta will love it," I said.

"And you? Do you love the guitar player?"

"Sometimes I surely do," I whispered in his ear, smiling as he set the guitar down.

He drew me to him and whispered in my neck, "I know that feeling, but it passes. And then I love you almost completely," he said with a grin. As he stood and blew out the lantern, he hummed that "Leaving" song. But I knew for certain we would never leave each other, only "should death do us part."

CHAPTER 17   THE OLD SOULS

"And a little child shall lead them." Isaiah 11:6

Sarah was coming to love Baby James, or Jimmy, as she called Fancy's baby. Because Fancy was needed in the kitchen, Sarah and I were left to care for him, and sometimes I was too busy to tend to him, even though I was in the house. It worried me some that she was so attached to him because I felt the good doctor would return someday.

He was a beautiful, happy baby, until he was hungry, and then Sarah would run to the kitchen to fetch Fancy. All in all, everything was working out well. Loretta moved in with us, John and his family moved into Loretta's house, Jasper was helping his father run the ranch, and things were looking up, financially and otherwise. I was feeling content except for that nagging feeling that Dr. Billings would come and take Fancy and James away. We would all be devastated.

Sarah fretted over Baby James because his nappies were wet most of the time and he smelled stinky. But that was the case with all babies and we had three in our compound, so washing and boiling the clothes was a continual burden. And then there was the rash on the babies' bottoms. At one point in time, Elizabeth and I had made perfumed corn starch that we used on our babies and ourselves, to boot. But we had not had corn starch in a while.

"Why can't the grist mill grind us some corn starch and we can grind up some orange blossoms at the same time?" Sarah asked me one morning.

"Sarah, my darling, you are a very bright young lady. If they can grind it fine enough, that would be a good solution," I said.

Loretta was drinking coffee at the table and almost dropped her cup. "Sally, that's the answer to many of our problems. Nathan is not a good business man and we have been losing money at the mill. But if we made little bags of perfumed drying powder, I believe we could make ends meet," she said.

Sarah jumped for joy, not only that she had had a good idea, but that we could keep the babies dry.

"We'll call it Elizabeth's Drying Powder," I said.

And so it began. We started sewing little flowered bags for the corn starch. We gathered all the blooms off the sour orange trees and Nathan began making the corn starch, which took a bit more time than making grits or corn meal. The blooms had to be dried in the hot sun so they would not mildew in the starch. They were added to the cornstarch to be ground once they had dried completely.

After the first batch came out, we dusted the babies' bottoms and our underarms to be certain it would work. And sure enough, it did, including making us all smell better. Why hadn't we thought of this before now? We were giddy with happiness and relief. Then Jasper asked why we didn't use oil cloth on the babies for nappies and we looked at each other and laughed out loud. My children were so brilliant; they were truly old souls. Of course, the oil cloth could go over the nappies and be wiped off and put back on after the change. With pen and ink we wrote "Elizabeth's Drying Powder" on the bags and tied string around the top when the bags were filled. We would sell them for .15 cents a bag, with refills costing .12 cents, and we made 100 bags. Some we sold to the general store in La Crosse and some we sold at the mill. Once word got out, we had a high demand and had a hard time keeping up with the sales. The biggest problem was the orange blossoms, as they only bloomed a couple of times a year and we didn't own that many trees. So we began planting and harvesting gardenias to keep up with the demand. We also gathered magnolia blossoms from the woods, which were extremely potent, and one flower was large enough to make a whole batch of starch.

This solution solved more than one problem; the grist mill was now doing so well that money was coming in faster than we could fill orders. And all of us smelled like blossoms of one type or another, even the men. Just a little dusting under the arms and we were much more pleasant to be around. Lani even bought a bag for the bunk house.

"At least the men will use it when they go to town on Saturday night," he said, laughing. "I know some ladies who will be thanking us."

Of course, any grist mill could have done the same thing, but we found that other mills were not interested in feminine things, and concentrated on food items. The women in our area were so grateful to us and stopped me on the street anytime they saw me, just to thank me for the new invention. I gave Sarah and Jasper the credit. The mothers also were using oil cloth, but we couldn't capture those sales as it was just a matter of buying oil cloth and cutting it to fit the baby.

Old Mrs. Langford caught me by the arm on a Sunday morning after church, thanking me for my new invention, whispering in my ear, "And I use it in places other than my underarms."

I'm sure I blushed at this information but I had never thought of dusting my drawers. However, I knew I would try it as soon as I got home.

One day I received a letter from a Tampa general store, placing an order for 500 bags of Elizabeth's famous drying powder. We raised the price to a quarter and shipped them off to the store on the train. But I knew I had things to do other than make bags, so Nathan hired a girl to help Loretta and Rebecca. And Sarah continued helping, too.

To celebrate our success, the family gathered on a Saturday evening for supper at our house. Everyone brought a food dish and we ended up with quite a feast. The babies played on the floor and

occurred on the ranch. I asked Lani if he would play Loretta's song and her eyes lit up like stars. Of course, he was proud to pick up the guitar and sing for all of us.

By the time he reached the second verse, however, Loretta's face had reddened and she began to weep such as I had never seen the like. I reckoned that finally she was grieving, but not what she had planned to do at such a joyous event. She retired to her bedroom and Lani was stricken.

"I'm so sorry," he said.

"Uncle Lani, it's just what she has needed. I think she will be able to live her life now," Rebecca said tearfully.

It was a cleansing cry for Loretta and we were all thankful, even though she was embarrassed, but a person can't hold all that grief inside forever without getting sick. I knew it was good for her.

Leave it to Jasper to lighten up the room. His next remark made us all laugh. "Sam says his ma uses a cherry switch when he doesn't mind. And I say, 'A cherry switch will make you do right.'" Even Loretta, who had returned to the room, had to laugh at that sentence. My Jasper was truly a wise boy to make us all merry once again.

Lani was stashing money away for our trip to Colorado. We would go north to Lebanon, Tennessee for a few days and then head straight across the country to Denver, where Harry would pick us up and take us to the ranch. It would be a long and arduous journey, not something to look forward to, especially with two 9 year-olds. And I worried about Jasper's health; at times he looked a little jaundiced. He truly lit up all our lives. Some nights while he slept, I laid my hands on his chest and prayed that his little body would be healthy and strong.

CHAPTER 18   AND THE MAN COMETH

*W*hile settling in on a cool winter evening in December 1889, with just a few more months until our big adventure to Colorado, Lester came in the back door with Lani. The fire in the fireplace was popping, the children were reading to each other, with Jimmy asleep between them, and Loretta and I were working on some quilt squares.

"Howdy, Lester, pull up a chair and grab some cookies off the table," I said, feeling as contented as possible.

"Ma'am," he stuttered.

"What is it, Lester?" I asked.

Lani spoke up, "Doctor Billings is here to take Fancy and James to Cuba."

"What? In this cold weather, on a cold ship, to a foreign land?" I asked.

"She's bound to go," Lester said pitifully.

Glancing at Sarah, I saw the distress on her face. She pulled James closer to her and cried, "Mama, don't let them take him away."

I stood and left the house, marching to the little cabin where Fancy and Lucy lived, Lester and Lani on my heels. There was loud talking between Fancy and Lucy coming from inside as I knocked on the door. Doc Billings slowly opened the door, holding his hand out to me, thinking I would shake it. I stormed by him, and walked to the corner of the cabin where Fancy was packing her carpetbag.

"You would do this?" I asked her. "You would leave us short-handed, dragging your baby out in this weather to a land unfamiliar to you, where they speak Spanish, with a man who cares not about your welfare?"

"Mrs. Walton, that is not fair," Doc blustered. "I love my family. We will marry on the ship and I have secured a position in Havana as head doctor in a hospital."

His wispy blonde hair was sticking straight up after he had taken his wool cap off and he looked down right ridiculous. Trying to stay serious with his image before me was not an easy task.

I turned to Fancy. "What say you?"

"I must go with my man, Missy. You been good to me but we deserve a life where we can bring up our boy together," she said.

"I have booked a passage out of the Port of Tampa in a week. It's the right thing, ma'am. Where is my son?" the doc asked.

Oh, it was the moment I had dreaded, when Sarah would see James taken away by his parents. It would break her heart and all our hearts. How we loved that baby!

Lucy stormed out of the cabin. Lester stood with his arms hanging loose as if he were powerless. Lani said, "Fancy, you go to the house and get the boy. Do not tell Sarah what you're doing. Bring him back here. Spend the night and then leave tomorrow. The weather is too cold to be traveling with him tonight."

"Yessir," she whispered as she brushed by me and went out the door.

"Thank you, sir," the doc said to Lani, extending his hand. They shook hands and Lani said, "You better do right by this woman and that child. Please write to us when you are settled. We will have a lot of broken hearts here tomorrow. Sally, let's go home."

When we returned home, Fancy was stepping off the porch of our house and I grabbed her and the baby and hugged them to me. "My God, Fancy, we will miss you and James. We do love you

94

both." She cried into my neck and made me cry, squeezing that little boy between us. I broke away and went inside to comfort Sarah and Jasper, a hard job.

"Oh, Mama, what will he do without me? He needs me," Sarah moaned. Jasper patted her hand and he cried, too. At that moment, I hated Doctor Billings. I prayed he would do right by them and not succumb to the pressures of society.

Once again, we watched Dr. Billings and Fancy leave down our driveway, only this time they took a piece of us with them, James, our sweet child. Only he was not our child and I determined not to allow my children to get close to another baby that could be snatched away at any time, leaving them hurting and empty.

Sarah could not be consoled, no matter how I tried. "He needs me," she said over and over.

"Sarah, he was not ours. He is with his parents and they are who he needs now. You did a wonderful job with him, but you must let him go," I said.

And so, for a week, Sarah moped, red-eyed and listless. Of course, Jasper could not be happy if Sarah wasn't happy. Then, Suzanna walked into the house one day, carrying her baby, and announced loudly that she was going to work in the kitchen and needed help with Fereby and wondered if there was anyone around who could help.

Hiding my joy, I realized she had, once again, come to save the day. Sarah's eyes lit up and she shyly said she was up for the challenge. We all laughed then and were filled with joy that our girl could find a nurturing purpose once again. But Suzanna solved more than one problem because Loretta and I were tired of cooking in the kitchen and washing clothes over a boiling cauldron.

Suzanna whispered to me, "Did you know that Lester is about to jump the broom again?"

"What?" I said, maybe a little too loud.

"Yep. Fancy said he met her at church and they have been courting and she will be coming to live here, if you don't object. I imagine he's getting up the courage to talk with you and Lani."

Goodness me! I guessed change was imminent, but I sure wished for a little peace and quiet every now and then. And I was hoping I would like this woman, knowing no one could take Abi's place.

☼

Love must have been in the air because Loretta was being courted by Mr. McNeil, a widower from our church. But I thought she would never marry again unless he came to live on the ranch, because she wouldn't leave her family. And there was no one like Samuel. But I was encouraged that she was living her life again, no matter the end result.

Lester did marry a younger woman, Izzie, and I did like her, but I was pretty certain Lucy cared little for her. Because of that disharmony, we gave the lake house to Lester for the time being. And even though I knew he would want his wife to work in the kitchen, I also knew better than to put two wrangling women together. I was starting to think that Lucy was mad at the world, with no smiles on her face for anyone. Suzanna said Lucy felt everyone in her whole family had betrayed her, especially Fancy, and now her father, too.

And then one day Lucy was gone, with no word to me or her father. I felt a little betrayed as we had always been good to her and her family. Lester was distraught and left to find her but when he returned he said she didn't want to be found.

Watching the evening breeze scour the sky of clouds, I thought how strange life was that we could never get completely comfortable because some new change was always about to occur and we either had to go with it or stay in a state of agitation. But it did make me concerned about our long trip to Colorado, hoping John would be able to deal with the many changes on the ranch, a man who was constantly grumpy about the least little thing.

Turned out, Izzie was one of the best cooks in the county; her canned peach cobbler actually made the ranch hands smile, closing their eyes as they pulled the forks from their mouth, not to mention her crackling bread. And she and Suzanna truly liked each other, laughing together a lot. What a relief!

☼

"Mr. McNeil is just looking for a cook and housekeeper," Loretta confided in me one day. "And I'm not good at either."

"Oh Loretta, you don't need to be good at anything because you are so good-hearted. But it's better to know these things before you jump the broom," I said, laughing.

"Well, my broom jumping days are over. We'll have too much to think about here with you and Lani gone. I want to help as much as possible."

And so, as things settled down on the compound, I hoped the status quo would remain when we left, but I knew that would not be the case. I would have to trust John, Suzanna and Loretta to handle things because I would be off on a big adventure to Colorado.

PART 2

1890

COLORADO

CHAPTER 19   COMMENCEMENT

*T*he big day had arrived, May 15th, 1890, the day we would take the train to Atlanta, Georgia, the start of the long journey. It was also Jasper's 10th birthday, and he, of course, thought all the hoopla was in celebration of his birth day - and we would make it so. Even though Sarah wouldn't be 9 until August, she was taller and stronger than Jasper. His boundless spirit was what made him strong, and the determination to keep up with her. They were bursting with enthusiasm.

As we stood on the wooden platform at the Alachua depot, staring at the peeling painted walls, I was filled with exhilaration, but also trepidation to be traveling along the area that I once had journeyed in a covered wagon some 26 years earlier in 1864, leaving behind my home, not knowing what lay ahead. I wondered if Atlanta was still a burned-out town or if it was rebuilding. In order to save money, we determined to spend a night in Atlanta, and forego a sleeping car on the train. From there, we would travel on to Lebanon, Tennessee, where I was born and raised. That thought made me weak in the knees, thinking about my ma and pa and my three brothers. And then there was Beatrice: how would she greet us?

None of us had ever been on a train before. Lani had never even been out of the state of Florida, nor had the children. I felt like a world traveler compared to those three. But I had only traveled from Tennessee to Georgia to Florida, and then I had stayed put. Although my carpet bag was packed with food, when we passed through the dining car the smells were inviting. I thought perhaps we could afford one meal, maybe a hot breakfast.

Jasper peeked over the seat in front of us, Sarah with her nose pressed to the window. His eyes were sparkling, his grin wide. I knew he was so excited he could hardly contain himself. Even though the clackety clack of the wheels was noisy, it seemed to lull us. But I wanted to be awake to see the spot where Lani and I had first met on the trail, when he and David had come to guide us to our new home. Of course, at the time, I hardly noticed him, so anxious was I to get to La Crosse with my new baby and await the homecoming of my husband, Jacob Henry.

As we rode through the red clay country of southern Georgia, my heart was filled with memories of hard times, good times, and the love of my fellow travelers. Lani squeezed my hand when we were near the area, even though it was hard to know the exact place. We had sat around a fire, so comforted by the feeling of safety at last. There had been many times on the trip to Florida when I had wondered if we would ever arrive, especially with my being in the family way, and walking most of the trail behind the covered wagon. We had endured two-legged and four-legged varmints and had come out of it victorious. Such bittersweet memories.

Our stopover in Valdosta gave us about an hour to stretch our legs. I bought a bag of peaches from a farmers' market right next to the depot, for our trip, since we had mostly beef jerky and jarred goods to eat, with a few biscuits. The children had never had fresh peaches and slurped them down, juice running all over their clean clothes. As they were giggling and laughing, I thought, "What are a few stains on a train trip?"

Although I had never been in the city of Valdosta, I had waited patiently outside the town for Jake to return in the old days of the journey. In my mind, I could picture him coming back to our camp and telling us there were no goods to buy. Disappointed and hungry as we had been, we were determined to continue on our trip to Florida.

As we left the station in Valdosta, I wondered if I would recognize the road to Montezuma. Watching closely, I saw a sign on the side of the tracks that pointed to the west, with large letters, "MONTEZUMA." I never want to go back there, I whispered to myself, thinking of the awful time we had experienced there on our trip south.

Lani jolted me out of my reverie, saying, "How about some roast beef, mashed potatoes, green beans and coconut cake for the boy's birthday?"

"Oh my, yes. Anything for the boy," I said smiling, knowing I would enjoy that meal for my birthday, which was a few months away. He laughed and said, "For the boy, huh?"

Lani had reserved a table for us in the dining car without mentioning it to Sarah and Jasper. We washed up in the lavatory, where soap and water were provided, also utilizing the drying powders. I wiped the peach juice off as best I could but I think the children were proud of the stains. Sarah said they smelled good, like perfume.

When we entered the dining car I watched Jasper closely, wanting so much to please him on his day. I didn't think this event could ever be topped, no matter how many birthdays he had, and the look in his eyes made it all worthwhile. He was speechless, for a change. It was like his mind couldn't register the idea that we had planned a fancy dinner just for him. Of course, I was ravenous, as we all were, so it benefited all of us.

As we sat at the white-clothed tables, waiters in white coats and caps brought our meals, and I couldn't help but give thanks to God for such an experience. Jasper and Sarah sat silently taking it all in, smiling the whole time.

Sitting on the west side of the dining car, the setting sun's rays shone through the stained glass window, drenching the four of us in a heavenly glow, like angels. I had never seen anything so beautiful, not even in a church. The glass pieces were so small and colorful and the reflection on the table was a replica of the window. The signature at the bottom was Louis Comfort Tiffany, whoever he was. It was a moment I wanted to freeze in time, a fleeting moment I tried to grasp.

Jasper's face was a golden color, while the side of Sarah's face was green. The children moved their hands all over the table to see the change. "You're purple, Mama," Jasper exclaimed gleefully. I was seated across from Lani next to the window and he reached for my hand before we hungrily dug in, hoping not to lose our manners.

"This beef is so tender, it might be one of ours," Lani said, breaking the spell.

"Well, don't tell Sarah and me which one or we won't be able to eat," I said.

"Good Lord, woman. You're a rancher," he said with a laugh.

"Mama," Sarah whispered. "I think I just saw Lucy."

"Where?" I asked.

I scrambled to get to the area where Sarah had pointed her finger. Funny thing, I thought those mashed potatoes tasted just like Lucy's, the best in the state of Florida. Catching a glimpse of a young, diminutive woman moving toward the kitchen car, I called to her. As she turned to me, my heart raced, realizing I had missed her so much. She ran back to me, hesitant to hug me until I grabbed her and held her to me, both of us crying.

"Cain't talk right now. It's the dinner hour, but I'll find you later," she said, hurrying to the kitchen.

When I returned, the coconut cake was being served, large slices of pure heaven. That's what Jasper called it, as he closed his eyes and took a bite. I knew that was Lucy's handiwork also. Nobody made coconut cake like her, light as a feather, with an icing that was divine on the tongue, sprinkled with large amounts of coconut. How I had truly missed, not just her cooking, but Lucy herself – and that coconut cake.

☼

Later in the evening, the conductor asked me if I would mind following him to a staff sitting room where Miss Lucy awaited. Lani was concerned but I told him I had my pea shooter in my dress pocket, not that he was worried about Lucy, but other strangers. Smiling, he patted his holster under his vest. "I know you can take care of yourself, Miss Sally."

We didn't expect to be in Atlanta until midnight and I surely would be happy to lay my head down on a pillow, but I truly wanted to find out what Lucy had been up to. I didn't think her pa, Lester, had heard from her since she left our place.

Nervously, she greeted me again. As we talked for some time, I realized she had been terribly hurt by her mother's death, her sister's actions, and her father's marriage. She felt abandoned by her whole family. I had known that fact, but not the depth of her despair. So, I forgave her for leaving us without notice, which I had already done.

"Your papa loves you and misses you so much. Please write to him and let him know you are all right," I said.

She looked tired and I thought she might be overworked on the railroad, with hardly a chance to rest, working long hours. Her home was in Atlanta, where she lived with a family and paid rent. I wondered at her decision to leave us, but realized quickly she was becoming an independent woman, a rare thing for a black woman in post-Civil War days. There was a pride about her, which I admired.

She asked about everyone and wanted to see Sarah, so we asked the conductor to bring her to us. Sarah ran to Lucy and embraced her. It was a true moment in time, when a prodigal (Lucy) was reunited with a family member. Sarah had taught Lucy and Fancy to read and write and had taken care of Fancy's baby and had worked in the kitchen with Lucy. They had a tight bond. When we parted, however, I didn't know if we would ever see her again.

CHAPTER 20   PEACH STAINS

$\mathcal{M}$y hair is so long and I am drifting in a clear river, with my hair floating around me like river grasses. My face is the only thing out of the water and the sun is warming it, but the rest of my body is cold. I'm not afraid, but I'm wondering if I should swim to shore before the current carries me too far downstream. And someone is shaking my shoulder, someone in the river with me. That frightens me.

"Sally, wake up. We're pulling into Union Station," Lani said softly.

I awoke with a jar, not knowing where I was until I heard the sound of the wheels on the rails.

"You were dreaming?" he asked.

"I'm afraid so." We had slept sitting up for quite a few hours and my body felt stiff and my joints painful.

"One of the gentlemen in the next car said the Kimball House Hotel was across the street from the depot. We'll stay there tonight," Lani said.

The brakes screeched as we pulled into the station, which woke the children. We were a bedraggled foursome, our hair sticking up and out, which I tried smoothing on all of us, except Lani, who simply put on his hat.

The only other folks in the station were the ones getting off our train and as we walked through the front entrance to the street, I realized I had needed a breath of fresh air. The night air was cool and pleasant and we simply had to walk across the street to the beautiful hotel.

A doorman opened the front door for us, looking down his nose. "Oh my," I thought. "Do we look that bad?" We did. Sarah and Jasper had peach stains all down the front of their clothes, their hair badly rumpled. I was in a cotton travel dress, which was wrinkled in every square inch, my hair needing a comb. And then there was Lani, looking every bit the country hick, cowboy boots and hat and shirt. He even had some peach stains on his shirt.

"I'm sorry, sir. We have no openings tonight," the agent, a puny-looking young man, said.

"You're telling me that you have 500 rooms and not one room open?" Lani asked.

"You can try the Markham House Hotel down the street," the agent said.

"I believe we will," Lani replied.

As we exited the hotel, Lucy came running up to us. "You don't want to stay here. They are uppity. Follow me. My friend is the housekeeper at the Markham," she said.

Honestly, I could have dropped down on the sidewalk and rested for a few hours, but we trudged after Lucy as she carried Sarah's bag for her and put her arm around her.

The Markham was a much smaller hotel, but very nice, and the beds were comfortable. None of us bathed or bothered to remove much of our clothes. We plopped down on the beds and pulled the covers up over our heads. Bone-tired, we were.

Golden sunlight flooded the room before my eyes were opened. Glancing around, I noticed Sarah and Jasper were still asleep. Lani came through the door then and sat on the edge of the bed, saying, "Your bath awaits you, my princess." Stretching luxuriously, I thought the one thing that would make me feel better was a warm bath and a privy.

Sarah and I were taken to the bath area, where we received royal service: a privy room in the hotel. Imagine that. And two tubs with steaming water and toiletries. Sarah seemed shy to take off her clothes but there was a screen between us and once she settled into the tub, she giggled. As I sank down, my hair floating about me, like in my dream, I determined to make our baths at home more comfortable, if not luxurious.

Lucy's friend, Margaret, the housekeeper, asked for our clean dresses so they could be pressed before we went down to breakfast. I felt like a princess, as no one had ever ironed my dresses for me but myself. When she brought them back to us, she said, "Miss Lucy sets a high store on you and the young lady, Miz Walton. She said to give you the best service possible."

"Thank you, and thank Lucy for us, too," I said.

"Yes ma'am. She a good girl," Margaret said.

As we entered the dining room, I could see Lani and Jasper all spruced up, with Jasper drinking a cup of coffee along with Lani and I laughed right out loud. "Like father, like son," I said. Jasper beamed.

"Mister Walton," a voice from behind said. "May I speak with you? I am the manager at the Kimball and I wish to convey my apologies for the treatment given you last night. The night clerk did not realize who you were."

"Who I am?" Lani stood and shook hands with the man, the night clerk hanging back behind the manager.

"Yessir. We buy our beef from your ranch for our restaurant. We would like to offer you a room tonight at no cost to you," the man said.

I was impressed with Lani's composure. "Thank you for your hospitality, sir, but we are most comfortable here. We may take you up on your offer at a later date, however."

"Thank you for the opportunity to serve you, and again, my apologies."

And with that, he handed Lani his card and turned and left the room, the clerk following on his heels. As our breakfast was delivered, I was proud that the children had seen their father be an example of true grace and gentlemanly behavior. If that had been me talking, I'm afraid I would have said, "I wouldn't stay in your ratty hotel even if I had to sleep on the street." Thank goodness I did know when to be quiet.

☼

Atlanta's Union Station was a very busy place by the time we got there. With our train leaving at two o'clock in the afternoon, we had little time to see the city. Rebuilding was still going on 26 years after the un-Civil War and I knew I would not want to see Jacob Henry's childhood home, either burned to the ground or some squatters living there.

Lucy came to say goodbye, especially to Sarah, upon whom she doted. Sarah said, "Lucy, please come for a visit. You know we all love you."

The tears welled up as they hugged each other. "I will," Lucy whispered. And she was gone from the station that quickly, practically running out the front door.

Our next stop: Chattanooga, Tennessee. My heart was pounding in my chest just thinking about going back to my home state. The train was crowded with travelers but the children stayed put. I had given orders they were not to leave our car as some of the folks onboard were not what I would call upstanding. I could see Lani felt a little threatened by some of the rough company as he rested his hand on his chest where his holstered pistol was. Instead, I had Sarah and Jasper focus on the scenery, as we would be pulling into the mountains of north Georgia and south Tennessee. We could feel the slowing of the train as the engines strained on the inclines, and I knew it would get worse when we headed west and over the Cumberland Plateau.

My memory was flooded with the love of the mountains and hills of Tennessee, which I had all but forgotten about. Jasper and Sarah sat facing us and I watched their faces brighten when we climbed the hills, as they were definitely flatlanders. May was a beautiful month for Tennessee because the spring rains had left the foliage a vibrant green. The dogwoods and the rhododendrons were in bloom and morning glory vines hung from the pine trees. It was a whole world away from Florida.

By eight o'clock in the evening we arrived in Chattanooga where the station also was called Union Depot, and was where we would change trains. I was astounded at how fast a train could take a person to another destination, compared to a horse and carriage, and with much greater comfort.

Jasper asked the obvious question: "Why are all the depots called Union Station?"

I had been wondering that myself, but Lani, who made a trip to the bar every evening, talking with other, more experienced, travelers, said, "Because that's where all the different company train tracks come together." Well, that made sense to me, but I thought they could have been a little more inventive with the names, and it satisfied Jasper's curiosity.

We surely were happy to get off that train and stretch our bodies, even the children. And then it was on to Nashville, where we would catch a train going east to Lebanon. Thinking maybe I should not have planned to go back home, I thought of the money my brothers and I had sent to Beatrice and I knew I would continue.

Even though we slept most of the evening on the train to Nashville, we awoke to painful cramps and stiff bodies. Sleeping while sitting up definitely was not restful. Arriving at six o'clock in the morning, I begged Lani, no, insisted, that we stopover at an inn before we traveled on to Lebanon. He said he had asked around in the bar the night before, and was advised to go to the Maxwell House Hotel, about a mile from the station. Breathing a sigh of relief, I wondered if we would have to walk that mile, but he said there were cabs right by the station. And sure enough, horses and carriages were lined up on the street right outside the front door. I did, however, wonder about getting all our travel information from drunks at the bar car.

The Maxwell House Hotel was as big and beautiful as the Kimball House Hotel in Atlanta and I was concerned they would turn us away again as before, since we were still road-weary and looked it.

Breakfast was being served as we checked in to the Maxwell House and we were all famished. Jasper ordered coffee with his meal and promptly said, "Good to the last drop." We all laughed at that silly boy who said the most clever things.

Later in the hotel room, when Sarah opened her bag to retrieve her nightgown, she found a journal-book and two lead pencils. Inside the cover, Lucy had written, "You are my favorite girl, who taught me to write and read and I will never ever forget you. Love always, Lucy." Sarah was so touched by that kindness, but I think she felt a little sad, thinking she might never see her again.

After we put the children to bed, Lani took my hand and led me to the bathhouse where he locked the door and we stripped and climbed into a large steaming tub. He massaged my shoulders and back, and I leaned back against him and relaxed for the first time in days.

"It's broad daylight, Mr. Walton," I said.

"And I like what I see, Mrs. Walton," he whispered hoarsely.

"Well, so do I," I whispered back.

Sleeping soundly till three in the afternoon, we then decided to take the next morning train to Lebanon. I wanted to be refreshed when I saw my sister after so many years. It was considered very bad manners to go calling without sending a notification of some type, but I wanted to catch her unawares, just to see what the situation really was. Feeling that my brothers and I we had been swindled, I wanted to have a report when I arrived in Colorado. After all, $300 was no small amount. And although Beatrice had said the farm was in the family, I knew our names weren't on the deed.

As I worried about the $4 bill for the hotel, Lani reminded me that all meals were included, which made me feel better…and hungry. Lani and I were like two youngsters since our bath, smiling and gazing at each other. He made me weak in the knees. It was not easy to find time for each other, traveling with our children. I believed when we showed love for each other, Sarah and Jasper felt more secure and content. At least, that's what I told myself.

CHAPTER 21   CEDARS OF LEBANON

$\mathcal{A}$s the train pulled into the small station in Lebanon, Tennessee around mid-morning, my heart was pounding. The heady smell of the cedars as we rode the train from Nashville filled me with such nostalgia. Closing my eyes, I pictured our little farm with my pa working the mule in the corn fields, the sun shining on his straw hat and shoulders and my brothers and I following behind. I could hear Ma calling us to supper and Pa turning to me, smiling, saying, "Better quit right now. Your ma won't be happy if we're late, and we got to keep her happy or else she'll make those biscuits as hard as rocks next time." A tear made its way down my cheek. Lani squeezed my hand and scooped the tear away with his other hand.

The livery stable rented us a horse and carriage for the day, as we planned to be back on the train heading west by the end of the day. Lani asked for directions, being as it had been so long since I had been to my grandparents' place. Everything was an adventure for Jasper and Sarah. Oh, to be that age again, when everything was new and exciting, I thought.

We headed west again on a road outside of Lebanon and I remembered driving that road many, many years ago. Turning up the long driveway, I was astounded that the property was so well-manicured, not how I had pictured it atall, but perhaps in decay.

Once we stepped down from the carriage and climbed the steps, Lani knocked on the door. A beautiful lady, dressed in a silk gown, with pure white hair, came to the door.

"We are not hiring at the moment," she said harshly.

"That's good," Lani said, "Because we're not looking for work. We are looking for a Mrs. Beatrice Scruggs."

"I am Beatrice Scruggs, now Lamberton. What do you want? I'm busy."

And that was when I recognized Beatrice, not because she said so, but because of the harsh tone to her voice. Feeling this trip had been a mistake, I turned to go.

"Wait. Sally, is that you? Why are you leaving? I didn't know who you were. Please stay," she called.

As we turned back, she said, "We have to be careful these days. It's not the way it used to be. Please come in." And so we did, but still I did not feel comfortable.

Once I had introduced her to my family, my sister offered tea and cookies to us; I could see she still had a black servant, probably a carryover from the slave days. On and on she talked of having to save the farm, and needing money for taxes. She had married a man from the north who had planted tobacco and they were waiting for their first crop to go to market. Feeling a little guilty for judging her too bitterly, I explained that we were heading to Colorado to visit the brothers. Her eyebrows shot up at that statement so I assumed she didn't want me to know she had asked them for money also.

"And why are you really here?" she asked, bitterly. At that, Lani took the children outside and said, "Call me if you need me."

When we were alone, she said, "Are you here to claim your inheritance? Because if you are, you may leave right now."

"So, you haven't seen me in 30 years, and that is your question to me?" I asked.

"Why else would you come all this way – surely not to ask after my health?"

"Actually, I was curious to see how you have spent our hard-earned money, and I can see by the dress you are wearing that you have spent it very well."

"Mother always did say she couldn't believe Jacob Henry would marry a plain jane like you."

"What does that have to do with the money you requested from my brothers and me?" I asked, angrily.

"You went off and left us all so that you could be well-to-do. Mother died here, a pauper, while you were living the good life," she spat.

I stood. "Well, I can see this conversation is going nowhere. I will give the boys my assessment, but I don't think you can count on us for any more money."

As I started out the door, Beatrice grabbed my arm and hissed, "You have always been a bitch."

"And you, my dear, have always been impossible," I replied. I pulled her hand off my arm and bounded down the stairs like an escaped convict. Lani was waiting to help me into the carriage, which was ready to roll like a getaway vehicle.

"Mama, who was that awful woman?" Sarah asked.

"Well, she used to be my sister, but she is no more," I said

"She sure is mean," Jasper added.

"Meaner than a one-eyed snake," Lani said.

"It was a mistake. I knew it, but I had hopes that she had changed. Still, it's good to know, so that I don't climb fool's hill again," I said.

"Plain jane, my ass," he whispered to me.

Driving north of Lebanon, we headed toward the little homestead where I had grown up. As we drew closer, I could see the fields planted in cotton, advice Jacob had given my pa so many years

ago. A young man was walking the land with his children trailing behind him and a moment of peace passed over me – to know that a family had taken up in the place where I was born and raised. The cabin was well cared for, the yard raked, the logs newly chinked. A woman on the doorstep waved to us and we all waved back. I couldn't have asked for more. I did wonder if Beatrice had benefited from the sale of the property, but I realized quickly I couldn't think like that and put it out of my mind, the way I was putting her out of my mind, forever, I hoped.

We settled in to our seats on the Lebanon train and, finally, felt we were on our way west. The worst part of the trip was over, what with the run-in with Beatrice. I was relieved and we were finally adjusting to train travel.

"Mama, be very careful in the privy room because the wind will blow your water right back up in your face. And did you know it goes right on the tracks and you can see the tracks?" Jasper said on the way to Nashville. I glanced around to see that no one was listening.

"Jasper, these are things we don't discuss in public and in front of ladies," I said.

Lani's shoulders were shaking and his face was red from trying not to laugh. I elbowed him.

"Oh, right. Ladies sit down to relieve themselves, but still, you need to be careful," Jasper said.

With that, Lani stood and walked away, almost chuckling right out loud. Sarah and I were having a hard time refraining from laughing too, but Jasper was already distracted by the landscape coming into Nashville.

"Thank you, Jasper," I said. "For the warning, I mean." But I thought, "Thank you for the good laugh, too."

Looking at Sarah's smiling face, a gush of love passed over me. There were times when I felt guilty for all the attention I had given Jasper due to his weakened state, but I loved my Sarah with all my might. I determined to give her an equal amount of my attention. She came and sat in the crook of my arm and I squeezed her to me.

CHAPTER 22   THE DISEMBARKMENT

We had to run to catch our train in Nashville. Our next stop would be St. Louis, Missouri, a long trip of about 12 hours. Lani said we would be crossing the mighty Mississippi River in that city and from there we would be on a train at least two weeks, maybe longer. Lani said on the straight-of-way, the engine could get up to 100 miles per hour, which I found hard to believe. But we were finally getting adjusted to train travel and had budgeted one meal a day in the dining car. We could barely contain ourselves when the dinner hour arrived, so hungry were we.

Our information continued to come from different patrons at the bar, and it was recommended that we get a sleeper room for the trip to Denver. Thinking that was a good idea in spite of the cost, I agreed, but first we had to get to St. Louis, sleeping on the hard seats. The gentleman had said a sleeping room would be the most comfortable unless we could afford a Pullman, which we couldn't.

Lani had a money belt strapped around his waist and I had sewed some bills into the lining of my petticoat, and had a few gold coins in a carpetbag. A private sleeping room would make our funds so much safer - or so I thought - because robberies were reported weekly on the railroad. I had even sewed a few bills into Sarah's petticoat.

As the train pulled out of St. Louis, what luxury it was to look out our private window and see the mighty Mississippi River flowing underneath the railway bridge. Jasper asked why it was so muddy and neither his Papa nor I could answer that question. I reckoned that information would have to come from the bar later that evening. There were times I wished I could join in the conversation in the liquor car, but women were not allowed in there, and I figured the language was probably distasteful, so I decided it was best anyway. Lani was restless the whole time we traveled, worrying about the ranch. Pacing from one car to the next to the next, I wondered that people didn't get tired of seeing him passing by. He also spent long hours on the back end of the caboose, thinking about God knows what. Bringing his guitar would have brought a little peace to him, but it was too bulky to carry.

Sarah had met a young girl, Lily, who had been waiting to get on the train with her family in St Louis, and later had asked to visit with her. Once we figured out which car they were in, she was allowed to go and spend time with the family. Of course, Jasper was not happy about that, but I had noticed his coloring was not good and I felt he should rest. All the traveling had plum tuckered him out. He was not happy about that either, but once he was in his bunk, he slept soundly. That boy worried me to death, but I prayed for him constantly.

Cinchona root was a medication I always carried with me, since Florida was usually dealing with either malaria or yellow fever. Laudanum was another medicine prescribed by doctors but I did my best to stay away from that awful stuff. I tried it once and slept almost 24 hours.

Once Jasper awoke, his color was better, so I allowed him to find his papa and pace with him. When Sarah didn't return for several hours, I went searching for her. The girl's mother said the two girls had headed to the caboose to stand on the back stoop. Alarmed, I ran toward the back of the train, knowing there were unsavory characters onboard, not to be trusted with two little girls. What kind of mother would allow two young girls to wander off by themselves?

As I passed through the caboose car, I asked the conductor if he had seen two girls. He said he had, but that they had headed back to their passenger car. I wondered how I had not seen them unless they were in the privy room. In a panic, I searched for Lani and Jasper, and found them seated in one of the cars. I scooted between the two of them and told Lani that Sarah seemed to be missing. At that moment, the conductor handed us a note, from a gentleman, he said.

"I will trade your daughter to you for the gold you carry," was all the note said, written in an awkward scrawl.

Lani jumped up and grabbed the conductor by the lapels, frightening the man near to death.

"Where is he?" Lani yelled.

"I don't know, sir. The note was delivered to me by a porter," the conductor said.

Scrambling over legs, I headed to our room to retrieve the gold. My thought was, 'what was a little gold compared to the life of our girl?' Panic-stricken, I dug the bag of coins from my carpetbag, as I threw clothes across the floor, knowing this might not be enough. A hand pulled my shoulder back and Lani said, "We will not play this game. I will find him and give him his due."

"You cannot jeopardize her life. I will give him the gold," I shouted.

"Sally, for once, let me handle this. Trust me. Stay here with Jasper," Lani said sternly.

"No. I will not. Jasper, lock the door after us. There's only so many places on a train that a man can hide with two little girls. I'll start at one end and you start at the other," I said.

A knock on the door startled all of us. A porter handed another note to Lani, who grabbed the black man and growled, "Who gave you this note?"

"A gentleman in the first car."

I sensed he was lying and spoke up, saying so. "No ma'am. I ain't lyin'," he said.

His eyes were saucer-round and his body trembled under Lani's hand on his throat.

"You will go to prison if you don't fess up, or maybe be hanged," Lani growled again.

"Just deliverin' the note. But he in the privy room," the man stuttered.

Lani slammed the man against the wall, then ran toward the area the porter had pointed out to us. I was fast on his heels, grabbing my pistol out of my pocket, seeing Lani's gun pulled from his holster, too.

The door to the privy was locked and Lani stepped back and kicked the handle with his boot and it went flying. A scrawny, scruffy, white man was startled by the entry and redirected a shaky gun at us that he had held on the two girls. Lani shot the man's foot and rushed at him. The man howled in pain and his gun went off. I grabbed the hysterical girls and pulled them into the hallway.

Once the door fell open again, I pointed my pistol at the opening, placing the girls behind me, but it was Lani who emerged alone. I looked at him questioningly, and he said, "Oh, he decided to disembark through the window."

I had to smile inwardly, but I was pretty sure that man wouldn't try that trick again and I was pretty sure, also, he didn't disembark voluntarily. I tried to calm the two girls down. Soon I delivered Lily to her hysterical mother and father, and took Sarah to our room. Our hearts were beating like drums; Sarah was near to fainting. Jasper hugged her and patted her back, saying, "It's all right, Sarah-girl."

Later, I said to Lani, out of ear-shot of the children, "You took a big chance that he could have shot the girls."

"Nope. I knew he was a coward the moment I laid eyes on him. The children will not leave us again."

"Yes sir, bossman," I said, managing a weak smile. A very slight smile crossed his worried face.

"I am not doing this again. It's too hard to protect my family when we're this far from the ranch. Once we get home, I'm not leaving anymore," he said. His hands were shaking and I held them to stop the shaking in both our hands. I knew relaxing would be a little harder at that point, but I also wondered how that scrawny man knew we had gold, even though it was only a small amount.

     The porter was taken away in handcuffs when we reached Kansas City, although I thought he was simply paid to deliver the messages, but he had to have known the man was holding two young girls at gunpoint. It was not my call anyway. The railroad would deal with him and I thought it would not be pleasant. A detective boarded the train and asked us a lot of questions, saying they had picked up the kidnapper on the tracks and that he was safely in jail, although he was badly bruised and shot in the foot. I was relieved that he was not dead, but did wonder how he was even still alive.

CHAPTER 23   BEHOLD THE MAJESTY

"*I*t was me. I told Lily about the gold, and that man overheard me." Sarah snuffled as she spoke when we were back in our room.

I didn't think she could have felt any worse, so I didn't scold her, but I warned her not to do that again. She quietly nodded her head, tears dampening her cheeks.

"Mama, look out the window. There ain't no trees," Jasper exclaimed.

"Aren't, Jasper," I corrected.

"Aren't no trees," he said.

Laughing, I said, "There aren't any trees."

"That's what I said," he said.

The four of us stood at the windows and marveled at the endless wheat fields, the landscape so vastly different from Florida – no lush, verdant vegetation, not a tree in sight, no waterholes.

"Lord have mercy," Lani said. "You can see for miles. Imagine that!"

The wheat was a beautiful golden color, such as we had never seen the like before, softly moving throughout the fields, blown by an unseen power, like a hand brushing the heads of the wheat. Mesmerized, none of us moved for several minutes. The knock on the door startled me, and Lani jumped too. I reckoned we would be skittish for some time yet.

Lily and her mother stood on the threshold, both looking very shaken.

"Just wanted to thank you folks for what you did. Lily told us all about it and we couldn't be more appreciative," Lily's mother said.

"Come in," I said, even though there was no room for six people. Lani grabbed his hat and Jasper, and exited into the hallway.

"We'll be leaving you at Topeka, but I just wanted to say how sorry I am for letting the girls go off on their own. I should've known better. Please forgive me."

Lily's mother, Mrs. Langley, was a petite woman, with a plain face, but a lovely smile – when she smiled. The guilt was readable on her face, but who could've known what kind of evil a man was capable of? I hugged her and told her, "Don't blame yourself. We are living in a dangerous world. You might want to carry a pistol when you travel, however."

"Oh, I could never do that. Our faith forbids us to murder anyone," she said.

"I see. Well, perhaps you could carry a big stick then, because there are some bad folks out there and you need to protect your children," I said, hoping that I wasn't too harsh.

After she left, I thought about people who would rather see their child shot than carry a gun to protect that child. It was a mystery to me and I patted my pocket to be certain my pistol was still there.

Lani became more and more restless, rambling with Jasper through the cars. The scenery that we had considered so beautiful had become monotonous because the Kansas landscape was the same for miles on end. My eyes longed to see a tree, and the lush green vegetation of Florida. It was hard for me to think that Harry and my brothers had made this long journey just to be certain we were safe from the epidemic. Sarah and I made several trips daily to the caboose railings just to break up the boredom. And then we entered Colorado and became excited to see the mountains in the distance. The conductor pointed out Pikes Peak to us and we were exhilarated, just to be able to look at that great mountain, which was still so far away. He said we were drawing close to Denver. As we went looking for Lani and Jasper, they came through the door, Jasper jumping up and down, pointing at Pikes Peak. A smile broke across Lani's face and I knew he was relieved to almost be there.

"The mountains are white on top." Jasper said.

"I believe that might be snow," Lani answered. "I've heard about snow, but I've never seen it."

"So many mountains," Sarah whispered.

We were all awed by a sight we couldn't picture in our mind's eye, having only seen drawings in books. It was majestic and made me feel humbled to be a part of this earth. The whole trying trip was worth every minute to see that scene.

We had been traveling northwest and then made a more northerly turn which displayed the extent of the mountain range even more. Being late in the afternoon, the mountains took on a purplish tone. My heart was surging, the air was dry and cool as the winds whipped around us, and my man was smiling the biggest smile I had ever seen in my life. Never ever would I forget that day, that moment, and the three precious people standing with me, experiencing the same elation.

"Never in my born days have I ever seen anything like those mountains," Lani said.

Jasper repeated, quietly, "Never in my borned days."

CHAPTER 24   DENVER TOWN

*G*oodness me! What a hubbub the Denver Union Station was! My eyes scoured the crowds of mostly men for my Harry or my brothers.

"Mrs. Walton! Telegram! Mrs. Walton! Telegram!" a voice rang out.

"Here," Lani called.

A telegram for me? I had never had a telegram in all my years, and fear struck my heart that it might be bad news. Lani gave the delivery boy a nickel and I held the paper message several minutes before Lani took it and opened it up.

It read, "Take cab to Windsor Hotel. Stop. All paid for including dinner. Stop. See you tomorrow. Stop. Harry. Stop."

Disappointment was my word of choice, in that I wanted to see my boy's face so badly. I reckoned everyone could read my emotions and then tried to comfort me. The hansom cabs were waiting by the curb, horses patiently waiting, and we hailed one to take us to the hotel, as suggested.

However, upon entering the hotel, our breaths were taken away. There was a huge courtyard in the center of the hotel that reached all the way to the top, which was five stories high, with live plants in big planters placed about the floor. And even though the sun was setting, the area was flooded with light. A porter grabbed all of our bags and took them to the reception desk and we followed. Lani walked backwards just to look into the courtyard, almost falling down.

Jasper said, "Never in my borned days." And we all laughed.

Truly feeling like country bumpkins when the porter took us to the elevators, I felt trepidation at setting my foot on that floor. The children were thrilled when we rose to the second floor, Sarah squealing with delight. Whatever kind of contraption that was, it surely was exciting, but I preferred the staircase, which I would use in the future.

The bellhop used the key to open the door of the room, and of all things, it opened from that incredible courtyard, so we could walk right outside the room and there it was for us to admire. Then there was the room, luxurious as could be, with a marble mantle around the fireplace, an iron grate, hot and cold running water, beautiful carpets and silk, overstuffed chairs, which I only recognized as silk because my grandmother's dresses had been made of that fabric. I would not let the children sit on the chairs and planned not to let Lani either, or myself. How on earth did they pipe hot and cold running water to that place?

"Your dinner will be served in the dining room after you have had a chance to freshen up from your trip," the bellhop said.

Lani tipped him a nickel and we wandered around the room, totally astonished by the magnificent furnishings. Starved as we were, each of us had a bath before we went down for supper, a hot bath for which we did not have to boil the water. "I want this in my house," I told Lani and he smiled, but made no commitment. Our clothes might have been shabby but our bodies were squeaky clean and smelled like lavender soap - even Lani.

A Mr. Hughes of Hughes and Keith Sanitary Supply Company had ridden in the bar of the train with Lani from Topeka. He had given him his business card and told him Denver was about

100,000 people strong, the second largest city in the west, behind San Francisco. Gold and silver mining had drawn people to Colorado, hence the large number of men I had seen at the depot. Mr. Hughes also had told Lani the city was lighted with electricity. I had thought the lights in the hotel were brighter than I had ever seen. It was a wonder to me and my family, although we had heard about that invention being used in Gainesville. We were country folk but this traveling experience had opened our eyes and educated us in ways we had not planned. The world was changing and my children would get to witness it.

One thing I could say about my family was that we had very good manners, taught from an early age, much more so than some of the people in the dining room of the hotel – even some of the more well-dressed folks. Ordering steaks for supper in a restaurant was a strange experience for a rancher, but Lani was interested in what these cattlemen fed their cattle to produce such tender meat. I assured him Harry would give him a full account. Longing to see that boy of mine caused me to look forward to the coming day and I could not wait to climb in bed, just to hasten the time.

When Lani asked why there were bullet holes in the ceiling of the bar, the waiter replied, "Aw, that was just ole Calamity Jane, mad 'cause they wouldn't serve a lady, which she ain't."

Early the next morning, before sunup, I heard a light tapping on our room door. Since everyone was asleep, I slipped my wrapper on and tiptoed toward the sound. Opening the door a pinch, I could see Harry standing with his hat in his hand, grinning ear to ear. Quietly, I stepped outside and grabbed him around the neck, my heart racing.

"Oh, Mama, you look wonderful. I'm so glad to see you, but why don't you get dressed and meet me for coffee downstairs. We don't want to scandalize the hotel patrons," he whispered.

As I threw my clothes on, and brushed my hair, I could hardly move fast enough, while trying to be quiet. I kissed Lani and told him where I would be. He grunted.

The staircase was wide and beautiful as I rushed to meet Harry in the dining room, holding onto the railing to prevent a fall. He sat in the corner next to a window, with hardly a soul in the room but him and the server.

"How did you get here?" I asked, after I was seated.

"Took the train from Greeley, but I was hoping to get here yesterday. Belinda is ailing and I just couldn't leave her. I'm sorry," he said.

"Ailing?" I asked.

"We've a child due soon. She's had a wicked time of it and hasn't wanted me to tell anyone as she doesn't think it will survive. Sometimes I think she feels she may not survive either, but she doesn't say so."

"Oh, that's terrible news. Maybe I can be of some help," I suggested, but I hadn't delivered a baby in many years.

"Her mother has been with her, but enough of that. How was the trip? How are you? I'm so glad you came."

"That's a mighty long trip and we had a little trouble on the way here, but you know Lani. He's good at handling difficult situations," I replied.

I recounted the story of the kidnapping and the early exit by the kidnapper. Harry laughed a relieved laugh.

"This coffee is just what I needed," he said. "Strong, black and hot."

"Ain't it so?" I replied, closing my eyes, savoring the aroma and taste of the jet black drink, filling my body with warmth and energy. I didn't even add cream and sugar.

"We'll take the UPD&G train this afternoon to Greeley and the uncles will pick us up there."

"UPD&G?" I asked.

"Union Pacific, Denver, and Gulf Railroad. Long name for a short ride," he said, smiling.

How good it was to see him. His eyes mirrored my own, but his smile and his way of speaking belonged to his Pa, Jacob Henry.

"I don't know if I told you how we valued coffee in the days of the war and the journey out of Georgia," I said.

"About a hundred times. You gave me the love of the drink from your stories. I miss you, Ma."

"Oh, Harry. I have thought of you every day since you left and I've missed you every day, too."

My heart melted and I had to work to keep back the tears. I had dreamed of this day and I knew I had to cherish this alone-time because once we reached the ranch we would be surrounded by family – lots of family. And it wouldn't be long before Lani and the children would descend on us this very morning.

Harry talked about the ranch, the cattle, Belinda, his children, my brothers, their wives, their children and grandchildren. They all lived within 10 miles of each other, but Harry was the one I had longed to see above all the others. This moment was *really* what made the long trip worthwhile and I reveled in it.

"How is that good-for-nothing brother of mine?" Harry asked with a grin.

"Grumpy as ever. I don't know how Suzanna puts up with him."

"I do," he said. "He's different around her and Fereby. I never thought he would find another woman after you-know-who."

"She whose name shall not be spoken," I laughed as I spoke.

"He's like an old man, but we all love him."

"Do you, Harry?" I asked

"I do. I always have. It took me awhile to understand that situation, but that woman was a witch who could cast a spell. I should know."

It had taken Harry a good long time to forgive his brother for running off with his first wife, Susan Marley, but in the end, Harry was the winner because he had found Belinda in Colorado. I thought the reason John was cantankerous was because he had never recovered fully from his awful sin against his brother.

"Here comes the clan," Harry said, standing to shake hands with Lani and Jasper, and hug Sarah. "Here's that pretty girl. Where did she get that beautiful yellow hair?"

Sarah beamed as they sat down around the table. Lani ordered a coffee for himself and Jasper and an orange juice for Sarah.

The conversation immediately turned to ranching and I slipped upstairs to properly comb my hair and put it into a bun instead of hanging down my back. I made up the beds and straightened our things. If I had had a broom, I would have swept the floor, but I did dust the vanity and dressers with my hanky. Running the hot water one last time, I marveled at that miracle, my fingers lingering in the warm flow. Such a luxury.

CHAPTER 25   GOD'S SPLENDOR

"The heavens declare the glory of God; and the firmament showeth his handywork." Psalms 19:1

I had lost track of the days. Harry told me it was a Sunday when we pulled into the Greeley station. As for how long we had been gone from home I had no idea, only that it seemed like months. Both my brothers, John and Henry, rode their horses alongside the train as we pulled in, like a pair of young whippersnappers, which they were not. Jasper and Sarah squealed with joy and I felt like squealing myself. They whooped and waved their hats in the air as if the president of these United States of America were riding in the railway car.

"Glory be!" Lani said. "These are my kind of folks!"

"Mine too," said Jasper.

"I believe my brothers might be wild and wooly," I said.

Harry laughed. "Yep. They are that! But they don't welcome everybody like that. You are going to get the royal treatment, Ma. That's what they think of you."

"We all do, son," Lani said, smiling.

I could barely wait for the brakes to be applied, I was so excited to see my little brothers, who were not so little anymore. Not only were they tall, but they were robust, all muscle, no fat. And were they ever horsemen. They had to have learned to ride like that in Colorado because we didn't own but one work horse and a mule in Tennessee. Their smiles were as big as my heart felt.

"You boys are quite the welcoming committee," I said, as I hugged them both.

"The Queen of Sheba, I would say. How 'bout you John?" Henry asked.

"I was thinking more like the first lady of these here United States," John said.

"Well, I was thinking more like your big sister, who is starving, along with her family. Where can we get something to eat?"

"How about the Winston Place? I hear they cook up a real good supper," Harry said.

"What about Belinda, Harry?" I asked.

"Everybody's coming with food, my dear. She won't lift a finger," he said.

"And how did the visit with Beatrice go, Sally?" John asked as he drove the carriage to the ranch.

"Just as expected," I replied

"Hah!" he laughed. "How was the old hag?"

"No change, just older and meaner," I said.

"Ah, and how was our investment spent?" John asked.

"You've invested very well in silk clothing and contributed some to a Yankee carpetbagger."

John threw his head back and laughed heartily. "Well, God bless her because we won't be blessing her again – unless it's blessing her out."

Harry, Lani and Henry rode behind on horses. I knew Lani had been missing being in the saddle and I smiled to see him so happy between my brother and my son, while Sarah and Jasper sat awestruck in the backseat, pointing out another mountain range to

was when I asked about Indians.

"Sad as can be, although they don't bedevil us anymore, stealing cattle and raiding homesteads. You probably heard about the Sand Creek Massacre, which happened in the 1860s, but these people are now defeated. They are reduced to begging, placed on reservations, a people who once were warriors. However, we don't worry about their assaults at this point in time. There were times when we had to move to a fort to protect our families. I am happy we don't face that threat, but we do have our own set of problems, namely feeding cattle on land that is being stripped of grass due to overgrazing. And don't get me started about water rights. How I wish we had the water you have in Florida," John said.

"I hear tell there's some trouble brewing in the Dakotas, however - with the Indians, that is," he continued. "I hope it all turns out all right – for all concerned and none of it spills over into our land."

I had heard about the Sand Creek Massacre from Harry, but John recounted the awful event where mainly Indian women and children were murdered. He said our train had passed to the north of that place.

"What is today's date, John," I asked, absent-mindedly.

"June 8th. Do you need the year?" he asked, grinning.

"I do remember that. Did we keep you from church?"

"Yes, praise the Lord, and I wish to thank thee for that," he said with a jovial laugh.

"You were always naughty, but I loved you anyway," I said as I hooked my arm through his.

"Praise the Lord! Good enough?" he shouted.

☼

The air was dry and the lower the sun sank, the cooler the air became. As we rode through the gate to Harry's ranch, a large fire loomed in the center of the yard. Thank goodness it was still light when I met everyone or else I would never have remembered their faces. Such a large crowd of people there was – all my relatives. It was overwhelming for me and I could see Lani's strained face as he was being introduced, not to mention that we were tired and hungry. Tables were lined up with piles of food on platters and we were not shy about eating, because we were ravenous.

John had warned me that his wife, Marina, was a fiery Mexican woman and his four sons had dual names; Juan for John, Pedro for Peter, Diego for James, and Roberto for Robert. Diego and Roberto, the youngest two, were unmarried and were wilder than blue blazes. His older boys were married with children, and were his best workers. Juan had begun a beet farm, which was unheard of in a ranching community, but not only did they sell the beets for sugar, the greens were used for silage. It was ingenious.

Brother Henry had a wife, Lillian, two daughters, Kathryn and Sarah, and two sons, David, and Jefferson, who was married to Martha, with one child. Of course my own grandchildren, Harry and Belinda's children, were so special to me and I ran to them when I saw them - John, Claire and Elizabeth. Oh how they had grown. Waddling toward me came Belinda, smiling, even though she looked extremely tired. We hugged for a long moment as I recalled what it felt like to be that big and miserable.

A setting sun was not something we always witnessed in Florida, due to the amount of trees on the ranch, but to watch the sun go down behind a mountain range was a sight to behold. The sky was a brilliant golden color, while the mountains were purple/blue and as we sat around the fire, all seemed right with the world, even though we were a long way from home. We felt comfortable with my people. Jasper fell asleep behind a hay bale and I felt like joining him, but everyone started drifting home and Harry took us into their very large log house.

Our family slept in the open loft, a nice-sized room with a log-framed bed. Snuggled in between a feather mattress and a down comforter, the only thing that made me want to wake up was the smell of coffee and the need to find the privy. Sarah and Jasper slept on the floor on pallets, Jasper snoring lightly. Dressing quickly, I stumbled down the stairs and out the front door toward the outhouse. Harry followed me with a lantern since the sun had not yet risen. The light bounced off the rocky ground as I hurried toward my destination, barely making it. The cold seat was shocking and I'm sure I squealed a little, with Harry laughing outside the door.

"It's cold for a June morning," I whispered.

"It's Colorado, Ma. Come inside and let's have some black nectar to get us going," Harry suggested.

"Oh yes. Have I told you about our trip out of Georgia?" I teased. He laughed heartily.

Norton, Harry's old hound dog, sniffed at my legs as I started up the steps. As I turned and sat to pet him, first light broke. I watched as the sun to the east lightly lit up the very tops of the mountains to the west as if the light flowed gently down from the peaks. My mouth hung open at the sight, while Harry handed me a cup of coffee and sat down beside me. Wrapping a quilt around my shoulders, he sat, barefooted, just like an old Florida boy. I was warmed inside and out, as I placed part of the quilt over his feet. We sat quietly watching the display of light and color until the family began to awaken.

I could see my father's hand in the building of Harry's log house. My brothers had helped build it, I was certain, and they had learned everything from him before he was killed. The small amount of chinking, the perfect joints at the corners, the pitch of the roof, even the loft, were all his designs. Wishing Harry could have met him, he read my mind and said, "Your brothers talk about their pa a lot."

"He was a man of great character. He taught me most everything I needed to know in life," I said.

Annabelle, Belinda's mother, brought us a platter of hot biscuits, buttered on top, at that very moment and I felt life couldn't get any better. Of course, Norton was feeling the same way and his soulful eyes begged for a morsel; I obliged.

"What kind of name is 'Norton' for a hound dog?" I asked.

"The children named him after their teacher, Mr. Norton, whom they love," Harry said.

"How is Belinda this morning?" I asked.

"Feeling poorly. I told her to stay in bed, but she won't. Hard-headed woman," he said with a smile.

"Everything will be all right," I said. As the worry returned

"That there's Horsetooth Mountain. That one is Long's Peak and all us Coloradoans call that one Mount Meeker," he said as he pointed toward the west, trying to change the subject.

The look on my face must've said what I was thinking. My son considered himself to be a Colorado native. I knew, then, that my heart would always dwell in two places, as he was as much a part of me as my own being. Hurting, I turned away from him.

"Ma, don't worry. I'll always be a misplaced Floridian. But my life is here now and I can't change that."

"I know, Harry. It's just hard to hear it, but I'm happy for you."

The peace and quiet was broken by the sound of little John, or Johnny, as he was called, coming through the front door and hugging me from behind, his small arms reaching around my neck. I pulled him around to my lap and tucked him into the quilt for warmth, but he was too energetic to sit still for long. Harry told him to put on his boots and they would go feed the animals in the barn. As Johnny was heading back inside, he grabbed a biscuit, grinning. I was left to myself, still astounded by the scenery, and still paining from information that I already knew to be true.

CHAPTER 26   JACOB'S LADDER

*B*lue is a weakling word to describe the skies of Colorado: azure, turquoise, teal, indigo, all of those words, in a cloudless sky, still could not describe the color. Looking up constantly, I had to watch my step or fall flat on my face. That's what the heavens looked like the day Belinda began the birthing.

According to Annabelle, everything looked all right but Belinda said she had had no movement in weeks, which didn't sound very good to me. Sarah remained with me while the men took to the pastures, doing what they did best, avoiding the situation. We surely didn't want them around anyway, but they could have stayed a little closer. Sarah and I cleaned the kitchen, boiled water for the birth, and made sure there were clean rags for bandaging in case there was a lot of bleeding. Of course, that took me back to my first birthing, when I almost bled to death in Georgia, as a young girl.

The brooms were handy, so we swept every square inch of the house, the walls, the front porch and steps. Belinda's cries could be heard outside the log house even though the walls were thick. Since Sarah was wringing her hands, I sent her to the barn to check on the animals and gather the chicken eggs.

Annabelle came outside after a bit and said she thought the baby would be stillborn and that's why Belinda was having such a hard time.

"What can I do?" I asked.

"Pray! I've delivered lots of babies but I've got to save my girl."

What did that mean, I wondered? Would she allow the baby to die? Was it already dead? Although the only experience I had had with midwifing was years ago, I still felt maybe there was a chance that the baby could make it. Entering the bedroom quietly, I crossed to Belinda and took her hand. Her eyes blinked open, blue as that Colorado sky outside, as she smiled weakly. She had now been laboring for eight hours. Once again, I went to the kitchen to try and make myself useful, feeling Annabelle was capable of delivering the child.

As Belinda's cries continued, I scrubbed the wooden table, the stovetop, anything to keep busy. And then Annabelle appeared in the doorway with a bundle and said, "Please prepare him for the burial while I clean up Belinda."

Gently I took the boy in my arms, holding him close to me for my warmth, even though it felt useless. I swabbed out his nostrils and his mouth and cleaned his whole little body, my tears falling on his blue-tinged skin. As I washed his small feet and toes, I massaged them as if he were just asleep. I held his hands as I cleaned them and worked his fingers back and forth, one at a time. Once he was clean, I bundled him in a blanket and sat in the rocking chair, singing, "Go to sleepy, little baby. Go to sleepy, little baby. When you wake, you shall have a cake. So, go to sleepy little baby." Just as I ended the song, I thought I felt him move, hoping I wasn't just wishing for it to happen, and then he made a tiny sound, so soft I hardly heard it. I almost fainted, my heart beating rapidly. As I held him up on my shoulder, patting him, he let out a loud cry. Annabelle came running into the room.

"Glory be! You mean he's alive? Thank you, God! He's alive!" she cried.

The boy was wailing by that time. Belinda leaned on the door frame, pale as a white sheet, not believing what she was seeing, either. Annabelle helped her to the rocker, where she sat and I placed her son in her arms, her body wracked with sobs. I don't know that anything has ever made me that happy in my entire life – sorrow turned to joy in a moment.

As Sarah came in, Belinda was trying to feed the baby boy. Sarah giggled with delight, not knowing how close we had come to losing him. Annabelle hugged me and said, "It was because you didn't give up. You are a saint, Sally."

"Not a saint, just stubborn as a mule," I said.

☼

When the men arrived, the scene was one of homesteaded bliss. Whether Harry would ever know the true story or not, I did not know, but I knew I wouldn't be the one to share that secret. I had a feeling he would not be told because of guilty feelings on Belinda's part – and Annabelle's, even though they were blameless.

So convinced was she that the baby would not live, Belinda had not come up with a name. Everyone had a suggestion, but no name seemed quite right to the parents. For a few days, he was simply called 'Baby.' When Jasper accidentally let Norton into the house and he got into the food pantry, Harry yelled, "You're going to be climbing Jacob's ladder pretty soon, you blamed old hound dog."

He looked at me and said, "Of course. Jacob Henry Winston." And I said, "At least he'll be in Colorado. Too many Jacobs in Florida."

Little Jacob Henry was a squaller. He may have been quiet and still in the womb, but he was loud and wiggly in real life. Everyone took turns walking him, but the person he was the best with was Sarah. Since she had had so much experience taking care of Jimmy, she was calm, and the baby responded.

The thought that I didn't want to think was that perhaps Belinda might not want more children and was secretly hoping the baby would not live. I prayed that wasn't the case, but I did tell her about Dr. Foote's womb veil, which I had used. Frankly, I thought there might be better products in this new modern age, but she said she would look into it.

CHAPTER 27   BARRELIN' TOWARD HEAVEN

*W*hen a woman's heart is divided, it is the lonesomest feeling – knowing that you will miss the folks you're with, but also missing the ones left behind. Truly, it's like never being totally comfortable because you're always feeling something is not quite right – someone is not there. Harry and I had a bond that couldn't be broken but that only made the pain a little worse. Now, I had also come to love little Jacob Henry and the rest of my grandchildren. Getting to know my brothers better was wonderful, too. However, had I never known them better, I could have missed them less. How I loved their wives and families, even those wild boys – especially those wild boys.

Between two of the ranches, Harry's and Brother John's, was an immense lake – one they used for irrigation and for watering the livestock. After we had been in Colorado for a week, a big Sunday picnic at the lake was planned after church. Jasper wiggled all morning long in church, so anxious was he to go to the gathering. He burst through the church front door after the services as if he were shot out by a cannon. It was an exciting time, since we had been house-bound taking care of Belinda and Jacob. Annabelle had gone home but she and her husband, Frank, would be at the event.

It was one of those cloudless days, when the air was crisp, and breathing was so easy. As we loaded the food into the covered wagon and began the journey to the lake, I slipped back in time a little. I could see Elizabeth and Loretta and myself walking behind the wagon, with the children waving out of the back. It was dizzying, and I stumbled as I walked.

"Sally," Lani called from atop his horse. "Girl, you all right?"

My face was warm and moist, my heart beating like a drum. I took hold of the wooden backing on the backend and allowed the wagon to pull me along. Lani stepped down and came to me, releasing my hand from the wagon.

"I'm ok. Just a little shaken is all," I said.

"What is it?" he asked.

"It was like a remembrance – kind of like the dreams I have – only I'm awake."

He pulled out his canteen and made me drink, saying, "Maybe you have not had enough water lately. With the air so dry, a person could get dried out. It's not like Florida here, you know."

"Ride with me," he said.

Once in the saddle, he pulled me up behind him and I wrapped my arms around his chest and laid my head on his back, looking west toward those towering peaks. Then, my mind calmed because I knew those mountains were not in Georgia or Florida and I think I had become weak due to not drinking enough liquids, as Lani had mentioned. Kathryn said it was called 'dehydration' – a big word I had never heard before.

Henry handed Lani a guitar as we sat around the fire after dinner and he sang a song he had never shared with me. That man constantly surprised me. Grinning, he began:

"You got your troubles.
I got mine.

Let's sit down and drink some wine,
'Cause we're all barreling toward heaven."

I had to laugh, along with everyone else, but that's all he had done on that song. Saying he had written it on the train, I realized he was a man of many talents – in more ways than one. And then he sang:

"Down in the valley,
Valley so low.
Hang your head over,
Hear the wind blow."

Everyone joined in singing that old folksong. It was one of those moments I wanted to hold onto and knew I would never forget. The next week would be our last in Colorado with our loved ones and every second had to count.

Sarah told me that Kathryn and Hannah, Henry's daughters, who were 16 and 17 years old, were starting at the Colorado State Normal School in October, studying to be teachers. She said that's what she wanted to do when she got older, too. They had spent a lot of time with Sarah, braiding her hair, and teaching her about wild flowers and wild herbs. She was very taken with her cousins and I wondered if she wanted to stay in Colorado, but I knew she couldn't be separated from Jasper and Jasper couldn't be separated from me and his pa – or Sarah.

Those wild boys, Diego and Roberto, put on quite the horse show for us. I never saw a rider run alongside a horse going full steam and throw himself into the saddle, then drop to the other side and land in the saddle again, with his brother riding in tandem. They whooped and hollered and made us all laugh and clap. Born to the saddle, they were. Their parents just shook their heads. Sometimes those brothers spoke perfect English and other times, they were speaking Spanish, although I couldn't tell if the Spanish was perfect or not. Lani was impressed with the riding and so was Jasper and I was totally impressed with their abilities, both equestrian and the bilingual talk. Their dark eyes flashed as they accepted the crowd's applause, their jet black hair tumbling out of their lifted hats.

I did notice that Jasper's breathing was better out in Colorado, but I surely didn't want him trying to ride like the brothers, although I could see he wanted to. The children all got into the lake water, but got right out, saying it was too cold, but I dangled my feet off the little dock and it felt right to me, happy we didn't have to worry about gators and water moccasins. I watched as seagulls, egrets, and herons fished for their dinner, thinking they should be in Florida, not Colorado. But Henry explained that this lake was a natural flyover pathway and many of the birds were on their way to Florida and would probably beat us home.

☼

It was a perfect day, weather-wise and otherwise. As I looked off in the distance toward the peaks, I could see dark clouds gathering. As my eyes followed the contour of the hills, I saw a ragged line of people slowly moving to the north. I had to strain my eyes to see who they could be, with no wagons, only a few horses, and walking at a dragging pace.

When Diego and Roberto noticed the group, they gathered up the leftovers from our meal in tablecloths, tied in a knot, and headed out toward the people, riding like the wind.

John said, "Indians heading to the Badlands. The boys know they're starving."

Those wild boys had good hearts, I thought, wondering how our government could let whole tribes of Indians go hungry. It was hard to know the right thing to do, with trouble brewing to the north. But people should not die from starvation - ever. That was not how I had pictured the mighty Indians of the West. I believed they had been brought low.

CHAPTER 28   THE COLOR

*H*arry was feeling hesitant about leaving Belinda and Jacob, but had wanted us to get into the mountains. He said the Cache la Poudre Canyon would be a good place for us to experience the 'hills,' as he called them.

"As long as we can be on that train in a week," Lani said. My husband tossed and turned at night and I knew he was worried about our ranch and the trip home. I wanted him to relax, so that our time with relatives was well spent.

Annabelle and Frank came to stay with Belinda and the children, while we loaded the wagon and started on our big adventure into the Rockies. The wild boys came along and I was glad because they were a joy to be around, bursting with life and energy. Jasper followed after them on his small horse, trying to keep up and they slowed for him. He was in hog heaven. I suggested they join up with Buffalo Bill's Wild West Show and they said those folks were amateurs. Laughing, I said, "Maybe you should start your own show."

☼

Camp Collins, as it was once called, was now Fort Collins, and it was there we stopped at the general store to buy a few supplies, including flour, salt and coffee.

"Just be careful of the rains, as flash floods can be dangerous," the store owner said.

"What's a flash flood?" I asked.

He looked at me in amazement. "You ain't from these parts, are you, little lady?"

"Florida," I answered, at which he laughed.

"Well, it's where the rain runs down the mountains and comes together in the canyons, washing everything in its path down to the plains. Just keep an eye out," he said.

"Thank you for that bit of information," I said.

The trail leading into the mountains was just that – a trail, rocky and steep, but Harry had hitched four mules to the wagon and they were hardy. As we ascended and looked back down the way we had come, I was awed by the view, looking toward the vast prairie and the ranches we had just left. The pathway followed the Poudre River, which was little more than a stream, but I guessed the rains the following spring would cause it to swell and overflow, as the store manager had stated.

Harry drove and I rode beside him, bouncing around like a rubber ball. By mid-afternoon we had reached a beautiful meadow, where we stopped for the evening. The boys, Jasper, and Sarah rode on for aways, but turned back after a bit, when Jasper had a difficult time breathing. I made him climb in the wagon and rest for a short while, although he didn't want the boys to notice. The altitude change was affecting all us flatlanders, but Harry said we would adjust.

"We'll make camp here and ride out on excursions each day – maybe pan for a little gold in the streams," Harry said. Lani's eyes lit up and I thought maybe he would start enjoying himself and forget the worries of our ranch – and the long ride home.

"What kind of trees are those surrounding the meadows?" Sarah asked.

"Aspen – the quaking aspens," Harry said.

"I love the quaking," I said. It was a gentle noise, not the whispering sound of the pines, but a rustling noise, calming to the ear.

Once the sun set behind the mountains, it got dark early - and cold - colder than down on the plains. We ate smoked beef and biscuits baked earlier, and apples. Goodness, the apples were delicious. Harry said they were grown in Colorado and were stored in their cellars. Appreciating that I didn't have to cook over an open fire, I settled in between Lani and Harry, stretching my legs out by the fire.

Roberto and Diego hoisted our food up in a tree, safe from the critters, especially bears. Sarah and Jasper's eyes were round as the boys told some tales about grizzly bears, and I had to admit, it made me a little jittery, too. The mules were hobbled and would be defenseless against a mountain lion or a bear, but I knew they would make a lot of noise if alarmed.

Pulling out a guitar, Diego played a Spanish tune, his hands all over the fretboard. I thought Lani had never seemed so excited, so enthralled was he by that way of playing. They sat together while Diego showed him the moves. Bonds were being made and I knew Lani would start to enjoy himself a little after this trip to the hills. I was relieved. After all, my family was his only family. The music lightened the heavy mood, what with the talk of predators.

After the excitement of the day, Jasper climbed into the wagon early, while the rest of us lounged around the fire, listening to the melodic songs played, first by Diego and then by Lani. It was another moment in time to savor, the music being like a punctuation mark. Closing my eyes, not meaning to sleep, I drifted off until Lani covered me with a blanket and slipped under it with me, kissing me softly on my cheek. Sarah cuddled up to my back. Indeed, I would be warm, I thought, drowsily.

As Lani stirred the fire in the morning, I stretched, and thought of all the times I had awakened to Jake getting the fire going in the mornings. I wondered why this trip, in particular, had brought back so many memories of those early days leaving Georgia, even though the surroundings were so completely different. But soon the coffee was boiling and I knew I was blessed to have all these folks in my life, especially when someone handed me a cup of coffee before I was out of bed.

"The best time to pan for gold is after the spring rains have washed it down from the hills," Harry said. "But we'll take what we can get."

"When can we start?" Lani asked with more enthusiasm than I knew he had for panning. Maybe he *was* getting the gold fever, I thought.

Harry passed out four gold pans and we walked to the river, while Diego and Roberto headed off on their horses, looking for dinner. As Harry showed us what to do, he leaned closer to me and said, "I know what you did, Ma."

"You mean…?" I began.

"If it weren't for you, we wouldn't have our Jacob Henry. How can I thank you?"

"Aww, Harry. It just happened. I wasn't responsible. It was God."

"Well, I am grateful," he relied. Tears formed in his eyes, he sat back on his haunches and wiped his face on his sleeve.

☼

Harry called the gold, 'color.' And truly, it was amazing how it could be seen in the pan as 'color.' Lani panned all day and came up with an ample little cloth bag full of powder and nuggets. For myself and the children, we became bored and went looking for blackberries for a nice cobbler. We strolled through the aspen trees, their tender little green leaves rustling, to a meadow in the distance. Although I carried my little pistol, I was still diligent about searching for scat and prints. I only knew that blackberries grew in the mountains because Annabelle asked me to bring her a bucketful.

When we did find the berries, only a few were ripe, but we picked them all because I knew I could add sugar to the cobbler, keeping it from being too tart. I leaned down and picked ripe berries at the bottom. When I stood up, a black bear also stood up on the other side of the vines. We were both surprised. The bear whimpered and I screamed and threw my cache in the air, grabbed the children and ran like a crazy woman. The bear ran the other way, just as startled as we were. As we looked back, we saw him run up a hill into the pine trees on the other side of the meadow. Once we got back to camp, we fell down by the wagon and laughed, mostly from relief. I had thought I was braver than that, but the bear probably thought he was, too.

"It was probably a young bear or else he wouldn't have run," Diego said in the evening.

"No matter. You must stay close to someone with a rifle. Your handgun would not kill a bear, just make him mad," Lani said.

The children had held onto their buckets of berries, thank goodness. The cobbler, cooked in a Dutch oven over an open fire, was so delicious. Of course, it would have been better with more blackberries, but mine were scattered over the meadow and beyond. Jasper relayed the story of the bear standing at the same time as me, and how I threw the bucket high in the air, screaming. The bucket had landed on the bear's head, which I had not known. Everyone laughed, including me. Jasper could tell a good tale, but Annabelle would not get any berries on this trip.

Indeed, my husband had caught the gold fever. He held his bag of gold as we sat around the fire and planned the next day.

"I'll be panning tomorrow, so you all go on into the mountains and I'll see you around suppertime. I'll keep an eye out on the mules," he said.

"I hate to abandon a flatlander alone up here, but I'll leave my rifle with you," Harry said.

"I may be a flatlander but I can handle myself. We do have critters in Florida, both two-legged and four-legged and some no-legged," Lani said, meaning snakes.

Diego and Roberto laughed, but Harry did not.

"Should I stay?" I asked.

"Goldurnit, Sally. Go! Have a good time while I pan."

When we turned in, I reached for Lani. "I'm sorry," I whispered. Tucking me into his arms, he said, "For what? Wanting to take care of your man? I should be thanking you."

☼

Early the next morning we saddled our horses and headed up the Cache la Poudre trail, as the light of day began its journey. I waved goodbye to Lani as he stood holding his newly acquired gold pan. I smiled at the image, grateful for such a good man in my life. God bless him, I thought.

Our horses were mountain horses, I assumed, because they were sure-footed. Jasper rode ahead with the wild boys while Sarah, Harry and I brought up the rear. The higher we climbed, the thinner the air became, until I had to ask for a breather. Stopping at a meadow, filled with wildflowers, I spread a saddle blanket and lay back in the warm sun and that's when I saw the snow-topped peaks that I couldn't see earlier as we had been in the canyon. What a sight to behold! How could I ever describe that vision to the folks back home? I wished for a camera to preserve the magnificent image, but alas, we did not own a camera, and probably never would. My mind would have to capture it.

"Mama, come see the beautiful flowers," Sarah called.

"That's a columbine," Harry said.

"Oh. Such a delicate thing, much like the ghost orchid in Florida," I said.

The columbines grew in the moist spots of the meadow, but the whole area was covered with blooming flowers. It was like a little corner of paradise. Colorado was the most beautiful place, but I would bet this meadow was covered with snow in winter and not near this pretty, rather, pretty in a different way.

148

In a far valley across the river stood a herd of elk, grazing on the verdant grasses. When Roberto wanted to ride out and shoot one to take back to the ranch, Sarah begged him not to kill the beautiful animal. We all agreed with her and Roberto smiled and said, "We won't ruin the trip for our pretty Sarah."

We ate our noon meal in that place, Jasper and Diego snoozing on my blanket afterward, while Sarah and I picked flowers. And soon it was time to head back down the hill, which would be as difficult as coming up. I walked beside my horse, as I felt he could trip and I would go over his head, but the rest of the group rode their mounts, but they were slow-moving, too.

When Jasper sucked in his breath and pointed to the cliff on the opposite side of the river, I followed with my eyes and saw an animal standing in an impossible position, with the most unusual horns I had ever seen. "Bighorn sheep," Roberto whispered. Once again, we marveled at one of God's creations, which could navigate that steep wall with so little effort. Then several more appeared, jumping from place to place, chewing on what little greenery was lodged in the rocks.

"Thank you, Harry, Diego, Roberto," I said. "You will never know how much this means to me, and the children, and my gold-panning husband."

The boys grinned big. I liked those two so much. When they got excited, they had a little bit of a Spanish accent to their English, which was so endearing.

As we turned the last corner before our campsite, a scene greeted us that was hard to comprehend after our remarkably peaceful day. A grizzly, old, bearded man was tied to our front wagon wheel and Lani sat by the campfire, drinking coffee and frying fish he had caught in the river.

"What in tarnation!" Harry exclaimed.

"This old geezer pulled a six gun on me while I was panning," Lani said. "So I took it away from him and tied him up. Figured I'd take him to the sheriff."

"You're on my goldurned claim," the old man said.

"The river doesn't need a claim," Diego said.

"Let me go. My mule needs me to take care of her. Don't take me to the sheriff. My mule, Sally, will die," the old man pleaded.

We all looked at each other and burst out laughing.

"What's your name, old man?" Harry asked.

"Sam McCall," he said.

"Well, Sam McCall, you need to be more careful who you pull a gun on. This here's a gator feller and not to be messed with," Harry said.

Lani took the bullets out of Sam's six gun, untied him and sent him on his way, grumbling and cussing, heading off to look after his Sally.

Sure enough, Lani had found a good sized gold nugget, which he said would pay for our whole trip, which made me happy. The nugget got passed around but Lani made sure it went back in his bag.

"We'll stop in at the assayers office in Fort Collins and see what it's worth," Harry said. Lani couldn't quit smiling.

CHAPTER 29   WILD WEST STAR

*T*oo soon it was time to leave: my grandchildren, my brothers, my son, the wild boys I had grown to love, and many others I had not had time to get to know. On Sunday, the day before we were scheduled to leave, dinner was planned at Harry's house after we went to church. My heart was heavy, but I knew I had to try to enjoy this one last day with my family. Sarah was already experiencing sadness from having to leave Jacob Henry and the girls, Kathryn and Hannah, and it was not easy to console her when I felt the same way.

After dinner, Diego announced loudly to the crowd that he had a performance for us to witness. I swear he should have been in a Wild West show, with a megaphone in his hand. My breath was taken away, however, when Jasper appeared in fuzzy chaps and a big hat, leading a pony to the clearing. "Diego!" I exclaimed, to which he held his hand up, silencing me.

Jasper turned the pony and as the pony began to trot, Jasper ran alongside him, finally throwing himself into the saddle. Our crowd went wild, whistling, clapping, and screaming Jasper's name. He rode in a circle and took his hat off, waving to his fans. His smile couldn't have gotten any bigger as he rode into the clearing. Lani was a proud papa, and me, I was relieved that he wasn't hurt. But he gave us several encores.

☼

"Seems like saying goodbye to you is getting to be a habit," I said to Harry.

"Didn't we have the best time?" he asked.

"It was the best time I've ever had in my life, but don't tell your brother that," I said, laughing.

He smiled as we stood at the train station in Greeley. "Come back anytime, Ma. We all love you and the family. Thank you for everything, especially Jacob Henry."

Squeezing my eyes shut, I tried to prevent the tears from coming, but it was too late and I cried as I hugged my sweet son goodbye...again.

"I love that you live in this wonderful place with all your friends and family. Colorado is a place I could live - except for the wintertime. Just keep the letters coming," I said sadly.

We had already said goodbye to the rest of the family, including my "little" brothers. My heart was full of love as we stood on the back of the faded red caboose and waved to my favorite child, Harry, watching him grow smaller as the train chugged away. But that didn't keep me from crying most of the way to Denver. I made up my mind that I would cry no longer than the trip to Denver and I was good at my word. After all, I wanted my vision to be clear when I laid eyes on Pikes Peak again.

☼

The nugget would not be sold and that was that. Lani said he wanted everyone back home to see what a real gold nugget looked like. He did sell the powder and small nuggets and splurged on a Pullman sleeper car for every leg of the journey home. If I had known what luxury it was to ride in a Pullman, I would have suggested it long ago. The weariness did not accompany a person into the Pullman.

"I reckon we'll never come this way again, and I want to remember every minute of every day," I said.

"Sally, you never can tell," he said.

Closing my eyes, I leaned back on the velvet chair and pictured myself in the mountains with the cool breeze blowing the aspen leaves, the elk bugling across the meadows, warm sun on my skin, and the columbines growing close by. It was hard to leave a place that was so beautiful and our experiences so rich. Slipping into a dream, I nodded out for a few hours. I think everyone did.

And then, we were home again, greeted by our friends and family members who had missed us so much. Fereby and Daniel had grown taller and older. We had been gone more than eight weeks and the ride home had made me realize how completely different Florida and Colorado were, both beautiful but diverse.

Loretta cried when she saw me, thinking I might not return, she said. Hugs were plentiful and we had lots of tales to tell, and not tall ones, except for Jasper, who might have exaggerated his rodeo riding a bit.

When John asked about his brother, I said, "He speaks fondly of you, son." It was all he needed.

Lani and John immediately left to ride the pastures and get caught up on the latest, but everything seemed fine to me. As a matter of fact, it looked a little bit better, but maybe that was because I had missed my home so much, and Florida – I had really missed Florida. Seems I was always missing something or somebody. It was the way of my life.

"Mama, we belong here. We're Florida folks," Sarah said.

Pleased to hear her say that, I had wondered if she weren't so taken with Colorado and our relatives, that she might want to move there for good when she got older. The thought of her one day leaving the ranch and me, was something I could not dwell on.

"Yes ma'am. We *are* Florida folks," I said proudly.

In spite of the fact that we loved Colorado and our Colorado family, we were Floridians and Sarah was right: it was where we belonged. I knew Lani would never return to Colorado, even though he kept that gold nugget in his treasure box and probably dreamed of going back to look for more nuggets, but he was relieved and happy to be home. It was the trip of a lifetime and though part of my heart remained there, I was glad to be where I belonged. Looking up into the Florida sky at the highest clouds, I pictured those mountains, and sometimes dreamed of being there. Harry suggested I do that in order to cherish our time together.

PART 3

1894-1897

I AM SARAH

CHAPTER 30   WHERE GOD LIVES

*F*rom my Lucy journal: "I am a chosen girl, chosen by my grandmother to be my mother, chosen by my Papa Lani to be my father, and chosen by Jasper to be my brother. And I have chosen them also and they complete my life. Having just turned 13 years old, I consider my life to be nearly perfect. The only thing that could make it better would be if Jasper could be healthier. My mama found him six years ago, dying of yellow fever by our gate, and nursed him back to health, but he seems to be going downhill these last few months. When he can't get out of bed, I read to him and we sing songs together. Sometimes I feel he might be my mama's favorite, but I don't care because he is my favorite, too. He is so funny and smart and he tries to make me laugh and is successful at it most times. Some days he feels good enough to play, though, and those are the days I love the most."

Mama ordered two ranch hands to build a wooden platform about 10 feet tall, so that Jasper could be at the top of the alligator pear tree, or the Jasper Tree as we all called it, since it wasn't big enough to climb. Sitting on that platform with him was delightful because we felt we were in the very top of the tree, the big, green, shiny leaves making shade and tickling our faces. Jasper kept looking for some fruit, but as yet, there was none. It was funny how far we could see from that high up, all the way to the lake and down to the verdant pastures that ran to the Santa Fe River. If it was warm enough, I brought a book and read aloud, which made Jasper smile.

"Will you marry me one day, Sarah?" Jasper asked, as we lounged atop the platform, our legs crossed over each other.

"We can't marry, you silly goose. You're my brother," I said, laughing.

"Oh well, I wouldn't want to marry you anyway. You're too damned bossy."

"What? Did you just curse, Jasper Walton? And I am not bossy. Mama says I'm a born leader. "

"Sam says 'damn' and words that are worse than that."

"And I suppose you want to be like cussing Sam. He's a terrible boy."

"He was our friend at one time. What happened to him?" Jasper asked.

"He got ruined somewhere along the way. You steer clear of him, you hear me?" I said sternly.

Unfortunately, Sam had grown into a mean boy and when he tried to join us, it ruined our time, as he threatened to throw Jasper off the platform. I didn't know what had got into that boy but my mama had caught him a couple of times and she was not to be messed with. But he sassed her, too. He might end up in jail someday .....or shot, I thought.

One day Sam caught me in the barn when no one was around and tried to press his wet lips on mine, but I am stronger than him and I slapped his face and pushed him to the ground.

"Sarah, you know you want a kiss," he yelled, his face a splotchy red.

"The next time you try that I will tell Papa and you will get a flogging. I mean it. What has become of you?" I said, standing taller.

Jumping up, he ran from the barn, anger emanating from him. I knew I would have to be much more vigilant because he might overwhelm me one day when he was bigger and stronger than me. I sure did miss that sweet boy he used to be. It was hard to sort out the two people, the one he used to be and the awful person he had become. One day when no one was looking, I saw him swat his little brother on the back of his head, causing him to cry out in pain. The subject was not something I could bring up with the family because it would make him worse, and I just couldn't tattle.

☼

The weaker Jasper became, the more Mama worried, becoming quieter and spending a lot of time off by herself. Meanwhile, he and I became closer, and he talked about his real mother, Miss Polly. Before that time, I hadn't known Papa was his sure-enough father and I was a little hurt that no one had told me, but I listened to him recount the days with his sweet, beautiful mother, which made him so contented.

"Sarah, don't tell Mama or Papa, but I think I am going to heaven to be with my mother. They would be very sad and I love them so much, I don't want them to be sad," he said wistfully.

"Don't be silly, Jasper. You're just having a bad day. How could you go off and leave me when you know how lonely I would be?" I asked.

"I'll wait for you there. I want to see my mama and I know it's a beautiful place, where God lives."

It was a confusing time for me; wanting to keep him with me and knowing he missed his mother so much. But I was selfish and refused to admit he might actually leave and couldn't bring myself to say the word, "die." Determination was one of my better qualities, or stubbornness as Mama would say. Sometimes she called me 'mule-headed,' and I decided right then and there, that he was needed on earth more than in heaven and I told him so.

"Jasper Walton, you stop feeling sorry for yourself. You have people right here who can't live without you. I will not let you go 'cause it would kill our parents...and me. Do you hear me? " I said in a strong voice.

"Yes," he said with a smile, his blue eyes flashing. I wished I could give him some of my mule-headedness.

We spent the rest of the day running through the piney woods with the beagle dog who was as good a hunter as any other dog, even though he had been spoiled, stopping to rest when Jasper tired.

When he turned to me, his face was flushed, from good health or fever I didn't know which. My spirit soared and sadness left me and I hoped I could keep him alive. Hope was all I had….and prayer. My mama said I was becoming a young lady and should quit tromping in the woods like a wild girl.

My real mother, Mary Elizabeth, was coming to see us and bringing her other children. Talk about confusion: how was it she had kept her other children, but not me? My life was very happy with my chosen family but I wondered how was I not chosen by my real mother. My step-father, Mary's husband, had not been nice to me and he had always frightened me, so I hoped he wouldn't come along. When I asked to go visit Aunt Annie during that time, Mama just laughed and said I could not avoid seeing my relatives. I thought maybe I could hide in the woods for a week or so but I knew that would worry Mama and Papa. So I prayed for patience and kindness to descend on me 'cause I sure wasn't feeling that way. I was talking to God a lot these days and I hoped he was hearing me.

CHAPTER 31   A ROYAL VISIT

*T*he preparations were underway for the relatives' visit, but I was not excited about it. Mama sent me to the kitchen to help Izzie and Suzanna as they were baking pies and plucking chickens: my least favorite job since I knew each hen as a pet and had named them. I thought I was plucking Matilda, which made me nauseated.

"Are you concerned about your mother and brothers and sister visiting?" Aunt Suzanna asked, as we sat around the fire, dipping the butchered chickens in boiling water.

"Yes ma'am. It makes me feel jittery, like a long-legged frog in a hot frying pan."

She laughed and said, "I understand completely. I had a stepmother one time who didn't like me one little bit and didn't want me around, so I left my home and family."

"You did? And came here and met Uncle John?" I asked.

"Yep. Best thing that ever happened to me. Look at all the family here that loves me. I believe your mama did the best thing for you even though sometimes it doesn't feel that way. Your grandma always says, 'Sometimes the things we dread the most become our biggest blessings'."

Thank you for talking to me about it. I feel better knowing I'm not alone," I said, feeling happier.

"Sarah, do you know how much you are loved? Your family here will support you," she said, giving me a warm smile.

☼

We were expecting our guests around one o'clock in the afternoon if all went well. My new dress that I sewed for the occasion was pink flower-printed and pretty, but itchy and uncomfortable. And in walked Jasper with a bow tie on, for goodness' sakes. He looked plain ridiculous and I told him so.

"Well, Sarah, that damned ole dress is ugly, too," he barked.

"It is not. I made it myself and sewed every single stitch. What has got into you, cussing all the time?"

He sat down on the overstuffed chair in the parlor and pouted.

"I am not leaving you, Jasper. Don't you worry about that," I said.

"You children stop arguing right this minute and go watch the road for the carriage," Mama yelled at us as she was putting on her nicest Sunday dress. There was a quiver in her voice and I reckoned she was a mite nervous, too. Surely she would not let Mary Elizabeth take me back with her. I grabbed Jasper by the hand and we ran out the back door, slamming the screen door as we ran toward the gate.

"You could throw that old bow tie away," I suggested.

Off it came and into the bushes he threw it. And we laughed as it got hung up on a palmetto scrub, dangling like a red wilted flower. The popping of a whip sounded long before we saw the carriage. I knew Mama would not allow anyone to whip a horse, whether she owned it or not. In fact, she had issued an order that if a ranch hand used his whip on a horse or cow, she would dismiss them on the spot. They could herd with the whips as long as they didn't make contact with the animal. As we turned to run and warn everyone, I hoped she had not heard that sound.

"They're coming! They're coming!" we called out in the center of our compound. People flowed out of all the houses and

162

barns and kitchen, waving dishcloths and hats. It was like the Queen of England was arriving. I stretched on my tiptoes to see what my real mama looked like and my brothers and sister. The man driving was a dark-skinned man with a mean-looking face, but Mary was smiling and jumped down immediately and ran to her mother, my grandmother. Smiles and tears at the same time; it was a wonder to me.

As Mary came toward me, I was shocked at how small she was. Since I was only 13, I thought she would be taller than me, but she was about four inches shorter. Her face was aglow and she smiled the sweetest smile as she hugged me to her.

"My darling girl, how I have missed you, but aren't you just the prettiest thing, with your blond curls and your beautiful skin," she said.

Feeling ashamed that I hadn't wanted to see her, I backed up a little as three young children ran to me and grabbed me around my waist and legs.

"This here's Emma who is 4 years old. Those two scruffy fellers are Jackson, 8 years old and Grady, who is 10 years old. They are your siblings," Mary said.

Since I had two mothers in one place, I decided to call them Sally and Mary (to myself, of course), even though Mary was called Lizzie by most folks.

"Sarah, where are your manners, girl? Give your sister and brothers a hug," Sally said.

Bending down, I looked Emma in the eyes and I knew I would love her. Her smile was so innocent and pure, and she was such a pretty little girl with big brown eyes. The boys were sweet-natured too, so I hugged all three of them to me.

"Jasper," I called. "Come meet your kinfolks." He had been hanging back but suddenly burst through the crowd, grinning ear to ear and hugged the three siblings, adopting them on the spot.

"Let's take them to the platform," he said.

"Not Emma," Mary called, as we started up the ladder. Emma cried, but Sally picked her up and said, "Let's go have some pie. And Jasper, where is your bow tie?"

He shrugged and I giggled.

Such a celebration took place, with piles of fried chicken and big bowls of potato salad and pecan pies. Both Sally and I could not eat chicken since we fed and nurtured the hens, their little murmuring noises at our feet.

Since it was September, it was perfect weather for a big dinner outside with all the children running and chasing each other and Charlie the beagle. I think Mama named all her dogs Charlie. The only youngster who didn't participate was Sam and he sat sullenly next to the barn door, watching the festivities, scowling. He was starting to give me the willies.

By nightfall, I was as tired as I had ever been in all my life, and as happy. Suzanna smiled at me, and winked, and I winked back. We made blanket and quilt pallets on the parlor floor and all the children collapsed immediately, our stomachs full and our hearts lifted that we had new relatives that we loved and enjoyed. Emma slept on one side of me and Jasper on the other. I squeezed his hand before we fell asleep to let him know he was still my favorite brother and he squeezed back.

The sound of adult voices droned in my head but nothing could have kept me awake that night. And the only thing that woke me the next morning was the fact that I had to use the privy. Everyone slept in that day, even though the roosters were crowing and the animals were waiting to be fed.

Sally poured me a cup of coffee when I returned from the privy, just like a grownup, and I could smell the bacon frying. Hordes of folks would be coming in for breakfast soon, with Izzie making biscuits and pancakes at the ranch kitchen. Mary and Rebecca were inseparable, as they had been when they were my age, giggling and snickering. I could tell Sally was in heaven and was back in a time when she was happiest, before Grandpa Jacob left us.

CHAPTER 32   SAM

"And if thy right hand offend thee, cut it off." Matthew 5:30

Wen all my brothers and I decided to climb to the top of the platform after breakfast, Jasper called out to me that it looked like the back leg had been sawed.

"Don't climb up there," he yelled, when I had one foot on the bottom rung of the ladder. I stepped down immediately and went to diagnose the problem myself and sure enough, someone had sawed almost all the way through the big log.

"Mama, Papa, come see what has happened," I yelled.

As they approached the structure, Papa said, "Well, I reckon we know who did this, but this is not a joke. Someone could've been killed."

"Who was it, Papa?" Jasper asked, but I knew who had done the dirty deed.

"Are you accusing Sam, Mr. Walton?" Uncle Nathan asked.

"Yes, I am, Nathan. It's just one of many tricks he's pulled lately," Papa Lani replied.

Aunt Loretta sat in the corner of the dining room, face paled. Aunt Rebecca was pacing and an angry vein bulged on her forehead.

"Where is the evidence?' Uncle Nathan asked.

"No one else would do this. You know Sam has been surly for a while now," Papa Lani said.

"Why would you accuse my son of such a terrible thing?" Aunt Rebecca almost screamed.

"Bring Sam in," Sally said calmly.

As Uncle Nathan went to get Sam, Mary and her children left the house and went to Aunt Rebecca's house to be away from the fray, I reckoned. Their eyes were big and frightened and I wondered if their own pa showed his anger to them.

As we waited, we could see Uncle Nathan dragging Sam across the clearing from the grist mill. Sam was cussing at his pa and fighting him.

"Goddammit, let go of my arm," Sam yelled at his pa.

We were all shocked and Aunt Loretta's hands were trembling. They entered the back porch with a loud banging and Uncle Nathan threw Sam into the dining room.

"Where's your respect for your father?" Sally asked.

"What do you old people want with me?" Sam spat out.

"Did you saw the leg of the platform?" Papa Lani asked directly.

"Why hell's bells, yes I did. And I would do it again. Miss Sarah sits on her high horse with all her brethren, and Jasper, you would think he was a little prince. He's so yeller he won't even fight me," Sam said, fists clenched.

Looking at every face, I could see the total dismay and surprise. Obviously, Sam had been ruminating on all these things for a very long time and had them bottled up until now. His mother and father were so taken aback they could not even form words. Aunt Loretta, a woman not prone to emotion, had tears leaking from her eyes.

"I am sorry to say this to you all, but Sam will have to be sent away. His behavior has been most unacceptable for a long time and we have swept it under the rug. But you will have to make a hard decision and stand by it," Papa Lani said.

"I don't want to live here anyway. You all hate me," Sam said, gritting his teeth, his voice breaking, trying to become a man's voice.

"I will take him to my parents' house today. Say your goodbyes, Sam," Uncle Nathan said.

And it was done. He was led away like a hardened convict and we watched with so much pain in our hearts that our friend had turned sour. But I knew this would not be the end of him; he would be back.

It was a blight on our happy reunion, with Aunt Rebecca being inconsolable. She locked herself in her bedroom even though she had a younger son to take care of. Aunt Loretta brought Daniel to our house and we all tried to pretend there was no problem.

Sleeping was not as easy that night with children all around me, squirming and sniffing. The low conversations in the dining room were hard to hear, so I scooted closer, since I was wide awake anyhow.

"What will become of him?" Mary asked.

"He's corrupted. I don't think his grandparents will be able to do anything with him," Sally answered.

"He should have never been put to work at that young age. If only Samuel were here," Aunt Loretta said with a sniffle.

"Loretta, I hate to say this, but he has a mean streak. I caught him beating a horse with a stick and I took it away from him and slapped him. Then I found a dead chicken with its neck wrung when he was seen behind the barn. You know I don't hold with animal cruelty. And Mary, tell your driverman if I catch him using a whip on your horses, I will see to it he loses his job," Sally said.

Mary was silent and I knew by her shyness that she would never relay that message. Papa came in then and pulled the whiskey bottle off the shelf and poured a three-finger shot in a glass. Mary scampered off to bed and Loretta was not far behind, but I continued to listen, curled up behind an overstuffed chair.

"Son of a damn bitch!" Papa said.

"It was the right decision, Lanier," Sally answered. Papa hated to be called Lanier as Sally only used that name when things were serious, and things *were* serious.

The whiskey gurgled out of the bottle again and I thought my papa might get drunk that night and I was wishing for a little myself, just to be able to sleep. As I peeked around the chair I could see Sally kissing Papa and pretty soon, they slipped off to bed, taking the bottle with them. I crawled back to my pallet.

Sometimes when I watched my parents, I thought I would like to be in love like they were. Even though Mama was in her 50s, she was still so pretty. When she took her hair down in the evening in their bedroom, Papa brushed it out for her because it was way down past her behind, and he gently caressed her hair and lifted it to his face and I saw he could hardly contain his feelings. Wondering how it would be to have someone love me like that, I took my hair out of the braid and caressed it. When I was in my bed, I could hear them talking low and the bed creaked for a while. I knew they were kissing.

CHAPTER 33   SAY YOUR GOODBYES

"And the recompence of a man's hands shall be rendered unto him." Proverbs 12:14

After my real mama and her three children left to go home, the conversations got very heated between Uncle Nathan and Aunt Rebecca and my parents. I could see that Rebecca was pushing Nathan to try to get Sam brought back. And I thought Aunt Rebecca was wearing the pants in that family.

"Now, Uncle Lani, I can see your point of view about Sam, but I believe we can get him straightened out here, if you will allow him to come home," Uncle Nathan said.

"He's a 13-year-old boy, for God's sake," Aunt Rebecca said, trying to remain calm, her neck and chest a splotchy red.

"You do realize he picks on Daniel and Jasper, Daniel who is smaller and Jasper who is not always well?" Sally asked.

"We can't take the chance that he will injure someone one day," Papa said.

A wind might as well have been blowing in the room when Rebecca stormed out. Papers and items on the table were blown about and it felt dark and dreary. Nathan followed after her.

"You don't think they would leave us?" Sally asked.

"Maybe," Papa said.

"Well, I won't be following them all over God's creation," Aunt Loretta chimed in, as she stepped out of her bedroom, and startled us. She walked with a cane these days and hit it on the floor, making us all jump. "Sam has turned out to be a most disagreeable boy, but he will not direct my life," she said sternly.

"Oh, Loretta, of course you can't leave us. I would mourn every day," Sally said as she went to her and hugged her. No tears were spilled that day; everyone was resolute.

Aunt Loretta was turning 67 and she had become a little crotchety – well, a lot crotchety. Her hair was pure white and she walked with a limp. She had not been happy since her husband, Samuel, had died a few years ago.

Jasper and I were relieved that Sam wasn't lurking around corners, waiting to punch Jasper or kiss me, that low-down rascal. But it was hard to think of him that way since we had grown up together.

Nathan and Rebecca packed their gear in an old wagon and headed out, I supposed to his parents' house. Poor little Daniel cried and waved to us as they pulled out of the gateway. Aunt Loretta limped after the wagon, sobbing, reaching for Daniel. Goodness me, what a terrible thing had just happened to our family. But Papa and

Mama had bigger things to think about and that was the running of the grist mill. Who would do that? The orders were still coming in for Elizabeth's Drying Powders and I was still sewing cloth bags for orders, but we didn't have enough manpower to run the grist mill. Papa had ordered a new Singer treadle sewing machine and I couldn't wait to try it out. My fingers were sore from pushing that needle all day long. I had wanted to say 'damn' needle but I was trying to be a virtuous woman.

"Looking for a strong man to run our grist mill. House included. Contact Lanier Walton," was how the poster read that Papa placed at the La Crosse Post Office. We soon had a drove of folks knocking on our door. They lined up twenty-strong for three straight days, until Mama and Papa made a choice.

"Lord have mercy. I didn't know there were so many people out of work," Mama said.

"I can only hope we made the right choice," Papa said.

The Lindsey family consisted of a father, Johnson, strong and willing to work hard, a mother, Lillian, who was a seamstress, and their three children. Their oldest son, who was 15 years old, was named Gale, which I thought was a very strange name for a boy, but he seemed nice and was enthusiastic about working with his father, and two younger boys. They were all smiles, lined up by size in our parlor. From their ragged clothes, I could see they had been out of work for quite some time. When Papa handed them the keys to the house, Lillian cried softly.

Johnson said, "You won't regret this, Mr. Walton. We will work hard to make the mill profitable."

They were well-spoken people and I wondered what could have happened that caused them to be so poor. It was a mystery at the time, but we would learn about it in due time.

CHAPTER 34   RENDERED HEART

*T*he La Crosse school was bulging at the seams with children. An extra building was added to house the older children, to which Jasper and I would be going. All the children from our compound would be going to school, with the exception of Gale.

He was aptly named Gale, a wind that blew through my heart, rupturing it. At family dinners his glances toward me caused my heart to pound so, I felt I might faint. Jasper would ask me what was wrong and I was alarmed that anyone noticed. Therefore, I stayed as far from Gale as I possibly could, not understanding my own feelings at that young age. It was most unpleasant and yet, I longed to catch a glimpse of him. My thoughts were constantly drifting in his direction. At 15, he was tall for his age and built muscularly. Dark thick hair grew down around his shoulders, until his mother chopped it off, which made him even more handsome.

After school one day, I was feeding the chickens and Gale approached me, smiling, a smile to break a heart - my heart.

"Hello, Sarah," he said, his voice already manly.

"Gale, you startled me," I said as I felt a blush creep up my cheeks.

"I'm sorry. I was watching you from the barn and wanted to ask where your Pa is," he said.

"I believe he's in the pastures," I whispered, unable to find my voice.

"You surely have pretty blonde hair. Would you mind if I touch it?"

"No. I wouldn't mind," I said, thinking of my parents.

Walking closer to me, he extended his hand and caressed my hair, lifting it to his face, as I had seen my father do. My knees almost buckled and I felt my face flush even more.

"You're the prettiest girl I've ever seen and that's a fact."

"I'm not really that pretty." What made me say that? I thought.

"I would like to go for a walk with you sometime, when we can both get away," he said.

"There's a lovely place down by the Santa Fe we could go one day," I offered.

The look he gave me was the same look my papa gave my mama, which I thought of as love. Was it possible Gale loved me? I was feeling like I loved him but I was only 13. Once he left, I touched my hair where he had put his hand, breathing rapidly. My whole body was trembling and I wasn't sure I liked those feelings atall. Maybe I should just avoid him, I thought.

Jasper was beside himself, asking me constantly what was wrong, why was I so quiet, why did I blush so much? He was starting to aggravate me; everyone was starting to aggravate me. And then, I had my monthly flow start for the first time. I thought, "What on earth is happening to me?"

Mama sat me down and explained everything and told me I should stay home from school for the five days that I had my issue of blood. I was provided with clean rags to be changed every day until the time was over. She told me that this was God's way of preparing my body for children someday.

"And sprinkle some of Elizabeth's Drying Powders in your drawers so you'll smell pleasant."

Unfortunately, my time at home from school was a time when Gale was free, because his parents had driven into Alachua for supplies. No one else was home when he knocked on the back door, asking me to walk to the river with him. Knowing I shouldn't, but wanting to so badly, I accepted the invitation.

His voice was like sweet cream, but I couldn't hear what he was saying as I was so filled with emotion. As we walked, he took my hand and held it in his, kissing my fingers and the palm of my hand. I couldn't breathe. Guilt flowed over me like water. I felt sneaky in slipping away, not wanting anyone to know what we were doing. What were we doing?

"Gale, I'm only 13," I said.

"And I am only 15. I love you, Sarah."

At the riverbank, he spread a wool blanket and we sat staring blindly toward the water flowing gently by, but I was not seeing the river. He leaned over me and kissed me on the lips and I knew I was in trouble. Pushing me to the ground, he laid directly on top of me, kissing my ears, eyes, and neck. There was no way I could resist him as I loved him madly and I kissed him back and wrapped my arms around him. But when he raised my skirts and touched me, I became alarmed. Squirming, I pushed him away and said, "You mustn't."

"I'm so sorry, Sarah. Please forgive me," he pleaded.

I could hear Papa calling my name so I jumped up and told Gale he should hide.

"Please stay away from me. You will get us both in trouble," I said breathlessly. Running toward the voice, I brushed leaves from my skirt and straightened my hair, which now smelled of pine needles and a boy named Gale.

Determining to steer clear of Gale, I spent a lot more time with Jasper and my mother. I also busied myself in the kitchen, helping Izzie and Suzanna with the meals for the ranch hands. Gale tried to get my attention but I would not even glance at him; to do so would weaken my resolve. It wasn't that I felt that he was dangerous, but I knew my feelings were dangerous, not being able to resist him.

He came to my bedroom window one evening as I lay abed thinking of him. Whispering my name, he stood eye level with my bed, only the screen separating us.

"Meet me outside, Sarah," he whispered.

"I can't," I whispered back.

"Please," he pleaded.

Wrapping a blanket around my shoulders, I tiptoed to the front porch, unlatched the screen door and stepped barefoot onto the cold step.

"Come with me to the other side of the oak tree, so no one will hear us," he said.

He took my hand and led me away from the house and backed me up to the tree.

"You're all I think of, Sarah. Please don't ignore me."

His breath was on my cheek as he whispered in my ear, his hand on my waist, my thin nightgown clinging to my body. When he moved his hand to my breast, I did not resist but gasped quietly.

"Do you love me? Would you marry me, if I proposed?" he asked.

"I'm too young to marry. I have strong feelings for you but I don't understand them. My papa would be angry if he knew you kissed me and touched me. Your parents would have to leave."

"I want you so much I can't eat or sleep. Have you ever had a boy love you? I mean has anyone ever had his way with you?"

"Of course not. I have never even kissed anyone but you. You are putting your whole family in jeopardy. You must stop this now. Leave me alone," I said sternly.

"Is that really what you want? If so, I *will* leave you alone," he said, teeth clenched.

"It's what must be. I do not love you," I said, telling a big fat lie.

He backed away from me and I had a sinking feeling that I would lose him forever, but I knew my parents would not approve of his actions and I wanted to finish school before I married. As he trudged toward his house, I quietly slipped onto the front porch, watching the silent shadow move across the moonlit clearing. I did not sleep the rest of the night, feeling his touch on my breast. When my mama came in the next morning, she said, "Sarah Walton, don't you ever go to bed with filthy feet like that again." I smiled inwardly.

By morning, Gale was gone. His parents said he was off to Gainesville for a few days and I cried down by the river so no one would see me. My heart was rendered. How could I love again and how could he love another? There was much discussion over the situation but no one knew of my part in it – or so I thought.

"That boy just wants some wicked loving and he'll find it in Gainesville. There's plenty of painted ladies there. And plenty of trouble in that rough old town. I hope he can handle himself," Papa said one evening, smiling at Mama. I had to turn my face away so the blush couldn't be seen but I don't think they even knew I was sitting in the parlor.

"I believe you might know all about wicked love in Gainesville, but you might be right about that boy. A boy that age has a powerful drive, but then most men do," Mama said.

"I only know about wicked love with you," Papa replied with a grin.

I was pretty sure they didn't know I was there or they wouldn't have been talking in that manner. Fleeing to my bedroom, I hoped they couldn't see the tears falling, but I knew Jasper would sense it. He had finally stopped asking questions, but he observed everything.

And sure enough, Gale returned to the ranch a week later, with a pretty little wife who had blond hair that was almost white and green eyes. Lana was her name. I didn't know how the situation could get any worse for me, as I loved him wildly and now had to see him with her every day. She was an older woman of 18.

My schoolwork was suffering, Jasper was suffering, but I was suffering the most. Avoiding Gale and Lana was hard work, having to plan my day around escaping their presence. I begged to go live with Aunt Annie and Uncle David.

"Sarah. Do you love Gale?" Mama asked at breakfast one morning as the two of us sat alone. I swear, she seemed to know every last thing I thought and yet she had never said a word.

"No. I hate him."

"Ah," she said. Then silence surrounded us.

"Hate is akin to love," she said a bit later.

"He's a married man now. How could I love him?"

"What has transpired between you two?"

"Just a kiss," I said, feeling it was a lie.

"Did you allow it?"

"I am ashamed to say I kissed him back."

"The Bible says, 'Who can find a virtuous woman? For her price is far above rubies.' Well, what's done is done. But you can't run away every time there's a problem. Do you want to go live with Mary Elizabeth?" Mama asked.

Alarmed, I said, "No! But I really want to be a virtuous woman."

"Then you must straighten up and behave yourself. Jasper needs you and I need you here. You are too young to know what love is anyway."

Not wanting to sass my mother, I thought that she should not have made that statement when she married at the age of 16 to a man in his thirties.

"I'll do better," I whispered.

"Go find Jasper and spend some time with him. He's heartbroken."

"Yes ma'am," I said quietly.

I knew there were times when my mother rode away alone – when she was troubled about something. And sometimes that worked for me, but I found that walking was a better choice for me since riding a horse was more visible to other folks.

When I could, I climbed through the fence and skirted the pasture that led to the Santa Fe. For some reason, the spot where Gale and I had lain was comforting to me. It was shallow water there, so I knew the danger of gators was less likely. Also, I didn't see how they could navigate all the cypress knees, their knobby points sticking up everywhere. It was coming on winter and the breezes were getting chilly.

"Take my coat," Gale suggested.

I swirled around, alarmed.

"No. I must go," I said.

"Let me explain, Sarah."

"You should not be here. You are a married man, or boy, I should say," I said sternly.

"I love you," he said hoarsely.

"Well, I don't love you."

"I think you do love me. But I want you to know I rescued Lana because she was starting to walk the streets of Gainesville for a living."

"What do you mean by that?"

"You do know what a woman of the night is? Goodness, you are so naïve."

Feeling stupid as a country bumpkin, I could only stare at him dumbly.

"It's a woman who gets paid for loving a man. But she's a good girl who has had a rough time of it," he said.

The tears gushed out of my eyes. I turned to leave and he took me by the arm.

"She gives me what you can't. You're just a child who looks like a woman. She *is* a woman."

"Then go be with your woman, your street-walking woman, who gives you what you want," I spat out.

Angrily he said, "I will and the devil with you."

Pulling away, I ran toward home, crossing the open pasture in broad daylight. I hated him and Lana and the fact that I *was* a child and had no idea what grownup folks did in their beds at night.

CHAPTER 35   FINALITY

"Excessive grief the enemy to the living" William Shakespeare

Winter was coming on and the nights were colder than ice. Jasper was seeming to be happier now that I was spending more time with him and I was not such a truculent person. Being embarrassed at my actions that centered around Gale, I concentrated all my free time on Jasper, evading Lana and her husband, whose name I was hard-pressed to mention.

Cold weather was hard on Jasper for some reason; his lips turned blue and his hands stayed cold, even when he sat by the fireplace wrapped in a blanket. Mostly, he was worried about the Jasper tree, especially since we had had a few flowers on it this year, even though there was no fruit atall yet. Papa built a fire in an iron pot close to the base of the tree when the nights got chilly, which caused Jasper to be joyous.

"Sarah, did you love Gale?" he asked me one day.

"I thought I did but it was all just me being silly."

"Lana's in the family way. I heard Gale's mother say so," he said.

My heart sank. I was pretty sure Gale had not shared Lana's past with anyone but me. And why me? I wondered.

"You do love him, don't you? I can tell because you're blushing," Jasper said.

"Jasper, let's not talk about this subject anymore. I am sick of it and I'm tired of thinking about it."

He sneezed then, and I noticed his face was flushed. As I ran to get Mama, I had a terrible feeling in my gut. Jasper was put to bed and was covered with a mound of quilts, but his teeth still chattered.

There was a new doctor in Alachua, who Papa rode to bring back to the ranch. Dr. Craig checked Jasper over and announced he had influenza. "Keep him comfortable and warm. It is contagious, so keep your mouth and nose covered," he warned.

I heard the doc talk to Papa in a whisper, "Normally a young boy can pull out of this, but his body was weakened by the yellow Jack. Watch him carefully and give him this quinine for the fever. And I have some belladonna to make him sleep."

Christmas, 1894, rolled around, but we stayed put. Several folks on the ranch bundled up and went to church in carriages. Mama and I waited on Jasper hand and foot, bandanas around our faces.

Jasper asked, "Sarah, do you remember that time we went to Colorado? Wasn't that the best trip we ever went on?"

I laughed and said, "It was the *only* trip we ever went on. But it was grand and I'm glad I got to share it with you. You were some rodeo cowboy."

"I love you, Sarah," he said. It sounded so final.

December 28th we awoke to tree branches popping off big oak trees, the noise as loud as a shotgun. Ice dripped from all the buildings and trees and a light blanket of snow carpeted the world.

"Look outside, Jasper. It snowed. Look how beautiful," I cried.

"How is my tree?" He lifted his head off the pillow and smiled, looking out of the bedroom window.

Running to the back porch I looked out to see the Jasper Tree broken at the base, ice weighing it down. As I touched the leaves, I thought, "There is no way I will tell him as it would break his heart." When I turned around, he was standing on the cold step, tears streaming down his fevered cheeks.

"It's dead," he cried.

Mama grabbed him by the arm and dragged him back to bed, scolding him for getting out in the cold.

By New Year's Day, Jasper was gone to heaven, 'where God lives.' It was the worst day of my life – and my parents'. I missed him with all my being. I held his hand until the ragged breaths stopped. Why would God take my chosen brother? Why would God hurt my mama and papa so? Mama could not be consoled.

"Did I save him from death for this?" she cried. Papa held her but he was suffering, too. No one could smile. People from the ranch came to say goodbye, even Gale and Lana, but there was no one I wanted to see....save Jasper.

And then there was Charlie, the beagle dog, who howled long into the night, missing Jasper, too. I wanted to bring him into the house to comfort him, but Mama said, "No, we can't risk having fleas in the house."

The only time I could comfort the dog was during the day – when I could find him. Once, weeks after the funeral, I did find him lying on Jasper's grave, his big sad brown eyes glancing at me when I walked up, his head tucked between his two front paws. Sometimes I could hear him running through the woods, looking for Jasper, baying. We cried together, wishing for our time with Jasper to return.

The freeze made digging the grave difficult, but Jasper was laid to rest in our small cemetery alongside Abigail and Samuel. Papa tried singing "Softly and Tenderly," a hymn that appropriately went, "Ye who are weary, come home," but his voice cracked and we all joined in while he strummed his guitar. Uncle John read several scriptures and we held hands and prayed.

As people started walking back down the path, hurrying to get out of the freezing weather, I hung back, not wanting to have to talk to anyone, not even feeling the chill atall.

"I'm so sorry, Sarah," a familiar voice said. I turned to see Gale, the one person I did *not* want to see.

"Thank you," I murmured.

"If it helps, my heart still belongs to you," he said.

"It does not help. Please stay away from me," I said sternly.

If he thought I was a girl in a woman's body, I thought he was a boy in a man's body. But he walked to me and wrapped his arms around me and I collapsed in his arms, sobbing, feeling somewhat consoled.

My mother stood in the pathway, watching. She called to me and I broke away and ran to her.

"Sarah, a virtuous woman would avoid that boy," she said.

"I know, Mama. I'm trying my best to be virtuous," I said through my tears.

Many of our cattle had died during the extreme weather, especially the younger calves and the pregnant cows. All the citrus trees died, and of course, the Jasper Tree was destroyed. Even the pine hyacinths down by the Santa Fe were drooping. Everything was brown and many of Mama's flowers were dead. But nothing was as dead as my heart...and Jasper. I had to stop thinking of myself, stop being selfish, and help my mama and others with their grief. It consoled me to know that Jasper was in heaven with his mother; however, he was not here with me as my constant companion. I had great guilt thinking how I had neglected him during the "Gale" months.

☼

In early February 1895, I awoke to the sound of what sounded like gun shots, only this time I knew the tree limbs were dropping, some already dead from the previous freeze. I looked to the far side of the room at Jasper's small bed, expecting him to be smiling at me, but of course, he was not there. Papa had been up all night, lighting fires in the pastures and rounding up the cattle into pens, so they would huddle together for warmth.

As I dressed in front of the fireplace, I could smell the coffee and could not wait to get my hands on a hot mug. Mama smiled at me as I entered the kitchen, the first time she had smiled since Jasper left us. My heart lifted and I smiled back. We would make it through this – together.

CHAPTER 36   BEING A WOMAN

I was happy to welcome in the year of 1895, as I would be 14 that year, a year closer to finding a husband and moving away from the ranch. Although I loved the ranch, I did not love seeing Lana grow with child every day. I saw Gale dote over her and slowly, I could see he was falling in love with her. No longer did he seek me out to confess his undying love, which I did not want but did want. So much confusion. I could only watch him from afar and dream of his arms around me.

How I missed Jasper when we rode to school in the mornings and home in the afternoons. So many times he would reach for my hand if he had felt insecure. I longed to feel his hand in mine and sometimes, I felt it was.

A terrible thing happened in early April. Mr. Lindsey just up and disappeared. When Papa called Mrs. Lindsey and Gale in for a sit-down talk, I left the bedroom door ajar slightly so I could hear the conversation.

"So, what's the situation here, Mrs. Lindsey? Your husband gave no notice to us of his leaving," Papa asked.

"Mr. Walton, he will be back. Sometimes he goes on a 'toot', but I know he will come back," Mrs. Lindsey said.

"You don't have to worry, sir. I can handle the mill myself. As you can see, I have been doing most of it anyway, since Pa suffers from some health issues," Gale said.

"Does your pa have a drinking problem, son?" Papa asked.

"He takes a nip or two every now and again, but as you can see, Ma and Lana have been turning out some beautiful bags for the drying powders and we are keeping up with the orders," Gale said.

"Please give us a chance, Mr. Walton. We love living here. I can keep the younger children home from school to work in the mill, if you want," Mrs. Lindsey said with a sniff.

"All right. We'll give it a try, but we must keep up with the orders. I'll move the sewing machine to your house so you can work faster."

"Thank you, sir," they said in unison.

And what about me? I thought. I was just starting to get a handle on that treadle machine. But I did understand Papa's thought processes. He did not want to turn a family out. At least, we now understood the mystery of the Lindsey family poverty – their pa was a drunk and a deserter.

Gale's voice had wrapped around me, like a cool breeze on a dry Florida summer day, trying to quench my thirst for him. It stayed in my head for days, softly whispering in my ear as on that night by the oak tree. Would I ever stop loving him and thinking about him, I wondered?

And then Papa told me to teach Mrs. Lindsey and Lana how to use the Singer machine. The only consolation was that I didn't think my papa knew about Gale and me or he would never have asked that of me. I was happy Mama had not told him, but still, I had to face Lana and maybe see Gale.

On my 14th birthday in August, I somehow felt older and wiser, more like a woman should feel, instead of that silly childish girl I had left behind. I realized I had to forget about my feelings for Gale and move on to someone else. Gale had moved on, especially with the birth of his baby boy. His pa still had not returned, but Papa was more than satisfied with Gale's work at the mill.

When I asked Suzanna about wicked love, she said my mama should talk to me, but I told her that would never happen. So, she sat me down and talked me through the process and I was stunned. Having no idea that was what Gale had wanted from me, I was glad he had chosen Lana. I couldn't imagine that a woman or girl would like that sort of thing. If that's how babies were made, I thought I would be childless and maybe even an old maid.

☼

Sean O'Hara, a new boy in our school, had taken a fancy to me. Of course, he was not Gale, in looks or personality, but he was very interested in me. He smiled shyly at me constantly and I did love his blue eyes. I started wearing my pretty Sunday dresses to school and I wore my hair down, which was to my waist by that time. Loving the attention, I smiled back at him.

Although he was older than me by two years, I didn't think he was as experienced in wicked loving as Gale. And I wanted to be a virtuous woman, like my mother, although I thought married women were not always that virtuous with their husbands, according to what Suzanna said. Mama said I was too young to think about marriage yet, and really wanted me to marry well. Sean was not well-dressed, so I thought his family might be poor and I didn't think he would be considered a good candidate for marriage by my parents. But I liked him and I liked the fact that he liked me. Slowly, I started to not think about Gale every blessed hour of every blessed day. When I went to sleep at night, I saw Sean's smile. It was a relief not to feel that strong passion, which was exhausting. Comfort was what I felt in his presence, not the constant upheaval of my spirits.

"I want to court you, Sarah," Sean said shyly one day.

"What does that mean? Would you take me for a carriage ride?" I asked.

"My family doesn't own a carriage, but I could come to your home and take you for a walk."

"You'll have to ask my parents," I said.

His family had started attending our church in La Crosse, but I believed they walked to church. I wasn't sure what my family would think of a family that walked everywhere. Sean and I talked together on the steps, waiting to go into the sanctuary and Gale watched me like a hawk hunting its prey.

Gale's whole family were now well-dressed folks, not looking like the poverty-stricken people they had been when first they came to our ranch. I could see he was looking down his nose at Sean's family. Was he jealous or just being a snob? I couldn't tell.

As I was heading to the privy behind the church after the services, Gale grabbed me by the arm and held me tightly.

"What are you doing with that boy?" he asked.

"The same thing you are doing with Lana," I lied, feeling mean as a diamondback rattlesnake. I twisted away from him but he held me.

"You are killing me, Sarah. That boy isn't good enough for you," he said.

"And you are? I intend to marry that boy and have lots of his babies. I don't intend to be virtuous with him."

Truly, I was trying to figure out how to marry and not have wicked love or babies.

"You are a spiteful girl. But I know one thing: you'll never be happy with him," Gale hissed.

"Would I be happy with you? You make me miserable," I spat right back.

"So you do love me?"

"Is that what love is to you – misery? Well, you've got Lana, so go be miserable," I retorted.

I swirled around and ran toward the front of the church, not getting a chance to use the privy, and we had a long ride home, so I really would be miserable. The conversation was troubling to me but strengthened my resolve to leave the ranch.

"Oh, Sarah, there are so many other boys out there who would be so much better for you. His family is dirt-poor," Mama said of Sean.

"I believe he would be good to me and that's important, isn't it?" I asked.

"How would he support you?" she asked in return.

"He just wants to court me, not marry me."

"Girl, you are still so naïve. You cannot live on love. But he may visit the ranch next Sunday for dinner."

If Mama had known what I was planning, she would never have allowed me to invite Sean home to court me. Never ever would she want me to leave her and Papa.

Sean's mother must have sewed him some new clothes because when he showed up at church he looked very handsome, with a sparkling white shirt and a broadcloth suit, even though his britches were a mite short on him. His worn shoes had even been given a shine. Proud as a peacock he was, and nervous to boot. His auburn hair was slicked back so that I hardly recognized him at first.

We rode home in the back seat of the surrey, Sean clearing his throat many times, sitting as stiff as a green oak board. I reached over and took his hand to ease his nervousness and he held it tightly. My mama cast a stern look at me, so I dropped his hand.

Once we reached the ranch, I gave Sean a tour of the barn and chicken houses. His eyes were big; I didn't know what he had been expecting.

"Sarah, are you rich?" he asked.

"I don't think so. We just work hard, all of us. Then, there's the grist mill which is run by Gale and his family. It does very well selling drying powders," I said.

"Yeh. I don't think Gale likes me very much."

"He doesn't like a lot of people. Don't worry about it," I replied.

I was hoping he hadn't noticed Gale's attitude and I didn't understand it either. After all, he was a married man.

Sunday dinners were always special on the ranch and especially if the weather was nice enough that we could eat outside because we were a large group. Sean and I sat close to my parents, since I knew Gale wouldn't misbehave around them. Most of the ranch hands left the ranch on Saturday night to be with their families or to spend time in Alachua or Gainesville, doing God knows what. But the few that stayed joined us at the table.

"I've never seen so much good food on one table," Sean whispered to me. He had a hearty appetite, which made my mama smile. His manners could have been improved, however.

"Do you ride?" Papa asked.

"Never had the opportunity, sir," Sean replied.

"Well, you'll have to come back and give it a try."

My heart did a flip-flop. That was not what I wanted; leaving the ranch was what I wanted, not giving Sean a job. I determined to talk to my mama to straighten this matter out. How could I do that without her realizing my goal, I wondered?

Sean and I straddled the fence to climb over, then ambled down to the Santa Fe, both of us smiling, sated from the delicious food. When we reached the "spot," I suddenly didn't feel right about being there with him, so we walked on to another place farther upriver. We had slipped away, as I knew my parents would want me to be chaperoned.

A big smooth river rock was warmed by the afternoon sun and we lay back on it, lazing in the warmth. Sean held my hand but he did not try to kiss me or touch me. It was a comfortable moment and we both fell asleep immediately. I awoke to a dark cloud shading our spot, the rock gradually cooling. Panicked, I realized we had been gone too long not to be noticed.

I shook Sean and whispered, "We must hurry back."

"Oh no. I don't want your parents to think I'm a bad boy," he said.

"Don't worry. I'll explain."

As we ran through the pastures, I could see he was panicked because he pulled ahead of me. But we managed to slip through the fences and into the barn, observing the tack in the tack room as if I were still giving him a tour. Most everyone was taking a nap also and I could see his relief.

"I better get on home. It's a long walk," he said.

"You don't have to walk. I'll have Lester take you home."

"Really? Sarah, you are such a nice girl. And the most beautiful girl I've ever seen," he said sweetly.

I had been hoping for a kiss but I could see he wanted to make a good impression on my folks so I realized that wouldn't happen. Thinking he might be overly impressed with my lifestyle, I hoped he cared for me and not the possibility of living on the ranch.

CHAPTER 37   A BREWING STORM

*O*ctober 19, 1895

Dear Mama,
It seems impossible that we have been gone a year. It seems even more impossible that someone else now lives in our home and runs our grist mill.
Sam has left to become a sailor, gone to the Port of Tampa. I hope they can straighten him out because it has become increasingly clear that we have failed.
Nathan and I would like to come home and Daniel misses his granny so much. Would you intervene on our behalf? We would like to live in our home and run our mill again. Please talk with Aunt Sally and Uncle Nathan. We are family, you know.
Love,
Rebecca

The letter was just lying on the table, spread out, so that I could read it without even touching it. I wondered how this would be handled, since Rebecca and Nathan had left us short-handed, and now they wanted to come back like nothing had ever transpired. I could hear Loretta and Mama coming up the walk, so I skedaddled to my room, leaving the door ajar.

"I can't just put the Lindseys out in the street when they have worked so hard to make a go of it, and with Mr. Lindsey still gone...." Mama said.

"I understand, Sally, but we are talking about my children. Is there something we can offer them?" Loretta asked.

"As I recall, Nathan was not much of a cowhand. I suppose Gale could use him at the mill, but would he take orders from Gale? Let me talk to Lani about this. Of course, they can come back. This is their home," Mama said.

Listening carefully, I knew there was going to be trouble. Rebecca was not about to allow Nathan to take orders from a boy, but Gale had made the mill more efficient and cleaner, much more so than it had ever been. Rebecca and Nathan had owned the mill, but they had also walked away in anger. A storm was a-brewing.

Aunt Loretta wrote back and told Rebecca they could come home but they would be living in the lake house (a two-room cabin) and Nathan could help Gale, and Rebecca could work in the kitchen. Whooee. I would not have wanted to be around when that letter was read. Trouble was on the way.

With all the 'whoop de do' going on at the ranch, I clean forgot about Sean until I saw him at school the next week. He seemed excited to see me and asked if he could come out to the ranch and try cowboying.

"It's called 'ranching,' Sean," I said, aggravated that that was the path he was going down.

Boys made me crazy; none of them did what I wanted them to. Maybe he was not the one for me, but there were slim pickings those days. Most of the boys were younger, the older boys having to go to work at an early age. Sean's mama wanted him to get an education so he could make a better salary for the family, being a railroad agent or something like that.

"Don't be mad at me, Sarah. I like you so much....and your family," he said.

"Yes, but do you love me?" I asked.

"Why yes." He took my hand and led me to the back of the schoolhouse and kissed me under the live oak tree. I was shocked but I kissed him back and I liked it. When he started kissing me harder, pressing me to the tree, I stopped him. He was breathing hard, like Gale, and his hands were moving over my body.

"What are you doing?" I asked.

"I thought you wanted me to love you."

"Is that how you love, by touching me inappropriately?" I croaked.

"I'm sorry. I thought that's what you wanted. Do you want to get married?" he asked.

Frustrated, I pulled away and returned to the playground. I didn't know what I wanted. Was I running to something or away from something?

My friend, Dory, said, "You're going to get yourself in a world of trouble if you're seen kissing behind the schoolhouse."

"Could you see us? I thought we were hidden," I said.

She laughed and said, "Sarah, sometimes you are just stupid."

The house on the lake had been empty since Lester and Izzie moved back to their cabin. Mama and I swept and dusted and washed the linens, hoping this would satisfy Rebecca, but we both knew she would not be happy in these surroundings. Trepidation was the word Mama used and I had to look it up in the dictionary, but I thought it fit.

The day they arrived everyone was nervous, especially Gale's family. I noticed the whole family watched the road for the old wagon.

"Do you think they'll throw us out, Sarah?" Gale asked me.

"No, I don't. You've done an outstanding job. You've done better than Nathan."

"But they're family. I'm worried. Don't know what we would do," he said. He paced back and forth in the barn.

Wanting to reassure him, but not certain of it myself, I slipped out of the barn and back to the house, where I found Mama wringing her hands. She liked harmony on the ranch but Rebecca kept things stirred up like a whirlwind in a pile of dry oak leaves, so I knew she was trying to reckon a solution. I realized that some folks were never satisfied, never grateful for their blessings, such as Rebecca and her son, Sam.

☼

Long toward evening, the wagon groaned into the compound with Daniel calling out, "Granny, we're home!"

Limping from the house, Loretta walked toward the sound, while Papa held a lantern up. She cried as Daniel jumped down and almost bowled her over. We followed them to the ranch kitchen, where Izzie had saved supper for them, and we sat and listened to the gruesome stories of how bad Sam had become.

"The cabin is clean and ready for you. I know you must be tired," Mama said.

"Yes, well, we'll talk tomorrow. I would like to be in my own home, but I am exhausted tonight," Rebecca said.

I thought, "Oh Lordy, this is really going to get rough tomorrow."

I knew my mama was as stubborn as a mule, but then, so was Rebecca. I believed this was called an 'impasse.' Nathan and Papa were steering clear, I could see that. They shook hands and headed in different directions.

☼

The hurricane, named Rebecca, blew in about eight o'clock in the morning. Everyone scattered but Loretta and me. It was going to be a sure enough showdown but I was not giving odds.

"That grist mill was given to my daddy by Jacob Henry Winston, your husband, Aunt Sally," Rebecca said.

"By my husband and me, Rebecca. I ran the grist mill long before the men returned from the war. You would not know that because you were a small child at that time. And it sustained all of us, including your mother and father, and yourself and your husband and children, but none of us ever walked away from the business like you and Nathan. While you were gone, the Lindseys have done a good job, with all profits going to your mother, except for their salaries. They will not be turned out. If Nathan cannot work with Gale, he can find a job in town and you are welcome to live in the lake house. That's the way it is going to be," Mama said, standing tall.

"You are not being fair to us. You know we had to try to help Sam. How could you be so cruel?" Rebecca asked.

"The way I remember it, you left because we would not allow Sam back here. And you left in anger. I don't see that Sam has improved atall and I believe Nathan told Lani that Sam was running from the sheriff," Mama said.

"What?" Loretta said, as she dropped her cane.

"It was a misunderstanding. He is now a sailor and everything is all right. But I want to live in *my* house that was built for me, not that dreadful little cabin," Rebecca said.

"You are welcome to make improvements if you want, but for now, that's your abode."

Mama was not mean but very matter of fact, not angry, just resolved. I wanted to be more like her in every way. Rebecca, on the other hand, was almost foaming at the mouth. She was red in the face and neck, and looked like she would explode.

"You are a hardened woman. I'm not sure I want to live here anymore with someone as mean as you. Mama, talk to her," Rebecca spat out.

"Rebecca, you have been very rude to your aunt. I will not intercede for you when you talk like that. She has been very good to me, to us," Loretta said.

I'm sure my eyes were popping out of my head, looking from one person to the next, my mouth standing open. No one had ever talked to my mama like that…and lived to tell the tale. But Rebecca had lost the battle; I just hoped there wouldn't be an ongoing war. Storming out, she slammed the door behind her, breaking the glass which shattered in a million pieces. She hadn't even turned around. We all sat quietly, stunned by what had just happened. I thought I knew where Sam got his disposition, and it wasn't from his pa.

"What in tarnation happened here?" Papa yelled.

Loretta, Mama and I had cleaned up the glass but we couldn't fill the hole in the upper part of the door. There was just no way to hide it.

Loretta said, "I'll gladly pay for it."

"Nope. You will not. Rebecca will work it out in the kitchen," Mama said.

"Oh boy!" Papa said, and did an about-face.

Every time I saw Gale the next day, he was smiling.

"Your ma is a force to be reckoned with. I so admire her and your pa. What a lucky girl you are, Miss Sarah. I'm sorry if I have been unkind to you; it's just that I have been jealous when I had no right to be. I should have waited for you, but I was a stupid boy. But I am a man now and I have seen the error of my ways, but alas, it is too late," he said.

"I believe we can be friends," I said.

"I do hope so, as I hold you in the highest regard."

"Then perhaps you can be kinder to Sean in the future."

"You do try me, Sarah," Gale called over his shoulder as he walked away.

CHAPTER 38   A QUANDRY

*E*very Sunday Sean came home with us, had dinner, and spent the afternoon with the hands, learning to ride and rope and crack a whip. There were things about him that bothered me - his table manners, his too-short clothes, his willingness to please my parents more than me. And then there was Gale, whose table manners were impeccable, as well as his politeness with all ladies. He was well-dressed for church, and when dressed for work, he always looked handsome. But he was unavailable and I had to admit, he had the cutest baby boy.

Sean had asked for my hand in marriage, even though I had not told him I would marry him. My mama said he was too accommodating and I agreed. She also said 15 was a better age to marry than 14 and she felt that was too young as well. So, he got no answer. She asked me if that was what I really wanted and I could only shrug. She said if I wanted it after I turned 15, she would give us her blessings. When Sean sneaked a kiss, I closed my eyes and pictured Gale. I wondered if I would always want Gale and felt again that we needed to leave the ranch if Sean and I ever did marry.

Meanwhile Nathan and Gale got along famously, working together, laughing together, which made Rebecca boiling mad. I felt sorry for Nathan when he went home in the evenings as I'm sure she gave him an awful earful. She, however, was impossible in the kitchen, working off her debt for the broken glass. As Rebecca kept slamming pots and pans around, Izzie asked that she be taken off kitchen duty, with Suzanna agreeing. But Mama put her to work washing dishes after the meals were over and we could hear her in the kitchen throwing things around while Izzie and Suzanna disappeared. She surely had a nasty disposition.

"I believe Samuel and I may have indulged her," Loretta said.

"It's called spoiled rotten," Mama said. "She called Gale's baby a brat and threw Lana out of the kitchen when she went after some milk. This can't go on. I hope you can help her understand, Loretta. We do not act like this in this family. I would hate to ask her to leave."

"Can't you just let her move back to her own home? That would make things better," Loretta said.

"You mean give in to her temper tantrums? I don't think so. And then what would she be demanding? Nope. No. Never," Mama said adamantly.

Well, if there was one thing Sean was good at, it was persistence. He had quit school and started riding on the ranch, but every spare moment he was on my heels, asking me questions like: 'When can we get married?' 'Do you still love me?' 'Why don't you spend time with me anymore?' He was really starting to aggravate me. And even if I married him, would he want to stay on the ranch, which was not in my plans? Gale and I, however, had come to a good agreement. We were cordial with each other and he didn't constantly watch my every move, but on occasion, I caught him looking at me in a longing way. I simply looked away and tried not to think about it. He was my love, my lost love, my unrequited love.

☼

Mama took my hand one day and said, "Let's go talk to Jasper." At first I was a little alarmed but quickly realized she wasn't losing her mind, just really wanted to spend some time with me...and Jasper. And the only way to do that was to go to our little cemetery and act like he was with us. When we got there, Rebecca was kneeling, placing flowers on her father's gravesite. Mama backed away, planning on doing an about-face back up the path, when Rebecca called to her.

"Please stay."

As we drew closer I could see she had been crying. "I'm sorry. I didn't know about Jasper. Selfish is what I am, selfish and thoughtless, not even asking after the little boy who filled our lives with joy. I only saw his grave today," she said.

Holding onto my mama, I was afraid they would tie into it again.

"Well, we were blessed to have him as long as we did. He truly enhanced our lives in his short time on this earth, and Rebecca, you are blessed also with that sweet boy Daniel," Mama replied.

"Yes, whom I've neglected. I am a fool. Can you forgive me, Aunt Sally?" she pleaded.

"The Bible tells us to forgive and it's already done," Mama said.

As they hugged, I realized I had been selfish also, thinking of my own little world and not considering the sadness others were experiencing. My parents didn't talk about their financial problems but my teacher had explained that the depression that had started in 1893 was still going on and was affecting our area. We shipped our cattle to the northeast and I'm certain the ranch had been touched by this event. Even though we were self-sufficient, we still had salaries to pay. I resolved to work harder.

After Rebecca left, we had a conversation with our Jasper, even though he didn't talk back - thankfully. But it was fun and we imagined what he might have said. I could picture him laughing, his blue eyes flashing. When we started back to the house, Mama smiled at me and said, "You are my biggest blessing."

How proud that made me and how I loved her, knowing she was my biggest blessing also.

CHAPTER 39   ENDURING

$\mathcal{B}$ecause our La Crosse school was losing older students to the work force in this time of depression, in order to help their families, my friend Dory and I were moved in with the little children, at which point we were simply going through the basics again. When I told my parents, they decided I should stay home and let Loretta teach more advanced studies, but I said I thought I had learned enough. Aunt Loretta was really grumpy in those days and I figured I could help out on the ranch more.

Thinking about marriage was discouraging, but I figured I had until I turned 15 to think about it. Sean lived in the bunkhouse and I knew he sent all of his money home to his parents. How on earth was he expecting to support a wife, or was he thinking his wife's family would support us? And on top of everything else, Lana was in the family way again. I didn't think Gale loved me that much if he was making wicked love with his wife. It made me want to scream – of course, I didn't. I simply endured.

And then one day, I saw Sean in a different light. He was shirtless, pumping water from the hand-pump to wash up with and he looked totally changed – more manly. Taller than he had been, I reckoned I hadn't looked at him in a while. His chest was thicker, more muscular, and his arms were strong-looking. He was no longer a boy and my heart skipped a beat as I approached him. I realized he was going on 17 years old. Handing him a clean towel, I stepped back and waited for him to look at me.

"Sarah, thank you," he said with a smile.

His smile was wide, with white teeth, and his hair was a beautiful warm auburn color. He grabbed his shirt and hurriedly put it on, seeming embarrassed.

"Haven't seen you in a while. Where you been?" he asked.

"Helping with the grist mill bags. I'm not in school these days."

"Good to see you. You're as lovely as ever," he said.

As he turned to leave, I said, "Where are you going? Your day is over. Can you talk a while?"

"I didn't think you were interested in talking with me. I quit trying."

"Shall we walk?" I asked.

"I. I don't know. You've been so distant," he said hesitantly.

"I'm sorry. I had a hard time when I lost Jasper." And I thought to myself, "And I've been crazy in love with someone else."

We headed down the path that led to the graveyard and circled the iron fence and walked toward the Santa Fe. The silence was deafening, except for the aquatic birds nesting on the lake and the occasional splash of fish jumping for mosquitoes and water bugs in the black tannic water. Sometimes when a snowy egret flew across an azure sky, I was so thankful to be alive at that particular moment, and on that day, when the bird passed overhead, I was feeling hopeful.

I grabbed up some lyreleaf sage flowers growing in the meadow to take back to Izzie, who used them in a salve and made tea for colds and sore throats. Instead I looked like a bride walking with a bridal bouquet.

"Are you being courted by someone else?" Sean asked.

He was much taller than me by then and I marveled that 'cowboying' had made him into such a comely man: more confident, more handsome, much more attractive.

"I thought *you* wanted to court me?" I said.

202

"I did. I do. Can I call on you?"

"You may and you may kiss me," I said boldly as we reached the river's edge.

Taking his hat off, he bent down and touched my lips ever so lightly with his lips. Well, I wanted more than that but he pulled away.

"I don't want to disappoint your family but I would like to court you."

There it was again – that eagerness to please my parents more than me.

Not wanting to be perceived as a wanton woman, I took his hand and we ambled back to the path that led to the barn. Surprised by my strong feelings for him, I once more took up the goal of marrying and leaving the ranch. Comfort was not a word I would use to describe my new feelings for Sean. He had definitely stirred me up.

As 1896 rolled around, the year I would be 15, I decided to marry Sean if my parents approved. Where we would live I had no idea; all the houses were full on the ranch and the thought of staying with my parents did not appeal to either of us. But he would have to have another job to go to before we could leave.

"You can live with us, Sarah. Your room is big enough for the both of you," Mama said one day, but I didn't want anyone to hear our bed creaking in the night as now I knew what grownups did at night. I was not looking forward to that process either. We had no other choice if we wanted to marry. When I talked to Sean about leaving the ranch, he asked, "Why would we do that?"

CHAPTER 40   DREADED THINGS

*A*nd so, we married in our little church on a Sunday morning in late September 1896, with friends and family gathered round. Since Lester and Izzie couldn't come to our church, we also had a celebration at the ranch. Mama had reserved us a room at the Alachua Inn and had paid for a wedding dinner and breakfast for us. Sean was overwhelmed with gratitude, saying he had never stayed at an inn before. He was extremely handsome in his new clothes and his manners had improved a lot since he had been working at the ranch, mostly by observing my papa. I was still filled with trepidation about the wedding night, but I had talked with Suzanna about it at length again and she said she actually enjoyed the act, which stunned me.

The drive from the ranch to Alachua was endless, but at least the inn had someone to take the carriage to the livery stable, which meant we could go directly to the dining room. After dinner, which we both ate very little of, we headed to our room, as nervous as school children about to get into some mischief. All the drunks from the bar slapped Sean on the back, calling out bawdy advice, one man handing him a bottle of some sort. "This'll help the little lady," he yelled, the whole bar breaking into raucous laughter. Darkness had descended and I was glad, so Sean couldn't see me blushing.

Our room was a single cabin set apart from the inn, with a gravel walkway leading away from the main building. The wind had whipped up, a slight mist falling from the sky.

"Looks like a storm brewing," Sean said and I thought, "Yep, in more ways than one. I had a storm brewing inside me."

His hand was shaking as he fitted the skeleton key into the lock and I could see a candle flickering behind the window shade. Once the door was unlocked and we stepped inside, Sean bent to kiss me. It was a sweet kiss, but I wondered when he would kiss me like Gale, with passion and fervor.

I took off my gloves and hung my chapeau, as Mama called it, on the bedpost. I walked around the room, noticing all the décor, and the turned-back covers on the bed, with two chocolates wrapped in paper on the pillows. I tried the bed out to see how comfortable it was and popped the candy in my mouth nervously, allowing the taste to melt on my tongue.

Sean poured a whiskey, from the bottle given him, into a glass and glugged it down, for courage I imagined. Wanting some courage myself, I took a swig, choking and coughing.

As he began removing his clothes, I became more uncomfortable, as I had never seen a naked man. He bounced onto the bed in his union suit, lying on his back with his hands under his head, looking confident.

"Don't be scared, Sarah. Come and lie with me," he said softly, patting the pillow.

I walked around a little bit more and then, fully clothed, I lay down beside him, shoes and all, staring at the ceiling. Turning to me, he began unbuttoning my jacket, his hands adept, making me think he had gained some experience at wicked loving. Slipping his hand into my jacket, he felt for my breast, causing me to gasp. That was when the kisses became passionate and I kissed him back, tasting the whiskey, and I thought it strange that I still had my shoes on. He took my shoes off and told me to stand and he removed my jacket and skirt. I stood in my bloomers and chemise and he wrapped his arms around me while sitting on the bed, nuzzling my chest. Oh my, Suzanna had not mentioned this aspect of loving. His hands held my behind, while he kissed my neck and chest. It was not so bad after all, I thought, and I knew then he was very experienced. I also knew I was not going to be a virtuous woman for very long.

As my clothes dropped to the floor, I was trying not to think about Gale, as I sometimes thought I was kissing him instead of Sean. At those times, I would open my eyes and look at my handsome husband. That was the only way I could keep Gale out of my thoughts. I reached for the glass of whiskey and took another big swig, which set me on fire. Courage was on the way, so I poured another…and another...and another.

Sean's hands were moving expertly, whether from the alcohol or experience, I didn't know which, and the whiskey had made me bolder than I would have been ordinarily. My hands began to roam also.

My face was feverish and my body longed for more than kisses, and that was when Sean committed the act that I had so dreaded. He was wise to wait until I really wanted it and cried out for it. Otherwise, I would have been scared. The bedstead creaked loudly and I didn't care. I liked wicked loving and I liked the taste of whiskey. The rain pattered loudly on the windows, the wind blew the trees around, and the storm raged within me also.

"I brought your breakfast, Sarah," a voice said.

"Where is that light coming from?" my voice croaked in return.

"It's morning," Sean said.

I pulled the covers over my head, my head that was splitting wide open. Oh, I felt awful.

"Come eat your eggs and grits," the voice said.

With that, I threw the covers aside and ran to the wash bowl, where I vomited profusely. As I stood there, totally nude, feeling as if someone had beat me up, I realized Sean was not being compassionate, but was smiling.

"You have a beautiful body, Sarah," he whispered.

Grabbing the sheet to wrap my beautiful body in, the memories of the night before came flooding in. Mortified, I was. How could all that have happened and I participated in it?

"You were wonderful," Sean said. "I didn't expect that you would like it."

"Did I? I can barely remember," I whispered.

"Well, you did down a little whiskey."

"My head is splitting."

Sean came to the bed and pulled the sheet back as if he intended to have a repeat performance, but I was having none of it, worried I might vomit again and embarrassed by all the carrying-on we had done. I couldn't imagine that my mother and Suzanna and other married women did that sort of thing.

"Well, you can't get drunk every time we make love," he said. I could not have agreed more.

Sean battled the wind as he brought the carriage around. Praying I would not be sick on the way home, I helped with the bags as he held the horse, who was prancing and neighing, disturbed by the storm. The carriage top kept the rain off our heads, but the wind whipped the water onto our clothes. Branches were downed, and the bouncing of the carriage caused me to lean over the wheel and vomit more than once. Wasn't that a lovely sight: the new bride smelling of whiskey and last night's dinner, not to mention the mixture on the side of the cab and wheel. I was certain Sean would want a divorcement.

Once we made it back to the ranch, I felt so wretched I went straight to bed. All the women had knowing looks on their faces, which aggravated me. They were all thinking I had had the same experience they had had, but I'm fairly certain they weren't drunk as skunks when they lost their virtue. And that's exactly what it was – losing virtue, when a girl could never be a virtuous woman again. It made me sad in a way, but also, I remembered that I had liked it and was hoping it would happen again, but not the drunkenness – Lord no, not the evil drink.

Mama knocked on my door a little later and came in and sat on the bed. She wanted to know if I wanted to talk about it. How could I tell her I felt like a wanton woman? And why hadn't she asked that question before the wedding night?

"Sarah, I know what it's like the first time. It's painful," she said.

"Yes ma'am," I said, but I couldn't remember the pain, only the desire and I was truly embarrassed.

"You will grow to like it," she added.

How could I say I already liked it? I just said, "Yes ma'am," again and turned my face to the wall.

The storm, called a hurricane, blew all day and the next two days and we heard through the grapevine that Cedar Key, a little fishing village, was inundated with stormwater. At that point, the storm in me was abating also.

Settling into a routine of work, meals, and sleep, Sean and I made time for each other. He told me how happy he was with me and how surprised he was that I wanted him every night. Sometimes we stole away to the river's edge for some privacy, which was even better than being in that creaky old bed. I avoided Gale's looks, of course, but there were times when he was next to me in the barn or the dining hall. And sometimes I had to help Lana with the sewing machine or deliver bags to the grist mill. Always those eyes bore into my skin.

"How was it?" he asked one day when we were alone at the mill, as I delivered the flowered bags for the drying powders.

"Delightful!" I said, blushing, wanting to hurt him.

"I'm certain that it would be with you. How I wish I could trade places with him."

"Well, you can't. Please stop talking like that." I dropped the bags and left to go when he touched my arm lightly. I pulled away and rushed out the door, but I still felt the burning touch of his hand on my arm as I hurried to the house.

"Sarah," Sean called to me from the barn. "Let's go to the river to eat our noon meal."

"I can't, Sean. I have to finish an order of bags," I lied, and I could see the hurt in his eyes. I hated Gale and myself at that moment. Somehow Sean and I had to leave the ranch.

CHAPTER 41   ENDING THE JOURNEY

*R*ight when my mama was starting to get happier, Aunt Loretta took sick and passed away. She had been ailing for a while, but had made peace with Rebecca and seemed to be less truculent. Mama often told me the story of how they had come out of Georgia, with homes being burned and all of Atlanta in flames. Other than her children, all the folks who had made the journey were gone. It had been a time of bonding and the bonds could only be broken by death, she said. Of course, Rebecca and her family were reeling from the loss.

Loretta was laid to rest alongside her beloved Samuel, from whose death she had never recovered. Our little cemetery was filling up. Mama and I stayed behind to talk to Jasper and Loretta.

"She was such a lady, Sarah, the finest in the world. I could never measure up to her," Mama said.

"You're a lady and I think you are the finest in the world," I said.

"Aww, darling, you are my shining star."

As we walked back down the trail, she asked me how things were with Sean.

"Good. I am a happily married woman."

"And do you love him?"

"I do," I replied, but thought, "Not in the way I love Gale, God forgive me."

As long as I steered clear of Gale, I could focus on my husband, trying to love him more. Some Saturdays I would pack a picnic and meet him at the river, spreading a blanket on the ground. If he was late, I slept in the warm sun, waking only when I heard the sound of horse hooves. He was always ravenous, for the food and for me. He asked me why I kept my eyes opened when we kissed and I said it was so I could see his face, which was the truth.

On one of those warm days, as I drowsed on a smooth boulder down by the river, I heard a horse neigh. Thinking it to be Sean, I stretched and remained where I was, waiting for him to come to me, as usual, hungry for my kisses.

"Sarah, you look beautiful, girl. Marriage has been good for you," a man said.

Sam stood over me, smiling. Panicked, I jumped up and started to head back to the ranch.

"Wait," he said as he grabbed my arm.

"What are you doing here, Sam?"

"Visiting my family. My granny just died, you know. Am I not allowed to do that? Let's just sit and talk, like we used to do," he said.

"My husband will be here shortly."

"I would like to meet him." He was politely restrained, but it felt like he was a belt about to snap.

"I heard you were running from the law," I said.

"Not anymore. I've been at sea and I am now a law-abiding citizen," he said, flashing a grin.

"What do you want with me?"

"Sarah, we had good times. I just want to be your cousin again."

"You've always been my cousin. But you were awful back then and treated Jasper terrible and now he's gone."

"I heard. I'm sorry about that. I had some growing up to do. Can you forgive me?" he asked.

His words sounded trustworthy, but he was not. As uncomfortable as I was, I felt I owed him something.

"I can forgive you, but it is hard to forget how you behaved," I said slowly.

A horse and rider came into view at about that time and I was more than relieved. Sam had grown bigger, with large, muscular arms, and I knew I wouldn't be able to fight him off. I waved to Sean. After I introduced them, Sam, hurriedly, jumped in the saddle and bolted off.

"I don't think you should be late anymore," I said, testily.

"Why? He's your cousin," Sean said.

"He's mean and he scares me. I don't know what might have happened if you hadn't shown up," I said with a small amount of genuine fear.

Sean ate everything in the picnic basket, but I couldn't eat a thing, feeling jumpy now that Sam had appeared. I made Sean walk me back to the house, even though he said he didn't have time.

At supper, Sean said, "It was nice to meet another relative today." He was making polite conversation but I had not mentioned Sam. I glanced at my parents, nervously.

"Who would that be?" Mama asked, smiling.

"Why, Sam, of course," Sean replied.

Papa stood and kicked his chair back. "We were not told he was coming. He better not be here tomorrow."

"He says he's changed and is all grown up," I offered.

"Sarah, you knew he was here?" Mama asked.

"He came down to the river at noon," I said.

I felt guilty, not having told anyone, but I knew it would cause problems if I did – and it was.

Papa rushed to the bedroom and came out holding his treasure box, shaking the contents out on the table. The language that came out of his mouth I had never heard before and I surely had not heard my papa talk like that. Mama sucked her breath in, not because of the language, but because the famous gold nugget was missing. Sitting, silently staring at the contents, Sean and I could not make a sound, our eyes bugged out. It was if we thought we could make the nugget appear by staring at the table.

The banging of the screen door was all we heard of Papa. He was headed to the lake cabin and I was scared what would happen if he caught Sam down there. But I reckoned Sam was long gone, once he had stolen the treasure. Mama paced and I cleared the dishes, not knowing what else to do. I hoped I wouldn't be blamed – or Sean.

When Papa returned, Rebecca was trailing after him, crying, "Please don't kill him."

"You should've told me he was here, Rebecca. This is your fault, along with your husband's," Papa said angrily.

As she crumpled to the ground, Mama bent to help her up and said to Papa, "You would not kill him?"

"Only in self-defense. John will be going with me."

We paced in the house as the horses rode past the window and Sean left to do some work in the barn. Once again, we swept the floors, dusted the furniture, and re-washed dishes, while Rebecca cried in the parlor. Finally, she left, which was a relief, because we couldn't console her. What could we say? Your son is a criminal and stole from family that had raised him?

"Lord have mercy. I would like some peace and quiet for a change," Mama said.

All we could do was wait...and wait. I took to my journal and wrote about my cousin, Sam, who had gone down a wrong road and might get killed for it. But I worried that Papa and Uncle John could get killed also. Mama took up her quilting, along with Suzanna and her little daughter, Fereby, my cousin. The candles would burn into the night, I was certain.

CHAPTER 42   THE TAKE DOWN

"$\mathcal{H}$e left a trail as wide as a cattle stampede," Papa said on his return home. "Tried to sell that nugget all over Alachua County, but nobody had that kind of quick money. We caught up with him yesterday and turned him over to the Gainesville sheriff."

"I am so glad Loretta is not alive to witness the trouble Sam has caused. I don't think she could bear it," Mama said. "Did you rescue the nugget?"

Papa pulled it out of his pocket and held it up in the light, smiling. "Yes ma'am. It will be going in a safer safe place this time," he said.

"I better tell Nathan and Rebecca," Mama said.

"That's my job," Papa said. And he left to walk to the cabin by the lake.

Of course, they did not take the news lightly and left the next morning for Gainesville, leaving Daniel with Suzanna.

"I'm sure it's not the first time he's stolen," Papa said at breakfast.

"Did he surrender to you or pull a gun?" Mama asked.

"We caught him unawares, coming out of a saloon, drunk. Luckily, he wasn't armed and still had the nugget on him. He was pretty easy to subdue, once he saw John," Papa said.

The tension eased as we realized Sam would not be back for some time, but eventually he would get out. When would he learn, I wondered, and would he seek revenge when he did get out?

Sean cut some Palmetto fronds for me to weave as mosquito beaters. Hanging outside the doors, they required anyone entering the house to fram their clothes, in order to leave the insects outside. It was a terrible thing to hear the whining noise of a mosquito once a person was in bed and it was too hot to pull the covers over your head in the summer, when the mosquitoes were the worst. The beaters really were a work of art once they were finished and sometimes I made fans out of the fronds to cool myself off in the heat of the summer. Of course, everyone wanted one and I was happy to oblige.

There was always a lot of work to do and I kept myself busy, still trying to avoid Gale, and he did the same, but there were times when it was impossible. Sunday dinners were awkward, with neither one of us glancing at the other. If Sean was openly affectionate, I became uncomfortable, which made Sean look at me, I'm sure, wondering what was wrong. When we were alone, I was always open to Sean's advances, welcoming them.

At night, I couldn't wait for him to slide into bed next to me, reaching for him in the dark. Feeling pretty certain it wasn't virtuous to have that kind of passion, I just asked God for forgiveness, because I had no intention of giving it up. The one thing I had worried about was getting in the family way, thinking I was not quite ready, since I was still young. Loving children like I did, I knew I would want a baby at some point, but not just yet. There were preventions available.

A positive thing started to happen with our relationship. The more we made wicked love, the more I loved him, and the less I thought about Gale. I could now close my eyes, even in the daytime, when we kissed. When he entered a room, I was conscious of his presence and wanted to be with him. Life and love were mysterious, as I once thought I would never get over Gale. Was I a fickle woman, I wondered? No matter: Sean and I were happily in love with each other.

☼

Rebecca and Nathan were standoffish with the family and took their meals in the lake cabin. Daniel was allowed to play with Fereby as Rebecca was still friendly with Suzanna, and the two children went to the same school together. Of course Nathan had to communicate with Gale and his family because they worked together, but that was the extent of it. The tensions were mounting, I felt, and I knew nothing good would come of it.

"Nathan has taken a position with the railroad in Newberry – as a clerk. We will be leaving and this time, I don't think we will be coming back. My mother would be very unhappy with your treatment of her grandchild," Rebecca said, when a meeting was called.

"I'm sorry to hear that. I guess you don't believe Sam should be punished for stealing from people who have been good to him," Mama said.

"I don't think the sheriff needed to be called into family business. He did give the damned old nugget back to you, after all," Rebecca replied, teeth clenched.

"No, Rebecca. It was taken from him by force," Lani said.

"So say you. No matter; we are leaving." And with that, she flounced out of the house and by noon that day their wagon was loaded and they pulled down the driveway once more, with Daniel calling out to everyone, "Goodbye, my good friends." His little voice waivered and we all cried, especially Fereby.

Mama said Rebecca was not only angry about Sam, but also the death of her mother, which had left her grieving for the loss.

☼

As Sean and I lay abed later that night, a thought occurred to me: the lake cabin would now be empty and he and I could move into it, perhaps. Oh my, the joy that generated in me was overwhelming. Reckoning I had been too sad seeing our family split apart, I had had no idea anything good could come from it. I whispered my thought in his ear, and he said, "Wouldn't that be grand? We could actually make noise at night."

Wishing I had thought of it earlier, I couldn't wait until morning, hoping my parents would approve of my new plan. I was too excited to sleep and so was Sean, but we made use of the time.

"Well, I hadn't thought of that," Mama said at breakfast.

"We need to hire kitchen help and grist mill help now."

"Unless we put Sean to work at the mill," Papa said.

I gulped, but Mama came to the rescue. "No. Sean is too good with the cattle," she said and winked at me.

My heart was in my shoes, thinking of Sean and Gale working together.

"I reckon we can handle that," she said. "But we may have to make some changes if we need that space."

"Yes ma'am," I said, packing my bags in my mind. Sean grinned at me and squeezed my hand.

All that morning I spent cleaning the cabin, as our fleeing relatives had left it a mess. Singing while I worked, I was happy as the mockingbird I could hear chirping in the treetop. Sweat rolled down my face in spite of the cool weather and I wiped my sleeve over my forehead, which was dirty from the dust I swept. Nothing mattered but the feeling of freedom that I felt, and the fact that Sean and I could be ourselves, finally. As I sat to rest on the decking, watching the birds fly in and out of the rookery, Gale rounded the corner of the cabin.

"Your pa sent me to help move whatever you needed from the house," he said quietly.

He stood, leaning, with one hand against the wall, handsome as ever, his dark hair glistening in the sun, his eyes penetrating mine. I felt faint, and embarrassed at my messy hair and dirty face and hands.

"Oh, thank you, but I think we will be fine."

"Sarah, I have to do what your father says. He is my boss."

"All right then. Help me move the bed, so I can sweep under it," I replied."

Thinking I had had no more feelings for him, I realized I had simply repressed them. My heart was beating out of my chest, my face was flushed, and I felt weak.

"Sarah, you look awful. I think you are over-heated."

He helped me to a chair in the cabin, with his hand around my waist, then loosened my blue hair ribbon and held my hair away from my head, his fingers stroking my scalp. And then, his lips were on mine and I did not fight it. He carried me to the bed and placed me on the feather mattress where I had just changed the sheets. Lovingly, he caressed me in all the right places. Then, he went to the door and locked it, which made me realize how wrong it was, and the sliding sound of that wooden bar over the door, caused something to go off in my brain.

Shame drifted over me like ocean water; I knew I had to end this action but I hoped I had not placed myself in a position to be harmed physically. I stood, a little shaky, and demanded that he unbar the door.

"Sarah, I love you," he said.

My mule-headedness kicked in then and I went to the door, removing the wooden bar. I opened the door, which allowed fresh air to flow into the room and demanded that he leave.

"I will tell Papa that you were a big help, but you must leave this very minute," I said.

My hair was a tangled mess and I had no way to calm it. I worried that we might have been caught, even though I had stopped it before it escalated. The anger showed on his face and I was sorry that I had allowed as much as I had.

"You constantly lead me on," he said.

"And I am sorry for that. It will not happen again. Please stay away from me."

"I would risk everything for you, but you, you just play games with me. I love you madly, Sarah."

"You must go." I grabbed the broom and began sweeping where the bed had stood.

"I won't be back...ever," he said, slamming the door behind him.

"Good," I whispered. But I had heard that before.

Collapsing on the bed, I found it hard to breathe. How could I have let it go that far? Still, I couldn't stop thinking of the thing that had almost happened. I tied my hair up with the ribbon and glanced in the mirror, seeing a flushed face, warm with shame.

Sean and I took our supper in the ranch kitchen that night, since I had worked all day bringing luggage and other items we needed. Sean whispered in my ear that he couldn't wait to be in our bed that night. What a quandary I was in. I had really messed up my life.

As Sean headed to the cabin, I went home to waste time and try not to join him until he was asleep, knowing he had worked hard all day. I sat with Mama as we worked on her quilt again.

"Did Gale help you with the heavy stuff today?" Papa asked.

"Yessir," I said. Mama watched as my color rose but she said nothing until Papa left the house, when I let out a sigh of relief.

"Sarah?" she said quietly.

"He helped move the furniture so I could clean. Papa sent him," I said.

"Why, then, is your face so red?"

"I did not ask him to help."

"Oh my God in heaven. You are playing with fire. You must stop this right now or I will let Gale go. I mean it," Mama said firmly.

"Yes ma'am," I answered.

Although I didn't confess to anything, she knew something had happened, and I felt I had let her down...and Sean. Determined to not let it happen again, knowing it would ruin a lot of lives, I made up my mind again to plan to leave the ranch. Sean would be the hard one to convince, as he loved living on the ranch.

It was dark when I carried the lantern down to the cabin, hoping beyond hope that my husband was asleep. He was, and I dropped my clothes, quietly slipping into bed, listening to his deep breathing, holding my own breath. I could hear the egrets and curlews in the rookery squawking to each other and I turned on my side, away from my husband, and dreamed of a man that I loved beyond measure, a man I could not have, ever.

CHAPTER 43   ENTANGLED TIMES

"Oh what a tangled web we weave, when first we practice to deceive." Sir Walter Scott

*T*he younger ranch hands were let go early Saturday, so they could go to town and whoop it up. The older ranch hands stayed on to work in case they were needed. I found Sean fishing off the dock, with a string of bream tied to a pole. Grinning, he said, "I'll clean 'em if you'll fry 'em."

"Come here, Sarah. Sit down. It's gonna be a fine evening for some fried fish and hush puppies," he added.

As I sat beside him, he looked down at me. "What's wrong? I thought we moved here for some nighttime privacy, but we haven't touched in a week," he said.

"I don't like it here, Sean. I want to move."

"Back to the house?"

"No. Newberry."

"Why would we do that? Our life is perfect here. You are a perplexing girl, Sarah. I don't think you're ever happy," he said, sounding puzzled.

"You could get a job on the railroad, like Nathan."

"What is wrong with you? I like ranching. I love this cabin, your family, and I love you."

"Uncle Nathan would help you," I replied.

Sean threw his fishing pole down and stomped away into the cabin. Sticking his head out the door, he said, "Does it matter what I want, or are you so spoiled, that it can only be what you want?"

"Spoiled? You think I'm spoiled?" I yelled.

"Yes ma'am. I surely do. Selfish is what you are. You are the most selfish person I have ever met."

It was an argument I could not win because it was the truth. I was a terrible, awful, no-good person, only thinking of myself. Tears dripped down my cheeks onto the bodice of my dress. He stood before me, apologizing for his words. I didn't know how I could feel any worse, mistreating two men.

At a time when I began to feel panicky, Aunt Annie asked if I could come stay with her for a week and help with her house cleaning. Mama and I rode over together in the carriage. She was very quiet, but then, so was I. I was afraid if we talked she would ask about Gale. Crickets were chirping, birds were singing, the horse was snorting, but no sound came from us.

When Mama said goodbye, she hugged me tight, and said, "I love you, girl. I want the best for you. Take this week and make a quality decision."

That statement made me think she had asked Annie to take me for seven or eight days, but that was all right with me, as long as Annie didn't know the situation.

Although I worked hard all week, it was more relaxing than being on the ranch, always dodging Gale, and feeling frustrated and guilty around Sean. I loved Annie and David, and Jake and his family. There was no tension and I really thought Aunt Annie was

222

getting old, because she couldn't see the dust and grime in her house anymore. It was a good thing, all the way round, even though the work was hard, but Mama always said, "If you want to get through a hard time, set your hands to work."

The thought occurred to me on a Thursday, while I was scrubbing the wood floors, that Gale wanted me because he couldn't have me, but Sean wanted me because he could have me. It felt like a character flaw on Gale's part, but on mine also, because I almost gave into him. My mind was clearing finally, and how smart my mama was to get me away. A weight was lifted from me with that thought. However, I had to face the fact that I had come close to committing a grave sin against my husband and God. If I confessed it to Sean, he might hate me forever and maybe even leave me. I had, after all, almost committed adultery. My good mood vanished as I thought about telling Sean, but soon realized this might have to be my forever secret. What good would it accomplish, and it would only serve to hurt him.

Annie said she had never seen anyone work harder and said how much she appreciated me. I believe I worked like a whirlwind because I was trying to think through my problems. On Sunday, we went to church and I met up with my family. Sean stood shyly outside the church doors, waiting for me to arrive. My heart melted when I saw him, knowing he hadn't understood why I had left.

"I've missed you," he whispered as we sat in the pew, next to my parents.

"And I have missed you, my husband," I whispered back.

Holding my hand in his, we sang the hymns, and when everyone closed their eyes in prayer, he bent and kissed me on the lips. So many emotions washed over me: love, guilt, pain, disgust at myself. But my confusion was clearing and I realized what I had to do.

Gale and his family were in attendance, but they were not my concern any longer. I realized my attention must be directed toward my husband and my loved ones, not some man who was looking for a way to cheat on his wife. My disgust turned toward Gale, thinking I never wanted to see him again.

After church, Annie and David invited us to dinner. Oh how they bragged on me, thanking my parents for raising such a good girl. And I thought that maybe now I could try to start thinking of myself as a good young woman.

☼

The aroma of the longleaf pine trees was something I hadn't noticed in a while, so involved had I become in my own selfish self. I inhaled the air slowly, so as not to forget the aroma again. As we rode home in the backseat of the carriage, Sean smiled down at me and tucked the quilt closer around my shoulders. What a fool I had been, I thought. I had a man who was so good to me and yet, I had not appreciated him. Mama turned and smiled at us.

Once we returned home, I set to working hard: helping clean the houses, working in the kitchen, washing clothes and linens, taking care of the farm animals. By the time I 'hit the hay,' as Papa said, I was as tired as a person could be. I believed I was doing penance. But also, the ranch was now so short-handed, everyone was overworked.

"I'm proud of you, girl," Mama said one day as I washed the dishes. "I knew as stubborn as you are, that you would make the right decision."

"Thank you, I think," I said. I thought it was a compliment but I wasn't quite certain.

CHAPTER 44   ALL IN THE TELLING

"Life can be understood backwards, but it must be lived forwards." Soren Kierkergaard

"Sarah, I feel you are always just beyond my grasp. Why is that?" Sean asked.

"Whatever are you talking about?" I asked.

"I'm not sure you love me like I love you."

"Is this about Newberry?"

"Newberry… and a feeling I have. I am the man of the house. It should be my decision where we live," he said, squaring his shoulders.

"I can work for a salary as a seamstress. We could make more money there."

"We would have more expenses," he argued.

It was an ongoing argument, one I couldn't win logically. I had written to Aunt Rebecca, asking about seamstress jobs and railroad agent jobs. She, of course, would do anything to take revenge on my parents, so I assumed she would help us. Knowing my mother would be heartbroken if I left, I knew Rebecca would be accommodating.

However, Sean did not know of this particular plan. It felt as if I was conniving, but what else could I do? At that point, I had been able to avoid Gale, but that couldn't last forever. And… would I give in to him the next time? Weak was how I felt, and disgusted that I might not resist.

"I am a person of low character," I thought. I prayed God would help me; after all, I was mule-headed.

☼

"Here's a letter to you from Rebecca," Mama said, as I stepped into the house to begin sewing bags for the mill. "Why would she be writing to you?"

"I…I am looking for a new job," I stuttered.

"Away from the ranch? Why would you do that?" Mama asked, concerned.

"We need more money in order to support Sean's parents."

"Why didn't you say so. You can have more money and stay here."

"We need to start our life and not be a burden to you and Papa."

"Sarah, you are not making sense. What is the real reason?" Mama asked, touching my hand.

Frustration must have been written all over my face because Mama got quiet then. I didn't have any good answers for her and the truth, it was lost somewhere in the telling. Too many people would have suffered had she known the real story as she would have fired Gale and his whole family. Mr. Lindsey had never returned; everyone thought he had been killed in a bar brawl or something.

"Read the letter," she said.

Dear Sarah,
There is a lady here in Newberry who hires out girls to sew for her. Most of her orders come from Gainesville, so she has a good business. Of course, you may come and live here with us until you

and Sean get on your feet. Nathan will help Sean get a job. Come on
to Newberry.
Love, Rebecca

"Well, of course, she wants you to come and live with her.
It's her revenge against us. I am not happy about this, Sarah. You are
allowing her to win a battle," Mama said unhappily.

The feeling I had then was of misery; I never wanted to make
my mama unhappy. I left the house feeling nauseated. Whatever was
I to do? As usual, I just said, "Yes ma'am."

And right when things couldn't get any more miserable, Lana
appeared in my open doorway. Since the weather had turned off
cooler and the mosquitoes were fewer, I enjoyed opening the door,
listening to the birds in the rookery across the lake. I thought to
myself, "I need to keep that door locked and bolted." I had had very
little contact with her, only to say 'Good Morning' on occasion.

"Hello," she said. "Can we talk?"
I wanted to say, "No." But I asked if she would like some coffee,
just boiled earlier. She took a seat at the table, and I poured us two
cups, my hand shaking a little.

"A little sugar? I have no cream this morning yet," I said.
"Black is good," she answered.

I could tell she was hesitant to begin the conversation and I
wanted to be turned into a lump of salt, to avoid the conversation
altogether.

"It's about Gale," she began, which sank my heart.
"Yes?" I said.

"I know he loves you. After he sees you, he won't come to
my bed for a few days," she said.

Wanting to run to the end of the dock, and jump in, and sink
to the bottom of the lake, I said, "I'm sorry. I don't know what you
mean."

"I would like you to leave him alone. The children and I have a wonderful life with him and he is so good to us, until you come into the picture."

"I want nothing to do with Gale. If you haven't noticed, I am married to a good man."

"I think you entice my husband," she said, angrily, her milk-white skin blotching.

"No. No, I do not," I said quickly.

"I am here to ask you to stay away from him."

"You do not have to ask. I will stay as far away from him as I can. I don't know what he has told you, but I am not interested in Gale."

Well, I didn't know if that was a lie or the truth. I was in love with him, but I realized he was poison for me and my family. I stood, hoping she would stand and leave.

"He tells me nothing and that is the telling. It's a selfish woman who will not leave a married man alone," Lana said with conviction.

Equally angry, I said, "I don't know how to say it any clearer: I do not want your man. Please leave."

Knowing I could have said something mean about her past, I didn't, feeling sympathy for her. She slammed her coffee cup on the table, cracking it, coffee flowing over the table cloth. As she stormed out the door, I gathered the cloth up and took it to the dock to shake it out over the water, my hands quivering.

As I looked across the lake, the storm clouds started gathering, black as smut, thunder rumbling, lightning flashing. I reckoned it to be a sign that I needed to leave this place soon, and I wrote the letter to Aunt Rebecca, riding into La Crosse before the storm hit, to be certain it was in the evening outgoing mail.

☼

Rebecca had secured a seamstress position for me and seemed eager for my arrival. I knew her intentions were not honorable but I was eager to move. At some point I would tell Mama and Papa, but I had to tell Sean immediately.

☼

Mama asked me to walk with her to the barn as we had a new colt she wanted to check on. We found Gale in the stall with the baby, feeding it with a bottle. That was not normally his job, but Papa sometimes called on him to do other things around the ranch. My face flushed and my heart raced as I watched how gently he treated the little animal.

"He's quite the beauty, Miz Walton," he said.

"Aww. He is so pretty, sassy, too," Mama said, as the colt bumped Gale's leg.

"Where's his mama?" I asked.

"She didn't want the little feller," Gale said sadly.

I stood on the bottom board of the stall, my arms draped over the top, watching with glee as the baby drank voraciously.

"He'll be healthy with that kind of appetite," Mama said.

When Suzanna called to Mama to give advice in the kitchen, it left me alone with Gale. I jumped down, turning to go when Gale touched my hand.

"Sarah? I'm sorry for the other day. I'm sorry for a lot of things, but mostly that I made so many mistakes with you," he whispered.

"It's all right, Gale. I will be leaving the ranch soon. I have taken a job in Newberry."

"Because of me? Please don't leave because of me," he pleaded.

He set the bottle down and came to me, looking me in the eyes with that soulful look, breaking my heart. And that was why I had to stay away from him. He took my hands in his, over the stall wall.

"You tear my heart out," he said.

Tears formed in his eyes, at the very moment Sean stepped into the barn. Gale dropped my hands and rushed to pick up the bottle and feed the colt again.

"What the hell?" Sean growled.

I rushed from the barn and down the trail to the cabin, Sean right on my skirts.

"Well?" Sean asked as he slammed the cabin door.

229

"He's my friend," I stammered.

"Is that why he has always hated me?"

"Sean, I am leaving the ranch. I was saying goodbye to him."

"You are the most aggravating woman I have ever met. You are leaving me?" he asked harshly.

"I would like you to come with me, if you will."

"Are you in love with him?"

"No," I lied.

"Is that why you're leaving, because you can't stand to be around a man who is married with a family – a man you love?" Sean asked, pain in his voice.

"I am leaving tomorrow. Either you can come with me or you can stay here on the ranch. I have taken a seamstress position," I said firmly.

"I am the man of this house and I say we are *not* leaving. Do your folks know?"

"I am telling them today. There is a job for you on the railroad if you come."

"God Almighty. You scorch my grits," he yelled.

He slammed the door again as he left the house. I hoped he wasn't going to confront Gale, but I heard his horse gallop to the pasture and he was riding hard. About ten minutes later, Mama showed up – no privacy here.

"Sean was riding that horse in a way I don't approve of. What is going on?" she asked.

"I told him I was moving to Newberry tomorrow," I said.

"Oh!" she said as she sank into a chair. "You must tell your Papa tonight. Come to supper at the house, you and Sean," she said, with sorrow in her voice.

"Yes ma'am," I said quietly.

☼

"All right, Sarah. I will go with you and take that job, but if it doesn't work out, I want a guarantee, from your folks and you, that we can come back here. And I want it known that this is not my idea and I am not happy about it," Sean said with conviction.

"We're going to supper at their house tonight, so I can break the news to my papa," I said.

"You do beat all – going off and leaving your family that loves you so much and dragging me along like you wear the britches in this family. You make me look the fool," he said angrily.

Sean walked ahead of me as we took the trail away from the cabin. I reckoned he was trying to wear the britches. I didn't care who wore the britches as long as I didn't have to face Gale and Lana anymore.

I helped with supper, setting the table and serving the food Mama had prepared. She was quiet and I was nervous, as was Sean.

"What the hell is wrong with everyone tonight?" Papa asked.

"Sarah has something to tell you, Lani," Mama said.

All eyes focused on me and I stuttered, "Sean and I will be moving to Newberry tomorrow. We have taken jobs there."

"Why would you do that?" he asked, incredulously.

"My sentiments exactly," Sean said.

"Wait. You are not on board with this, Sean?" Papa asked.

"Nossir. I am happy as a clam here," Sean replied.

"What brought this on?" Papa asked, staring at me.

"Rebecca found me a seamstress job and Sean a railroad job and I felt it was time," I said weakly.

"Ah, Rebecca. So, you are allowing her to get the best of us. Is that it?" he said, with hurt in his voice.

"That may be how it looks, but I truly think she's doing us a favor," I said.

"I won't have you living with her while she speaks ill of us," Mama said. "I will lend you the money and you can find your own place right away."

"This is all rather confusing to me," Papa said. "Have we not been good to you and Sean?"

"The best, Papa," I said.

My frustration was evident. How could I explain my situation to him without talking about Gale, who would lose his job, hurting his whole family? And how could I tell Sean that I could not stand to see Gale one more day, that I loved him truly. And how long could Lana go on, without revealing her information to my folks? Since I could not tell the truth, I stayed quiet.

"Sir," Sean said. "I would like to come back here if this crazy scheme of Sarah's does not work out."
Papa stood and paced the floor, ruminating, I reckoned.

"Allrighty then. But we will have to hire two folks to take your places. I can't promise a job for you, but you can return if it doesn't work out," Papa said, obviously still wondering at the true story.

"Thank you, sir," Sean said, shaking Papa's hand, leaving to do some chores in the barn. I went to Papa and hugged him, my tears dampening his shirt-front.

"I love you, girl. I don't always understand your mama or you, but I love you both. Don't be a stranger. Take the small wagon and the bay mare. You'll need a horse," he said affectionately.

Mama cried when I said goodbye, knowing we would be gone early in the morning. She slipped me the money and I was thankful, but my heart was breaking.

CHAPTER 45   GUILTY OF MISERY

As the small wagon rattled down the driveway, I saw Mama's light on in the kitchen window. She looked up as we passed and my sobbing began, lasting nearly to Alachua, as dawn was breaking. Sean was hot with anger; no comfort did I receive from him.

Feeling hollowed out, my eyes finally dried, as I had no more tears left. Leaving the only home I had ever known and the people I loved most in the world, I wondered why Gale and his family couldn't have been the ones to leave. Sitting on the cold, hard wagon seat, a brisk wind blowing, my husband furious with me, I thought things couldn't get more miserable. But, I found, they could.

Aunt Rebecca and Uncle Nathan were happier to see us than they would have been ordinarily. I knew she was feeling her revenge and I hated to be a part of that, but we needed them, for a few days anyway.

"Your eyes are awful red, honey," Rebecca said, while Sean and Nathan took the wagon to the barn. "I know just how you feel when you leave the only home you've ever known, but it's nice to have you here and you will bring joy to us because we have been a little lonely."

I didn't want to feel sorry for her because of the way she had left the ranch, but I found I needed her sympathy and company. Daniel asked me several times about Fereby, saying he missed her so much.

Needing comfort in the worst way, I was drawn to Rebecca, even as she was bad-mouthing my mama and papa. She was the only thing I could hold onto at the time…and she was kind to me. Sean was cold, hardly looking at me.

"This here's a rough old town – a railroad town. It gets loud at night and you will need to be in about dark. Gunshots can be heard outside the saloon, especially when the phosphate miners are in town," she said.

Even though their little house was on the edge of town, what she said was true – the noise in the evening kept us awake – not that we were asleep. Sean tossed and turned, sighing, until he finally left our pallet on the floor, slipping out the front door, quietly. I also arose and sat in the rocking chair in the small parlor, waiting for him to come home. Waiting until I could stand it no more, I fell into our bed and slept soundly. At dawn, he slipped in beside me, smelling of whiskey, and things kept getting worse in my life. He reached for me, groping my body, but I was disgusted, with him and myself, and stood to start my day, while he passed out.

Exhausted as I was, I went with Rebecca to interview for my job. Minerva Jones, the proprietor, was impressed that I could use a treadle machine and hired me on the spot. I told her I had to find a house that day and would start the next day.

When we returned, Sean was up, drinking coffee, getting ready to go for his interview. He neither smiled nor acknowledged my presence.

234

"There's a little house for rent about a mile or so down the road," Nathan offered. "However, Sean will probably be working nights since he's new – if he gets hired. That would put you alone and it would be hard to get to town unless you walked."

"How about the railroad housing?" Sean asked.

"Oh no. That's a rough area. Sarah couldn't live there," Rebecca said.

Well, didn't everybody have an opinion about where we would live? I reckoned I could find something on my own, with or without Sean. Folks were causing me to be peevish, making me wish my mama was here.

"I'll take a walk around town and see if I can't find something," I said.

"I'll go with you," Rebecca said. And I groaned inwardly.

Rebecca and I set out in her carriage, driving about Newberry and a little farther down some roads. It was a bustling town, with so many miners and railroad workers. The countryside was full of watermelon farms and we stopped and purchased a big green one for later. The little house that was down the road was quite a distance from town, but I felt that was all we could afford and it had good locks on the doors.

"I don't think this is a good idea, Sarah," Rebecca said. "I don't want Sally to think I lured you here and something bad happened to you."

"I'll show it to Sean and we'll make that determination," I said, but I thought 'lured' to be a strange word.

Overjoyed that he got the railroad job, Sean was finally getting back to the old Sean. He liked the little Cracker house, with the swing on the front porch. It was well-built, with a fireplace, and a cook stove, and a small bedroom. He smiled for the first time in a week, and bent down to kiss me. It was the only time I had felt positive in a while. The old bed was a creaker, but the mattress was soft and I spread new sheets and a quilt over it. It would be our first night in the house and I had much to do before Sean left for work at dark, but he was interested in that bed and before long we had tried it out, laughing and listening to the sound of the springs. Finally, I was filled with hope.

Rebecca, Nathan, and Daniel brought our supper that evening and I was so happy not to have to cook, with all the cleaning I had been doing. They stayed to eat with us and when they left they took Sean to the railroad station, leaving me alone. Sean said he would take me to work the next morning; the one-stall barn behind the house was where the horse stayed and he would have to hook the horse to the wagon.

By the time I "hit the hay," I was asleep, waking about midnight, wondering where I was. My first thought was of Gale and I cried as I clutched the pillow to my body. Would I ever stop thinking of him? I prayed I would not dream of him one night and call out his name, but then I fell fast asleep again, until Sean came in at dawn.

As I stretched, my body tucked in the quilts, he climbed in bed with me, clothes and all, and kissed me on my neck, saying, "This might work out just fine, Sarah. Maybe we did the right thing." I smiled while he took his clothes off and we made that bed creak some more.

CHAPTER 46   PIES AND LIES

Some days I had to walk to work, about a mile. When Sean came in from working all night, he was like a dead man. Thinking it would be easy to be a night clerk, he found that they used him on the tracks and on every other hard job out there, since he was young and fit. If I rode the horse, I wouldn't have any place to keep it for the day, so I just figured the fresh air was good for me. My skirts dragged in the dirt on the road and by the time I got to Minerva's I was kicking up a little dust cloud, which caused her to scream, "We cannot have dust in the sewing room."

I had to take my skirts off on the back porch, standing only in my bloomers, while shaking the clothes vigorously. Minerva Jones was not near as nice as when she hired me, yelling at the two other girls and myself if we didn't sew a straight line and if we weren't fast enough. I reckoned she was under the gun to get the rich ladies' dresses done in a timely fashion. Once again, I questioned what I was doing there when my beautiful life on the ranch had slipped away. The other two girls, Margaret and Helen, were pretty nice though. They, like me, were working to help support their husbands, who worked also. Once Minerva left the room, we talked freely and laughed about her awful nature.

When Minerva told me I had to work six days a week to finish an order, I told her I could not do that. Margaret and Helen were suddenly quiet, their eyes popping out. We had ourselves a standoff but finally she gave in, but that meant the other girls would have to work extra, so I gave in. Thinking I could find better work, I determined to talk to Rebecca, to inquire about other job openings.

Sean was outside the door at five o'clock sharp, with the horse and wagon, thankfully. But then, it was on to the cabin where I had to make supper. Oh, I missed my home and the ranch dining hall where I didn't have to do anything but sit down and be served. He was learning to cook a bit, and sometimes he had a stew boiling on the cook stove when we got home.

He was thoughtful, too, and allowed me to rest before I started cooking. Rubbing my shoulders and neck, which was where I pained, from bending over the Singer all day, he sang "Down in the Valley," just like Papa, which made me miss him so.

"Don't walk to work no more. It's gonna be getting cold soon. Just wake me up and I'll drive you," Sean said.

One morning Helen came to work with a big bruise on her neck and a black eye. She tried to avoid our eyes, but it was too noticeable, and I didn't know what other bruises she had with her dress hiding some areas. Margaret prodded her verbally until Helen broke down in tears and said her husband came in from the saloon, drunk, and beat her badly, saying he raped her, too.

"Can a husband rape his wife?" I asked.

"I reckon, if she doesn't want his advances," Margaret said. "I would shoot the SOB."

Now, Margaret was a sizeable woman, and strong. I didn't think anyone would mess with her, including her husband, but that question worried me for days. Should a woman have to submit to her husband no matter what?

We were all childless at that point, newly wedded, and young. When Helen talked about not wanting a child to come from that violent act, I recommended Dr. Foote's womb veil, which I had been using since my wedding night, as recommended by my mama. Helen's eyes lighted up and she asked where she could order it and I told her it was in the mail order catalog. She smiled then, and I knew she had solved one of her problems, but how could she keep her husband from beating her? Margaret told her when he came in drunk, she should roll him up in a rug and take the rug beater to him, which would be easy if you were Margaret's size. Minerva walked in then, and our discussion changed to style.

"What is the cost?" Helen asked later.

"Six dollars," I said.

"Oh, where will I get that kind of money?"

I walked to her machine and pulled a five and a one dollar bill out of my apron pocket and laid it on the wood of the machine.

"Thank you," she whispered, her eye swollen almost shut.

At home later, I asked what Sean thought of a man raping his wife?

"Good God, Sarah. You do ask the goldurndist questions. A man has needs and a woman has to submit to those needs."

"What are you saying? That a woman has to do whatever the man wants?" I asked angrily.

"Have I ever forced you?" he asked.

"Well, you make it sound as if it's all right to force a woman."

"Why are you so mad? I have never raped you. Honestly, you are starting a fight here over something that has never happened."

"And if it did, would you think it was all right?" I asked.

"Well, I reckon not. Who would want a woman if she was obstinate anyway?" he snorted.

"Well, that should have been your first answer, Sean O'Hara."

"Yep. It should have been. Please give me the correct answers before you ask hard questions," he said, trying not to grin.

I laughed then, and so did he, and I kissed him, knowing he would never force me.

Christmas was coming on and I wanted to be with my family, thinking we could ride the train to Alachua and someone could pick us up. But Sean said he would not be allowed to take the time off. I hadn't counted on not seeing my mama and papa during the holidays and it caused me no end of agony.

"If we were still living on the ranch, we would be able to celebrate with the folks. It's your doing, Sarah," Sean said.

Well, there's nothing like having your mistakes thrown in your face. He scorched my grits sometimes – lots of times, as a matter of fact. I glared at him.

"If you want to go on home and leave me alone at Christmas, go ahead. Being the selfish girl you are, it wouldn't surprise me one bit," he said.

I slammed the door behind me, wrapped my shawl around my head and walked to Rebecca's, steaming all the way. The wind blew me down the road and by the time I reached their house, I was chilled to the bone.

"Oh my darling, come in," Rebecca said, pulling me in and guiding me to the warm cook stove where she had an apple pie baking. She took my hands in hers and rubbed them until they were starting to warm, while the aroma of that pie drifted to my senses.

"What are you doing out on this cold day?" she asked.

"I was missing my folks and with Christmas coming on, I wanted to go home. Sean is the most ornery man I know, saying we can't go home," I said, as my teeth chattered.

"Oh, honey, you don't know ornery. We're going to have a big Christmas here and we're your family. Don't worry about a thing. Sam will be here with his wife; you will love her to pieces," she said.

"Sam has a wife? Sam is out of jail?" I asked, my voice squeaking a bit.

"He wasn't in jail that long. There was no proof he stole anything. He's working at the mines now and comes home on Saturday and Sunday. He's reformed, you'll see. We'll have a grand celebration," Rebecca said happily.

"Well, that makes me feel a little better. I'll plan on it," I said.

"You know your mama, Mary Elizabeth, and I were the best of friends growing up. How we loved each other. I miss her so much."

I sighed then and she said, "Your grandmother took you away from her and she was sorely grieved."

"What?" I was aghast. Did Rebecca forget that I was there and knew my mama had asked my grandmother to take me? But I couldn't question her for she was my only link to family and the upcoming celebration. I needed her for womanly consolation, but I really needed my mama, Sally, and I knew the truth and so did Rebecca, which made her a liar.

Right about that time, Sean knocked on the door and came barging in, shouting, "Why did you run off?"

"Come have some pie and coffee, Sean. Everything is okay. Aunt Rebecca is going to make everything okay," Rebecca said. And I thought, "The pie and coffee will make everything okay."

CHAPTER 47   ONLY TWELVE MILES

Since I didn't have time to make gifts for everyone on the ranch, I wrote a letter to each person, telling them how much I missed them, and making it seem like our life was so much better than it really was.

I had stayed on with Minerva, mostly because of Margaret and Helen. I was growing to love those two girls and I wanted to help Helen, but it seemed impossible as she still had bruises from time to time. Smiling, she said she was pleased with her 'womb veil' and I thought it was because she had some power over her husband. He was not aware that she worked at Minerva's and she had to manipulate her time in order to keep it a secret. She hoped to save enough money and planned to run away whenever she could buy a train ticket. Shame kept her from sharing the beatings with us, but we knew. I wondered how a woman could feel shame over something beyond her control. I hated that man.

I wrote again to my mama, explaining Helen's situation, asking if there was a place for her in the ranch kitchen or gristmill, sewing bags.

A big package from home arrived on the train a few days before Christmas, with gifts for everyone, including Rebecca and Nathan. Sean took the package to Rebecca's for opening on the big day.

On Christmas Eve, we attended church, without Sean, singing hymns of praise and worship. My heart swelled, but I was not with the people I wanted to be with. Deciding I should be grateful instead of feeling loss, my spirits lifted. The Lord said, "Make a joyful noise" and I sang as loud as I could, smiling all the while and holding Daniel's hand.

☼

Hoping that Sean could keep his eyes open while driving to Rebecca's, I patted the small presents I had made, mostly sewed little things, a quilt piece for Rebecca and a stuffed horse for Daniel. Sean had carved a pipe for Nathan and I had made pillow cases for Sam and his wife.

By baking all morning, I had three pies to take to dinner: pecan, apple, and canned peach. I was brimming over with excitement, jabbering up a storm, while Sean smiled quietly. I was a little nervous about seeing Sam again, but I had to believe he had changed. Nevertheless, I left my money at home and only wore my gold wedding band.

The weather was chilly, not unbearably cold, but I figured we would have to eat inside, around a small table. No matter what Rebecca said about my parents, I was happy to be included in this joyous occasion.

As Sean took the horse and wagon to their barn, I entered the front door, loaded with the presents, knowing Sean would bring in the pies. Everyone was smiling and happy, hugging each other. Daniel held my hand and pointed out the small Christmas tree in the parlor.

The men filed in the back door, Nathan, Sean, Sam, and behind Sam, his wife, who, when she stepped to the side, made me almost faint. It was Helen, whose eyes were as wide as mine and I realized I had to become an actress. Smiling big, I greeted Sam as if I were glad to see him, knowing in my heart who he was. I shook hands with Helen and we acted as if it were the first time I had laid eyes on her.

Sam was only a few months older than me, but he looked like a full growed man, with squint lines around his eyes, a permanent frown on his forehead, and a heavy moustache. He was surely glad to see me and he and Sean got on famously. I cringed.

"Sam is your cousin?" Helen whispered to me.

"Sam is your husband?" I whispered back.

She and I talked little the rest of the day, and I tried to enjoy my family, but knowing Sam was Helen's husband had changed things. How could I send her to our ranch, knowing Sam could cause so much trouble? I didn't know what he was capable of, but how could I not help her?

Sam cornered me in the kitchen, asking why I hadn't come to see them and meet Helen. "She's a good cook and a stand-up woman," he said, boastfully.

My skin crawled when he said that, knowing how he had abused her, and her being only about sixteen years of age.

"She's lovely, Sam. I hope you treat her well," I said.

"Why wouldn't I? I'm reformed, you know," he said, proudly

"So I'm told," I said.

"You don't believe it, do you? You're a damned snob, Sarah."

"Time to eat," Rebecca called out, saving me.

My appetite flew out the window, sitting across from Sam and Helen, who smiled meekly. But I determined to help her escape and hoped he suffered greatly at her loss, being the total horse's ass he was. I couldn't wait to be home in my safe little cottage, far from the people in that house.

"What was wrong with you today, Sarah?" Sean asked on the way home.

"Sam! Sam is what is wrong with me!" I shouted.

"I like him," he said.

"Do you remember I told you about a man who beat and raped his wife, Helen?" I asked.

Sucking in his breath, he said, "No. Sam and Helen? Oh, good God almighty."

"Will you help me to save her before he kills her?" I pleaded.

"Well, now, that is a dilemma. What about Rebecca and Nathan?" he asked.

"No one can know. Mama says she will take Helen in but she doesn't know Sam is her husband. I will have to clarify that."

"I'll have to do some ruminating on how best to get her out of town on the evening train to Alachua," he said.

And so, we became co-conspirators. It was almost exciting, but I was happy that he would be helping me, especially since he knew the train schedules and how best to shuffle Helen without anyone knowing. Since Sam worked all week down at the phosphate mine south of town, I thought it might work out. The only problem would be Rebecca and Nathan, but Sean said the midnight train would run when everyone was asleep. Helen would have to travel alone, however. We were cooking up a plan and I wrote to my folks explaining the Sam situation. My mama was tough though, carrying a pistol for most of her life, and she was just as stubborn as me. I couldn't tell Helen until I had confirmation, but I knew it would come.

Sean bought me a little lady's pistol to carry in my skirt pocket and he taught me to shoot behind the lean-to, even though I had learned years ago from Papa. Waves of exhilaration, coupled with fear, passed through my body. But when Mama wrote back, saying she would be proud to rescue that young girl from Sam, I knew we would move ahead. I wondered if Mama wasn't getting a little revenge on Rebecca, too. But no matter.

When I broke the news to Helen and Margaret, I thought Margaret was going to kiss me, but she gave me a bear hug instead. She had been trying to come up with a plan herself.

"Sean says Wednesday night at midnight would be best. He can take the train with you to Alachua for safety. I will ride with him so I can see my folks for a few minutes. We must keep this a secret," I whispered.

Helen was breathing rapidly, but she had a smile of relief on her face. I was hoping we could pull this off and swore Margaret to secrecy.

The train on Wednesday evening started at the phosphate mines south of town. After loading the phosphate ore, which was heading to the port of Jacksonville, it would wind its way northeast, stopping only for water for the steam engines. Sean had worked it so that we could ride in the caboose, claiming he wanted to be sure the trains were operating correctly, which his boss thought was a good idea. Even though the ride to Alachua was only 12 miles, the engines pulled a heavy load and the trip took more than two hours.

Before he went to work, Sean dropped me at Helen's house, saying we should be at the station by 11 p.m. Helen and I were both nervous, pacing the floors, thinking Sam might show up at any moment, unexpectedly. At 10:30 p.m., we grabbed her two bags and began the walk to the station.

Dogs barked as we passed fences and we were jumpy at each house. We even had to pass by Rebecca and Nathan's house, where a light was on in the kitchen. Helen grabbed my hand and we moved silently onward.

Stashing us in his office, Sean told us not to move or make a sound. Our eyes were big and we gulped more than once and cringed at the least little sound. Helen wore a cape with a hood, which she felt would disguise her if anyone she knew happened on us.

The noise from the locomotives shook the glass in the office window; in fact, it felt like the whole building quaked. As we left the office with Sean, Nathan walked in from the platform. Helen pulled her hood down over her face, scurrying outside by the side door.

"Nathan, what are you doing here?" Sean asked, nervously.

"Covering for you. Orders from the boss. Where are you going, Sarah?" Nathan answered.

Helen had dodged Nathan's notice, but Sean had to explain that we were meeting my folks for a few hours. Nathan smiled and acted like it was the most normal thing in the world. "Send them my regards," he said.

Once inside the caboose, we all collapsed, knowing that we were almost caught. "Whew," Sean said. When the train stopped for water in Alachua, we scrambled off the train to be greeted by my folks, so late at night.

I ran to them and hugged them to me, thanking them for saving Helen. I introduced them to her and Mama put her arm around her and I knew we had done the right thing.

I walked with my arm around Papa as they could not stay long, traveling at night, with only a lantern to guide their way. I hugged Helen and told her she would be in good hands. How she thanked me and cried as they drove away. I was a mite jealous that it wasn't me in their carriage, heading home.

We had to wait for the next train back to Newberry, which came at about daybreak, but we were two happy people, knowing we had done a good deed for Helen. Snoozing on a bench, we were wrapped in each other's arms. Sean was a good man, indeed.

CHAPTER 48   SECRETS, NOT LIES

*M*inerva came through the door, screaming at the top of her lungs, "I know you two girls had something to do with Helen's leaving. This leaves me short-handed for my orders to the Gainesville Dry Goods Store. Tell me where she is!"

Both of us lifted our shoulders and hands at the same time, but when she left, we giggled. "I'm sure she won't have trouble finding a new girl, with that sweet personality," Margaret commented. Laughing, we began our day, but we knew we had our work cut out for us. I hummed the whole morning, wanting to burst into song, but knowing I shouldn't show too much joy.

Along around noon, Rebecca entered the sewing room, motioning for me to follow her outside.

"A terrible thing has happened. Helen is missing. I sent for Sam this morning. I can only hope she wasn't killed by a road agent. I'm so distraught," Rebecca stated, wringing her hands.

"I'm sorry. What can I do?" I asked, my mind racing.

"It's a small town. If you hear anything, come to me immediately," Rebecca said.

"Yes. I will," I said, feeling a little guilty at seeing Rebecca so upset, but this was one time I didn't feel bad about being dishonest, knowing Helen was safe with my folks. What I didn't understand was how Helen had kept her job a secret from everyone, including Rebecca. If Minerva and Rebecca ever talked, they would put two and two together, making me nervous at the thought.

Then there was Sam. Everyone in town was talking of his destructive ways, his drunkenness on Saturday nights, carousing with unsavory characters and women. Sunday mornings would find him in an alley or passed out in a brothel, being thrown out like dirty water. Rebecca and Nathan were mortified, but of course, they blamed his behavior on Helen for leaving him. I hoped they never discovered our part in it.

One Sunday morning, a month after Helen's disappearance, Sam's body washed up on the banks of Watermelon Pond, south of town. As we were leaving church, the sheriff pulled Nathan aside and whispered in his ear, at which time Nathan turned away from us and shook with sobs. Rebecca asked me to take Daniel home while she ran to the two men. Daniel and I could hear her screaming as we walked toward the house, hurriedly. At that time I didn't know what had happened and could not answer Daniel's questions, but by the time his parents returned, we knew the full story. Of course they blamed Helen.

Mama always said a woman can have secrets, but not lies. Sometimes it was hard to distinguish between the two. Sean asked me if I was ready to start a family, which was my secret, but it was a lie not to tell him I was preventing us from having a family.

"When the Lord is ready for us to have children, He will make a way," I said and he smiled at me, making me feel guilty.

"The Lord knows I'm doing my best with you every night. I would have thought we would be in the family way by now."

Blushing, I said, "You do a fine job, my husband. Loving is not just for making babies."

"Aww, Sarah. You are the best lover I have ever had. I mean…" he stammered.

Cringing, I said, "Well, Sean, I had to have known there were others. You were too experienced."

"You don't mind?"

"I do, but hopefully, they were before me."

"And you? Did Gale have his way with you?" he asked.

The question took me by surprise, feeling the blood rush to my head. I couldn't answer right away.

"Well, I reckon your face says it all. I knew it."

I stammered, "He did not have his way with me."

"Well, I guess what's good for the gander is good for the goose," he said.

"I am not lying. You are twisting things."

"He wanted you though, didn't he?" he asked.

"Yes," I answered.

Not knowing how a conversation could get so tangled up, I decided to hoe some weeds in the garden, hoping to dispel any thought of Gale. There were still times at night when I wished he were beside me, but those were nights when I was alone. I tried to always be with Sean when we were in bed. Just the mention of Gale's name triggered my desire for him.

Rebecca took on the position of teacher in the Newberry School. She was like her mother, Loretta, when she was grieving, burying herself in work. She asked me to be her assistant, but I didn't think I could face her every day, knowing I had assisted Helen, which she thought caused the death of her son. Besides, I could make more money sewing for Minerva, even though she was hard to work for.

Mama wrote to me, raving about Helen, saying she was so much like me, in that she worked hard, didn't complain, and even looked a little like me, with her blond curls. Oh my, how jealous that made me, knowing that she was living in my bedroom. I felt I should be ashamed, and corrected my attitude with the knowledge that she had suffered greatly from Sam's abuse.

Rebecca asked me if I knew where Helen had gone and I lied outright. I was becoming a regular liar, but Sean said there are some situations that cannot handle the truth and I reckoned he was right, even though I lied to him, too.

In the spring, I planned to visit my parents for a few days since I had been missing them so much. Sean felt it was safe for me to take the phosphate train to Alachua in the daytime, and all I had to do was ask Minerva for time off. She had hired another young girl, unmarried, who was helping support her family. Chloe was her name and she was as shy as a girl could be, hardly smiling or speaking. Minerva said she could get some work done because she wouldn't be gabbing all day like Margaret and me.

CHAPTER 49   HOME

$\mathcal{M}$inerva had reluctantly allowed me to take a few days off. Actually, I thought her dress orders were down or she would have never let me go. Then, the day had finally arrived when I would jump a train to Alachua where Papa would meet me at noontime. I was as nervous as a long-tailed cat in a room full of rocking chairs, knowing I might get a glimpse of my love, Gale. My heart ached to see my mama, who had always been my sanctuary, the finest woman in the world, and Helen, whom I had rescued – hoping she had blossomed under my family's care.

Sean took me to the station in a drenching rain and saw that I was well cared for in the caboose, even though I was soggy. He admonished the attendant to take care of his precious cargo; the man smiled indulgently.

Riding in a blue velvet chair, I gazed out the window and thought of the trip to Colorado and all of a sudden, I missed Jasper in the worst way. When I began to cry, the conductor came to me and asked if I was afeared. I laughed and said no, but thanks for asking.

☼

Papa stood in the downpour on the Alachua train platform in his yellow slicker. Realizing Mama would not travel in the rain, I was content to hug the man who had been my father. Usually, his smile was as big as his heart, but today it was tentative. I wondered if he was hard-pressed to leave his workload, but he said no.

As the wind blew the mist into our faces, I jabbered up a storm, asking about everyone. He just nodded, which wasn't like him.

"Is Mama sick? What's wrong? Is everyone okay?" I asked.

"Your mama's all right. I'll let her tell you the story," he said.

"What story?" I asked worriedly.

He was quiet and I knew I would have to ride the eight miles in silence. Once he spoke, I knew he would not tell me the story, and then I was anxious, wondering if someone had died, or was sick. Then, I thought of Gale and prayed that nothing had happened to him. It was the longest two hours of my life, delayed by the rain and dodging the mud puddles and downed limbs.

The horse stamped and snorted as Papa drove right up to the front porch and I jumped down while he drove on to the barn. There at the front door stood the person I had missed the most, my beautiful mother, her smile warming me.

"My girl," she whispered. "Come and take off the wet clothes and dry out. Take your things into your bedroom."

Feeling things were askew, I had no clue as to the problem. Nothing was right with my folks; smiles were small, talk was limited, and attitudes were not up to par. There was no sign of anyone living in my bedroom and I hoped Helen had not met with illness or something worse. Quickly, I changed into dry clothes, anxious to find out the solution to the mystery.

"Let's eat breakfast. I've made biscuits, your favorite," Mama said. Papa did not reappear.

Quietly, patiently, I waited, buttering my biscuits without much enthusiasm. I knew better than to push her as she would

253

address the problem in her own time. She was not to be prodded, as I nibbled on the scrambled eggs and grits.

"I know no other way to say it kindly," Mama said sadly. "Helen has run off with Gale, leaving behind his wife and children, his mother and his brothers."

I didn't know what I was expecting, but it was not that. Waiting a moment, I found it hard to fathom what she was saying. After all, Gale loved me and only me. I was breathing rapidly and could not catch my breath. And that was when I fainted and fell out of my chair.

Gently, Mama laid me out on the floor and removed the chair. My eyes fluttered open and the story came flooding back to me, while I tried to understand.

"I'm sorry to have been so blunt, but I didn't know how else to start," she said.

"But Gale loved his family and he said he loved me," I whimpered.

"Oh, Sarah. You are a foolish girl. Gale loves all women and himself. He is a self-centered man, truly despicable. I think Helen is going to be very disappointed."

As I sat up, the tears flowed. She was right: I was a God-awful fool. So embarrassed was I, that I could not look her in the eyes, wanting to sink into the rug.

"But there is good news, too. John and Suzanna are in the family way again," she said weakly. "And Izzie, too."

Slowly rising, I asked what would become of Gale's family. "Well, we can't put them out, now can we? The boys are old enough to operate the mill and Lana and Mrs. Lindsey are sewing bags and keeping up with the orders. No. They shall remain," she said.

Drying my eyes, I determined to try to enjoy my short stay, but it was like I had been living a lie, thinking Gale truly loved me and I thought I loved a man with some honor. All lies. It shocked my sensibilities. And Helen, what a terrible thing for her to do when she had been helped by so many people. How could I ever forgive her...or him?

I thought of Sean, my good man, and how I had been dishonest with him. Always steadfast, I realized he would have never committed　that sort of deed. And I was proud that he was my husband. I missed him terribly at that moment.

My time was short with my loved ones, but I got to feel Suzanna's baby kick and sing with my papa and have a wonderful supper cooked in the ranch kitchen, with all the hands and even Gale's family. Even though they looked sad, I was happy they had jobs and could continue on with my family, which was the best family in the world.

The rain stopped the day Papa took me to the station, and I kissed him goodbye and told him I loved him.

"You got a good man there, my Sarah," he said of Sean.

"Yes sir. I know that."

He helped me up the stairs of the caboose in my new dress that Mama had made me, with my new quilt packed away in my bag. I watched him drive away and settled into the velvet chair, opening the window to let in the fresh air. Once the car started moving, I reached into my purse and pulled out a little silk bag that held my womb veil. The faster the train moved, the brisker the air flowed in my face. I flung that little bag as far away as I could fling it and watched it land in a briar patch, dangling. Relief flooded my body and I felt I could be honest with my man again, and never again think about Gale, who could not hold a candle to Sean. I thought, "I believe the Lord can work in mysterious ways now." Smiling, I could not wait to be with my husband and I knew I was going to my real home.

EPILOGUE   SALLY'S SAYSO

"The years teach much which the days never know." Ralph Waldo Emerson

*B*ereft I was. As Sarah and Sean had pulled away from the driveway that day a few months ago I felt my lonesomest ever. When a person you love dies and leaves you alone, at least you know they didn't want to go. But Sarah seemed to want to depart from the ranch and me. It's the way of the world; children grow up and fly away like little birds.

Since Jasper left us, I had had a hard time being happy and maybe that's why Sarah wanted to leave. Maybe she couldn't stand being on the ranch without Jasper or maybe I had become too cranky or maybe, just maybe, she couldn't be around Gale and his family anymore. I knew she loved him at one point but I thought she had overcome that feeling with the love of Sean. It did not make me feel any better knowing why she left; I still had a hole in my heart.

I don't know that I had ever loved a child like I loved Sarah, my namesake. A mother loves a daughter in a different way from a son.

256

She knows the heartache she will experience, the painful birth of her children, the loss of a loved one, sometimes a baby, the loss of a sweetheart, and she wants to defend her from all those things, knowing she cannot.

"You can visit anytime you want to. She's not that far away," Lani said.

I didn't know what was worse – brushing your feelings away or just feeling them and getting it over with. Having lost Jasper, I was pretty certain Lani was hurting, too. Men truly were a mystery, every last one of them.

Once Sarah was gone for a couple of months, I settled into a routine, working hard so I didn't miss her so much. Her letters were like manna to me, with her poetic way of writing. They nourished me until I could see her again. And then, I only saw her for a few moments when they delivered Helen to us. I wanted to hold on to her, but I could see she was an adult.

Sweet Helen was so much like Sarah that I became attached to her also and loved spending time with her, quilting and sewing and cooking, but she was not Sarah. When she left with Gale, it was a huge disappointment to me. The ranch was rocked with the scandal and I knew my Sarah would have never done that. When Sarah left to go back from her visit, I could see the calmness in her face, and I knew she was going home to Sean, who was her home now. Feeling blessed, I knew I would still miss her, but as Lani said, "You can visit anytime."

ABOUT THE AUTHOR

Sarah A. Younger is a native Floridian whose ancestors settled Florida in the post-Civil War period. In researching family history, a discovery led to the fact that she is seventh generation Floridian on her grandfather's side of the family. The stories Sarah has passed on in the novel, "A Bend in the Straight and Narrow," and the sequel, "Ye Who Are Weary, Come Home," were told to her by her grandmother, Granny O'Steen. Since the stories were a mere skeleton, she filled in the gaps with historical fiction. Much of the research done for this project was accomplished by visiting graveyards in the Bradford and Alachua County areas. The search for Jacob Henry's and Sally's graves is ongoing. Many of the markers revealed things not known previously in family history, such as an epidemic that killed three people in the family, including her grandfather's mother, one week after he was born. Last names in the books have been changed, but many of the given names remain the same. Sarah has a BA degree from Baylor University and an Education degree from the University of Southern Colorado. She has an avid interest in history and quilting. She lives in Merritt Island, Florida, with her husband and Charlie, the beagle dog.

CONNECT WITH SARAH!

Sarah loves to stay connected with her readers. Follow her author page on Facebook @sarahayoungerauthor for updates, special deals, and discussion. Visit her website at www.floridaheritagenovel.com.

OTHER WORK

<u>A Bend in the Straight and Narrow</u> is Sarah's other novel. Published in 2015, this was Sarah's debut novel and the first book in the series. It can be purchased at Amazon.com. For more information, go to www.floridaheritagenovel.com.